TH

THING

ABOUT

LEMONS

TASHA HARRISON

The Thing About Lemons is a uclanpublishing book

First published in Great Britain in 2023 by
uclanpublishing
University of Central Lancashire
Preston, PR1 2HE, UK

First published in the UK 2023

978-1-915235-55-8

1 3 5 7 9 10 8 6 4 2

Set in 10/16pt Kingfisher by Amy Cooper

A CIP catalogue record for this book is available from the British Library.

Printed and bound in Great Britain by Clays Ltd, Elcograf S.p.A.

THE THING ABOUT LEMONS

TASHA HARRISON

TO ANYONE WHO'S EVER MADE
A REGRETTABLE MISTAKE . . .
YOU'RE NOT ALONE.

PROLOGUE

The (subconscious) plan of how things were supposed to go

1. Jackson and Ava would eventually realise they had nothing in common with each other and would break up, but stay good friends. (They both had roaming eyes, so it was only a matter of time . . .)

2. There'd be a "cooling off period" (like a couple of months?) while everyone got used to them not being a couple anymore.

3. Me and Jackson would hang out more, becoming closer, the chemistry between us growing stronger by the day.

4. Me and Jackson would each talk to Ava in private and give her a heads-up that we were starting to have feelings for each other. (She'd really appreciate our honesty and respect.)

5. Me and Jackson would officially start seeing each other and everyone would be fine with it, and say things like, "You guys make a really cool couple." (Not in front of Ava, obviously).

CHAPTER ONE

Dumb And Dumberer ...

I couldn't believe what an utter idiot I'd been.

Dumb was not the word. Stupid was an understatement.

If there was a medal for Spectacularly Dumbass Mistakes, I was up for a gold.

If there was a Donut of the Decade award, the chunky golden ring belonged on my mantelpiece.

Muppet of the Millennium? Hand me the Champagne.

How could I (a normally intelligent person) have done something so unbelievably stupid?

That was the realisation slowly entering my consciousness as Ava screamed in my face, a trembling blur of ringlets, false eyelashes and perfect white teeth that looked ready to take a chunk out of my arm. Jackson, biceps tightening as he gripped her by the shoulders, did his best to steer her out of my front room towards the landing while the insults poured from her snarling lips.

'You scheming, deceitful BITCH!' she yelled at me over his shoulder, spit flying in all directions. 'Get off me, Jackson! We're SO OVER!' She looked me up and down in disgust. 'Look at you all dolled up – you *never* wear crop tops and mini-skirts!'

I glanced down at myself. I *did* wear crop tops and mini-skirts, just not usually together.

'Stealing my look *and* my boyfriend!' she screamed. 'What's next – my wallet? My Instagram profile? My whole identity?'

It had all happened so quickly, I felt like I was having an out-of-body experience. My body was just standing there in the front room doorway, an empty shell, while I looked down on the exploding drama from above. Meanwhile, my lips still thought they were attached to Jackson's. I needed to wake up, but I couldn't. Things were unravelling too fast.

'Where are the others?' she snapped. 'Did you tell them not to come and somehow forgot to tell me? Or did you *want* me to walk in on you?' Her eyes widened at the thought that this must've been my intention all along.

I held up my hands. 'No, oh God, it's not like that. Ravi's away, Zac couldn't make it and Daisy and Martha should be—'

'Ava, just hear me out, will you?' Jackson interrupted me. 'It's not how it looked!'

I cringed on his behalf. *That was such a cliché.*

Ava clearly agreed with me. '*Seriously?*' She shoved a curtain of ringlets out of her dark brown eyes. One of her false eyelashes had come loose and looked like she had a moth stuck to her eyelid. We'd sworn to always alert each other to any wardrobe or make-up malfunctions, and it felt almost more disloyal not to mention it than it did to kiss her boyfriend. I mean, what was *wrong* with me? Where had my morals gone?

'*Tell her, Ori,*' Jackson begged me, his gold necklace glinting in the light.

I opened my mouth but nothing came out.

Tell her it wasn't what she thought? But it *was* what she thought! She'd walked in on her best friend and boyfriend snogging. We were caught red-handed. Guilty as charged. We might as well just hang our heads, admit it, apologise from the bottom of our hearts and gear up for a rough few weeks as Ava unleashed her fury on us for betraying her. This was NOT how I'd intended things to go, but if we apologised enough times, *surely* she'd forgive us eventually?

'*Ori!*' Jackson dropped his hands from Ava's shoulders and turned to face me, his gorgeous green eyes now glowering at me. 'For Christ's sake, tell her what happened.'

'She *saw* what happened,' I replied, avoiding Ava's firey gaze. Whatever we said, it would only make things worse. We had no excuse, so it was best to just own it. 'Ava, I'm so sorry . . .' I searched for the right words, but Jackson interrupted me.

'You've misunderstood the situation, babe, I promise you,' he said, combing his fingers through his perfectly scruffed-up quiff. 'I thought you'd be here already. I thought the others would be here, too. But when I arrived, it was just me on my own, and Ori said you wouldn't be here for a while, so we were just sitting, talking . . .' He gestured towards the sofa behind me, the dent of his head still visible in my mum's favourite cushion. 'And then she just . . . she just . . . kissed me! It totally took me by surprise – and that's exactly when you walked in.'

'Good job I walked in when I did, then!' Ava sneered. '. . . Given how desperately you were wriggling and squirming and fighting her off!'

'I was literally about to do ALL those things the very second you walked in.'

Er, I don't think so, Jackson. Also, that SO didn't sound convincing. Ava rolled her eyes. 'Gimme a break, *you dick.*'

'I was caught off guard!' he shouted. 'Can't you understand? It took a few seconds for my brain to catch up with what was happening.'

I would've felt sorry for him if I hadn't felt so insulted. *Wriggling? Squirming? Fighting me off?* Those were *not* the vibes he'd been giving out – and even if, as he claimed, those vibes were nanoseconds from kicking in, the initial vibes had been totally the opposite. Admittedly he'd given off a "surprised" vibe to begin with when I'd kissed him, followed swiftly by a "confused but intrigued" vibe as I continued to kiss him. But this (and this is the important bit) was then followed by a "hell yeah I'm into this!" vibe, as he totally, one-hundred-per-cent, kissed me back! And *I know* I didn't imagine that.

All this in the space of about ten seconds. That's how long our kiss lasted – ten measly seconds. The magical moment I'd imagined for months, fantasised about daily, was over in the blink of an eye. If it wasn't for the strange taste of smoky mint from Jackson's vape pen, I might not have believed it had ever happened.

Jackson turned towards me, his normally pale face reddening. 'I don't believe this. I didn't ask for any of this. Why the hell did you do that, Ori? You *know* I'm with Ava. She's your best friend for Christ's sake! You've totally lost it.'

His anger brought my out-of-body experience to an abrupt end.

Ava's jaw softened a little. Finally he was on the right track.

'She's not my best friend any more,' she said, giving me

a death stare. 'She's *nothing* to me. She can't even look me in the eye.' That was mainly to do with the eyelash malfunction, but she had a point.

I looked to Jackson for support. Was he really not going to share any of the blame? Was he going to deny he had feelings for me? Feelings I'm *sure* he'd hinted at from time to time?

'I'm out of here!' Ava strutted down the stairs to our flat's front door.

'Wait!' Jackson grabbed her arm. 'I'm coming with you. We need to talk.'

She shrugged him off and yanked open the door, nearly knocking over a box of vintage clothes Mum was planning to sell.

'Ava, wait,' I called from the top of the stairs. 'I'm really sorry. I've been a total idiot. I never meant for this to happen.'

She cocked her head to one side. 'Didn't you?'

She stormed out the door, Jackson hot on her heels, grovelling all the way down the communal stairs and out onto the street, leaving the lingering waft of hairspray in his wake.

I closed the door behind them, praying the downstairs neighbours hadn't overheard all the shouting, and dragged myself back upstairs to the now-empty flat, where I stood on the landing, gazing at my zombie-like reflection in the mirror. I had mussed-up hair, a dazed look in my eyes, and an incriminating lipstick smudge.

'Who *are* you?' I asked myself. 'What the hell have you gone and done?'

I drifted into my room and eased myself gently down on the bed, as if I'd just climbed out of a mangled car. I was in a state of shock. Adrenaline was pumping round my body. I tried to calm my breathing. My eyes had misted up, but the tears weren't falling. Mum wouldn't be home for another couple of hours. I was going to have to tell her what happened. It'd be a whole lot worse if she found out from someone else – which she probably would, as our social lives often encompassed different generations of the same households.

And when the rest of my friends found out what went down tonight – which would be in a matter of minutes as Daisy and Martha would probably be walking slap-bang into Jackson and Ava any second now – my life would officially be over. I felt like I'd been punched in the gut. Not only had I just lost my best friend and the boy I loved in one go – I'd probably just kissed goodbye to my entire social life.

My breath caught in my throat as the realisation of what I'd just done began to sink in.

It was like I'd just woken up from sleepwalking along without a care in the world, only to find myself standing on a flimsy branch hanging over the edge of a cliff-top – just in time to hear it snap beneath my feet.

Nice work, Ori Reynolds. Take a bow.

If only I had a time machine, I could leap in, rewind a few hours, erase the moment where I lost complete control of my mental faculties, and no one would be any the wiser.

But there was no time machine, so I'd be hiding in my bedroom for the foreseeable future, losing myself in a blur of Netflix romcoms, while desperately applying to different sixth form colleges outside Brighton where no one knew me and

I could hopefully start again with a fresh slate in September.

In the meantime, prom night was off.

Camping in Cornwall was off.

Reading Festival – off.

Losing my virginity – indefinitely postponed.

My whole goddamn life was OFF.

I exhaled slowly, my heartbeat thundering in my ears.

I couldn't face telling Mum when she got in. Right now I didn't need to feel any worse than I already did. I'd tell her in the morning – depending on her mood. She was menopausal (as she liked to point out every five minutes) and flew off the handle at the tiniest things (i.e. me forgetting to put the dishwasher on, me losing a phone charger, me borrowing her eye shadow without asking). And this was not a tiny thing. This was a biggie in Mum's book, as she had strong feelings about lying and cheating. Depending on her mood, she wouldn't so much fly off the handle as launch into outer space. I could just picture her, hands on hips, trying to keep a calm voice, saying: "What the *hell* were you thinking?"

Fair question, I guess.

What the hell *was* I thinking?

That I could somehow poach my best friend's boyfriend from under her nose and everyone would be cool with it?

Oh God.

I tried to swallow but my salivary glands didn't seem to be working.

As ridiculous as it may sound, I guess that's what I *had* been thinking – although I hadn't fully realised it till now.

CHAPTER TWO

Atonement

As expected, Mum didn't take the news of my "mistake" too well when I broke it to her the following morning. I forced myself out of bed about ten minutes after I heard her alarm go off, slipped my dressing gown on and shuffled sleepily into the kitchen. While I was making myself a cup of tea to gear up for the impending shitstorm, she appeared in the kitchen wearing a knee-length summer dress and some bright yellow slingback cloggs – this season's must-have footwear for the over-forties.

'You're up early, Piggles! The summer holidays have barely begun – I can't believe you're bored of lying in already?'

"Piggles" was the super-embarrassing pet name I'd had to endure since the day I was born. It had begun as "Piglet" and over the years morphed into the dreaded "Piggles". On the bright side, I was unlikely to hear it much once I'd made my shameful confession.

'I didn't sleep well last night,' I mumbled, waiting while she scooped her hair up into a ponytail and polished her glasses. (It was true. I hadn't slept well last night. I'd tried to call Zac, Daisy and Martha, but no one was answering and no one was calling me back. I'd tried calling Ravi *twice*, even leaving a voicemail saying it was an emergency, but nothing. Had Ava got to him first? To be aired by the group was hard enough, but if Ravi wasn't talking to me either . . . ? Unable to bear my phone's torturous silence any longer, I'd finally turned it off around one a.m., knowing I stood zero chance of getting any sleep while I was waiting for it to ring.)

Finally I told her while she was applying her lipstick in the landing mirror – the last thing she did every morning before leaving for work. (I was hoping she wouldn't have time to hang around and annihilate me. Wrong.)

'You did *what*?' She spun around to face me. (It would've made a great meme.)

'I kissed Jackson,' I said a little louder, the shame burning my cheeks.

She put her lipstick into her handbag and eyeballed me over the top of her glasses.

'*Why* would you do that? There are hundreds of decent, good-looking teenage boys in Brighton – why *him*?'

'Because I'm in love with him.' It was the first time I'd said it out loud to anyone – including myself – and it felt both shameful and kind of liberating at the same time.

Mum opened her mouth to speak, but was lost for words.

'That's not all,' I said, clenching the inside of my dressing gown pockets.

She shielded her eyes. 'Go on.'

'Ava walked in on us.'

'Please tell me you're joking?' Mum flung up her arms and dropped them again, her hands slapping onto her thighs.

'That was a really uncool thing to do. She must be *so* upset.'

"Apoplectic" was the word that sprung to mind. Not a word I'd ever used in a sentence before, but now I couldn't get it out of my head. It was the POP bit. Ava's eyes had kind of *popped* out of their sockets, like in a cartoon.

'I suppose I'd better call Lucinda and make some kind of apology.'

'Why? It's nothing to do with you or Lucinda.'

'Lucinda's a friend of mine! It's called damage limitation – ask Chuck, it's what he does for a living.'

Chuck was her new boyfriend. American. Impossibly white teeth. Penis-extension car. Also known as #chuckChuck by non-fans (i.e. me).

'If Ava had done the same to you, I might appreciate a text from her mother offering some kind of apology on her daughter's behalf.'

'You don't even *like* Lucinda!'

'Just because we don't always agree doesn't mean I don't like her. Besides, we have lots of mutual friends.'

She'd clearly forgotten the time she'd got back from book club raging that Lucinda had made yet another dig at her job. (Mum was a meetings and events organiser, but Lucinda always called her a "party planner" which, according to Mum, made her work sound fluffy and shallow.)

'I don't get it,' I said. 'It's between me and Ava. It's MY fault.'

'Damn right it's *your* fault. That's not how I brought you up. You know how I feel about that kind of thing – it affects other people and they can end up in therapy for years.'

She was referring to herself growing up with a serial womaniser for a dad. Whoa! Was she comparing me to *her dad?* I felt slightly sick.

'I know I screwed up – there's no need to rub it in!' I shouted.

My eyes welled up. What I could really do with right now was a hug. Some words of comfort. Someone telling me that while this wasn't my wisest moment, I was not an evil person. But no, that would be too much to expect from my perfect mother who never put a foot wrong. My lips started to twitch and quiver but Mum didn't seem to notice.

'What about the prom?' she asked.

'Guess I'm no longer going.' A rush of self-pity pushed a tear out of its duct. I wiped it away swiftly.

'But it's a landmark occasion! You need to sort this mess out, *Aurélie. Fast.*'

'Really? You don't say.' Why couldn't she just hug me? I'd never felt so alone my entire life.

'And cut the sarcasm. You have no one but yourself to blame for the way you're feeling right now.' She pulled her phone out of her pocket and checked the time. 'When I get home this evening I want to hear that you've apologised profusely to Ava. Got it?'

Yes, MA'AM! I resisted clicking my heels and saluting.

'We'll talk about this when I get home. I invited Chuck over tonight – guess I'll have to cancel him.' She pursed her lips.

Normally cancelling Chuck would've been cause for celebration. But if it was a choice between his hundred-decibel laugh and overpowering aftershave honking out our flat and me getting a lecture that dragged on for hours,

I'd definitely opt for the former.

'And don't forget there's some plumbing work being carried out downstairs so the water's being switched off between nine and one. You'd better shower and fill the kettle now, got it?'

'Loud and clear.'

'And finally, *for the umpteenth time*,' she gritted her teeth, 'can you tidy your dump of a room, pick your dirty clothes up and put them in the laundry basket, and wash up that mountain of plates you've left next to the sink for the scullery maid?'

She flounced down the stairs and slammed the door to our flat shut behind her.

That bastard door. The only way to close it was to slam it. I *knew* that. So when I'd let Jackson in and he'd closed it gently behind him, I should've known it wasn't shut properly. I wasn't to know the front door to the street also hadn't been closed properly – either by Jackson or one of our neighbours downstairs – but still. It felt like life was teaching me a lesson: *you do the dirty on someone, life will do the dirty on you.* I just didn't expect to get my comeuppance quite so quickly. The tears I'd been trying to suppress for the last five minutes exploded out of me like a dam bursting.

I dragged myself into the living room and forward-flopped over the armrest of the sofa, my head buried in a cushion, my feet suspended in mid-air like a human see-saw. There I remained, upside down and crying, until so much snot had gathered in my sinuses, I could no longer breathe. When I finally got up and went to retrieve my phone from my sock drawer, I had loads of new messages. I braced myself as I read each one.

Daisy: Ori, WTF??? Ava's devastated. So's Jackson. What the hell's going on?

Martha: So not cool, dude. Talk about breaking the girl code and killing the group vibe in one go.

Zac: Holy crap I've just woken up and it's like the world's gone mad. Please tell me I'm still asleep having a very bad dream?

Ravi: Sorry I didn't pick up last night — it was my auntie's birthday. Whole family was there. If you need to talk, I'm here. Well I'm still away but you know what I mean. Funny. Had a feeling you liked Jackson.

I exhaled heavily. Thank God Ravi was still talking to me.

Nothing from Ava though. Not surprising, seeing as she'd said it all last night and it was still ringing in my ears.

And nothing from Jackson. Not that I was expecting to hear from him either, but a part of me was secretly hoping that our kiss (which was unplanned, I swear) had made him realise he had feelings for me. It wasn't like he backed away when I kissed him. He kissed me back – even if it was just for a few seconds, till Ava walked in, taking us both by surprise. Who knew how much longer that kiss would've lasted or what things might've been said if she hadn't walked in?

I swear I never consciously planned to steal Jackson from Ava. I genuinely hadn't meant to treat my friend like that. I had, admittedly, invited him to come round earlier than the others so that we could just hang out and talk for half an hour, so that he could notice me a bit more. But that was all. The moment I leaned forward and kissed him – that wasn't in the script.

I literally don't know what came over me, because I'm generally not that brave. We'd been sitting really close together on the sofa and I'd just felt this spark between us. Or had I completely imagined it? If I hadn't gone and ruined everything, if I'd just been patient, he would have lost interest in Ava eventually – or the other way round – and pretty soon would've started taking an interest in me. Of that, I'm pretty sure.

And that would've been fair enough, as I honestly believed Ava wouldn't be *that* bothered about breaking up with him. This was because Ava had had crushes on more boys than I could remember. In Year Seven she liked Jacob; in Year Eight, Kai; Year Nine, Malik; Year Ten, Harry. Now, in Year Eleven, all previous crushes officially gave her "the ick", and lately she'd been cracking jokes about what she'd like to do to *Hot Boy*, who moved into her street a few months ago. (All we knew about him was that he went to the local sixth form college and from the T-shirts he wore, had a taste for 90s grunge bands.) I'd seen the way she looked at him when we walked past him in the street. Her body language was all *It'sOnlyAMatterOfTimeBeforeYouNoticeMeHotBoy*.

That's the thing about Ava. She *knows* she's pretty. She could have her pick of any of the boys at school – or rather, she'd *had* her pick. She chose Jackson. And who wouldn't? He was like her white male equivalent. *Jackson Crowley and Ava Etoundi.* They looked good together – like a couple off *Love Island*. He was all quiff, biceps and dimples, and she was all bouncing black ringlets, film star cheek bones, and bags of confidence.

I know I might sound jealous right now, but I promise you I'm not. I know I'm not as drop-dead gorgeous as Ava, but I'm not down on my looks. Me and Ava have been best friends since Year Seven. She was pretty ordinary back then – not the goddess she is now. We bonded over the annoyances of wearing braces and a mutual appreciation of *Dance Moms*. It was mainly just the two of us (and occasionally Ravi, who'd been my friend since reception) until Year Nine when we were joined by Daisy (the new girl) and Martha (a lone goth). Then, at some point in Year Ten, Jackson started hanging around with us. (It was obvious he fancied Ava.) Zac followed soon after. (He fancied Jackson but soon realised it was a lost cause). The seven of us slowly merged into a group that just kind of worked – and luckily continued to work even after Ava and Jackson got together.

Occasionally there was talk of Ravi fancying me – although I'd never seen any evidence whatsoever to back this theory up. In fact, he'd hinted to me a few months ago that he liked Maya from 11R, and even though he'd done nothing to let her know, he wouldn't be telling me that if he fancied *me*, would he? Besides, I was totally happy with our friendship the way it was. Ravi was one of my best friends. We'd pretty much had each other's backs ever since Reception when Olivia Mason had accused him of stealing her bobble hat. (I could see she was sitting on it so I grassed her up.) And if I forgot my packed lunch (or couldn't bear its boring contents) he'd share his with me. He was like a brother. And as I didn't have any siblings, it was a friendship I really valued.

Anyway, there only one person I fancied and, unfortunately, that was Jackson.

My friendship group had basically been my entire life since the beginning of Year Ten. They'd become more of a family to me than my real family. In fact, I didn't even feel like I had a real family anymore. Dad had moved to Bristol after he and Mum split up ten years ago. I used to visit him more regularly and stay for longer in the holidays, but these days I just spent the weekend with him and his girlfriend every six weeks or so. Often Zelda would "give us some space", although I actually didn't mind her company cos me and Dad never had much to say to each other anyway. Those weekends always followed the same routine: walk into town, get a fry-up, spot a Banksy, go to the cinema, get a takeaway, watch TV, bed. And we always talked about the same things: vinyl vs streaming, Star Wars vs Marvel, school in the Eighties vs school today. It was so predictable I could pretty much write the script. It always felt like we were just doing our duty till it felt acceptable not to bother any more.

As for Mum, we got on pretty well (when she wasn't nagging or lecturing me) but I was fairly certain she was just waiting till I moved out so she'd finally be free to come and go as she pleased and move in with #chuckChuck. Other than that, I had a few cousins on my dad's side who I barely knew and one remaining grandparent – my mum's dad, who lived in France and who we rarely saw because, according to Mum, he was "generally a bit of an idiot".

My phone buzzed.

Mum: Have you apologised to Ava yet?

Jeez. Give me a chance!

Me: Not yet. I'm still working out what to say.

Mum: Stop procrastinating. The sooner you deal with it the better.

I disagreed. Rushing would not be clever. I needed to choose my words carefully otherwise I could make things even worse.

I wandered into the bathroom and stared at my pale, blotchy face and long, boring, doormat-coloured hair in the mirror – it was time for a radical change. Something that marked the end of one chapter and the beginning of another. Something that made me look a bit more noticeable, and a bit less in Ava's shadow. In the meantime, I needed to concentrate and think about what to say to her – and what she'd probably say back to me. As I imagined how the conversation would go, my heart started racing, my stomach churned and my bowels kicked into action. I wasn't used to dramas and confrontations with friends. I went to the loo and practically exploded – with sound effects I'm glad no other human being was around to hear. This was worse than any of my pre-exam nerves.

I'd barely pulled up my PJs before there was a loud thump on the door. Who was that? Why were they knocking on our flat door rather than buzzing up from the street? It wouldn't be Ava this early in the morning would it? Or what if it was Jackson coming round to tell me they'd broken up?

I went to wash my hands but no water came out of the tap. *Weird.*

I ran down the stairs to our front door, put the chain on and opened it. A bald man in overalls was standing there on the communal landing looking damp, bedraggled and not very happy. And sweet baby Moses in a basket – *he stank!*

'Can I help you?' I asked.

'Did you not get the message *NOT* to use the water between

nine and one?' he said gruffly.

'What message?' *Oops.*

He sighed like teachers do when you tell them you thought the homework wasn't due in till next week.

'Listen, yeah? I'm fixing a pipe in this flat here.' He pointed to my neighbour's front door and gave me the iciest look. 'So kindly do *not* turn on any taps – *or flush the toilet* – until *after* one o'clock. Yeah?'

'Cool. One o'clock. Got it.'

I shut the door to our flat, scurried back upstairs, threw myself on my bed and died.

Life really wasn't going very well at the moment.

I'd basically just shat on someone's head. This was beyond embarrassing. I wouldn't be able to go out anywhere till he'd left the building. Ava would have found this completely hilarious – well, twenty-four hours ago she would have. We would've laughed about it for weeks. But now, thanks to my epic mistake, things were different. She wouldn't find anything I said funny ever again. She'd probably say: "Yeah, I *also* know how it feels to be shat on from a great height by Ori Reynolds."

I turned onto my back and fiddled with my fingernails while the memory of last night played out like a film on the ceiling above me. Some time later I turned to see a cluster of torn-off white crescents on my bedside table.

What had I gone and done to my life?

CHAPTER THREE
Can You Ever Forgive Me?

Ava, I am SO sorry. What I did was the stupidest, dumbest thing I've ever done. I totally hate myself. I should've told you I liked Jackson. I didn't mean to try and steal him from you – I never planned to do that, I swear. I've been such an idiot. I've ruined our friendship and messed everything up. I wish I could take it all back. I know it'll take time for you to forgive me, but I hope we can be friends again. I miss you already.

It was nearly two weeks since The Day I Committed The Crime, and Ravi was sitting cross-legged on the floor of my bedroom, holding my phone in one hand, and a melting Twix in the other. I'd made us iced coffees to cool us down – it was a baking hot day, and being on the top floor, our flat was like an oven.

I sat opposite him, leaning against my wardrobe door while he read the message I'd sent to Ava the day after I'd kissed Jackson. I watched him closely, searching for signs of disapproval on his face. Ravi's opinion of the situation mattered because he was known for being the calm, sensible one in the group, the one who could always see both sides of an argument and get people talking again. Not that my "side" had a leg to stand on, but I knew he wouldn't turn his back on me like the others had. Ravi liked to make up his own mind in his own time, and his measured opinions about things would often make the others reconsider their own strong, quick-fire views. As I watched his eyes scouring my text, I knew that whatever words were about to come out of his mouth, it was probably exactly what I needed to hear.

He stretched out his legs and squinted at the screen. He'd been away visiting relatives for most of the last two weeks, during which time he'd had a major haircut. Gone was the horrendous bird's nest he'd been so proud of – now it was short at the back and sides, a little longer on top. I told him it looked way better. He hadn't been quite so complimentary about *my* new look, but then mine was more radical and people seemed to need time to get used to the new colour (pink) and length (pixie-ish). By people, I meant Mum and #chuckChuck, as I hadn't seen anyone else since that fateful day, and I was trying my hardest to convince myself that all this time spent on my own was good for me – that I wasn't lonely, that I was actually training myself to be more independent and self-sufficient.

He passed the phone back to me.

'So what do you think?' I asked him.

'Yeah . . . You sound genuinely sorry, but still, I don't think anything's going to change anytime soon.' He finished off his Twix and washed it down with some iced coffee.

'I sent her that message the very next day. I've had *zero* replies. She's basically ghosted me.' I didn't mention how painful this was, or that I'd cried my eyes out on several occasions – usually when I was home alone, which was most of the time, as Mum was hardly ever here.

'Yeah, well. Guess you can't blame her, really,' he said, giving me a judgey but sympathetic look, like I was a dunderhead rather than a dickhead. 'What *were* you thinking, Oreo?'

That question again.

He frowned at my crestfallen face. 'Maybe it's my fault for dropping you on your head in the Year Four sports day wheelbarrow race.'

'Well we blamed "The Braver The Flavour" on that, so why not this too?' I joked, remembering our Year Six business enterprise plan, when I'd persuaded him to do an alternative sandwich stall with dubious fillings like jam and lettuce and pesto and marmalade. We'd been the most successful stall that day, but the bins were full of barely touched sandwiches and Ravi had wisely pointed out that our business would've been short-lived without any return customers.

'Seriously, Ori, this is *not good*.'

He was no longer smiling, so I decided I'd better do my best to explain my uncool behaviour.

'I thought Jackson liked me. He sometimes gives me that impression – like a flirty look now and again, or he'll say something a bit flirty, you know? I'd always kind of liked him, and then after a while, I realised I liked him *a lot*. I kept it to myself cos I didn't want to cause any trouble. I just thought they'd break up eventually – Ava's *always* eyeing up other guys.'

'Eyeing up is one thing – snogging is another,' he said.

Except that she *had* snogged someone else. Just once, briefly, at a party about six months ago, a few months after she and Jackson had started seeing each other. And no one else knew about it except me. It was the first time she'd ever got drunk, and somewhere between jumping up and down on the sofa and spewing up in the bathroom, she'd snogged some random guy from another school. As we'd walked back to her place, she'd sobered up and started crying, while I'd reassured her it wasn't *her* who'd kissed a random guy at a party, but the vodka. I'd sworn never to tell a soul, and I'd kept my word.

'Yeah,' I replied. 'You're right.' I felt the dimmest glimmer of self-respect flicker within me, but it faded pretty fast, like a dud match. I couldn't even use this example of my loyalty in self-defence. Ava drunkenly snogging a random guy was not the same as me soberly snogging her boyfriend. If you were to weigh the two things side by side on the scales of justice, mine would crash to the ground like a kettlebell, catapulting Ava's mistake across the room like a fluffy meringue pie. So, much as I was tempted to, I couldn't tell Ravi Ava's dirty secret. I'd already betrayed her once, so this would be like kicking her in the gut after I'd already knifed her in the back.

'Have you heard from Jackson?' he asked me, glancing at his phone.

I shook my head. I'd messaged him, apologising for making a move on him, and asking if we could still be friends – even if that meant being fairly distant friends for a while. I'd given up imagining he had feelings for me, but was still stupidly hoping he'd say it wasn't *all* my fault, that he *had* kissed me back, but all I got was a blunt reply saying: "You betrayed your best mate and you nearly broke me and Ava up. Friends don't do that to each other. I think we should keep our distance from now on."

'So when you saw everyone at the beach yesterday, did anyone mention me?' I asked.

'Not really.' Ravi fidgeted with his phone, turning it over and over in his hand like a coaster. 'The atmosphere was a bit awkward. We talked about the tent situation, now that you're not coming to Cornwall. I mean, they're guessing you're not coming... Or are you...?' He looked at me.

'Seriously? I'm not a total masochist, you know.'

We sat in silence for a few seconds. I watched as Ravi's eyes browsed the vintage film posters Blu-tacked to my bedroom walls. I'd managed to cover nearly two thirds of my room in different sized posters, making it look like really cool wallpaper. My friends – or rather *ex-friends* – liked to use it as a background for taking selfies.

'Have you seen *Trainspotting* yet?' He nodded towards the poster.

'I was going to watch it the other night but it cost extra.'

He tutted. 'Excuses, excuses, Oreo. What about *The Blues Brothers?*'

'Watched it a few days ago. *We're on a mission from God!*' I quoted from the film in an American accent.

'Hallelujah! *Have you seeeen the light?*' He quoted back.

'Yes, I've seen the light! Absolutely loved it – especially that scene in the church with James Brown. So have *you* watched *Thelma and Louise* yet?' I challenged him.

'Watched it with my auntie the other day.' His lips twitched.

'Lies!' I kicked his foot.

'I'm still in the lead though,' he teased. 'And you are *way* behind.'

'Whatevs, Ravioli. Anyway I thought we were going to watch *Trainspotting* together?'

'Sounds too depressing – the film, I mean, not watching a film with you. What is it about Jackson anyway?' he asked suddenly. 'I mean, I know he's got that whole baseball jacket and retro quiff thing going on, but you're so different. I just don't see what you've got in common.'

I snorted. 'It's got nothing to do with his *look*, give me some credit!' I wasn't about to tell him that Jackson sent a high voltage current running through my body whenever he looked at me with those magnetic green eyes. That he made me have a physical reaction to him that was completely beyond my control. That I probably spent several hours a day fantasising about rolling around under a duvet with him. This was highly confidential, super-embarrassing stuff. I couldn't tell anyone. Not Ava. Not my mum. Not even Ravi, who knew who all my celebrity crushes were.

'I just started having feelings for him . . .' I said pathetically.

'And do you still have feelings for him now?'

I looked down. 'Well they're not going to vanish overnight. But I'm doing my best to move on.'

Ravi sighed, leaned his head back against the wall and stared up at the ceiling.

'What?' I asked. I felt like I was being judged.

'Well I was thinking, why don't you come to the prom with me tomorrow night? Not as my prom *date*, but as my prom *mate*?'

I blinked. 'Er . . .' Was he mad?

'It'll make it look like you've moved on.' He tapped his forehead with his index finger, like he was a genius who'd come up with a wily plan to bring me back from the social wilderness.

'I just couldn't face it, Rav. I'm a social piranha.'

'*Pariah* – it's social pariah. A piranha is a fish with sharp teeth.'

'Whatever. No one wants me there.'

'*I* want you there.'

I shook my head. Nothing on Earth could make me go to prom night. Not even with Ravi's support.

'It's too soon. I did the crime, now I'm doing the time. It's only been two weeks. Like you said, nothing's gonna change anytime soon. In fact, I don't think Ava or Jackson will ever speak to me again.'

'They will eventually. Zac and Martha are over it now.'

'So they say, and yet they've gone *strangely* quiet.' They'd both gone from messaging me a gazillion times a day to just once or twice a week – and those were replies to my messages, often sent after a long delay and consisting of significantly less words and emojis than usual.

'They just feel awkward and don't wanna take sides – which is understandable.'

'Daisy's not speaking to me *at all*.'

'Yeah, but you know what Daisy's like – there's always *someone* she's not speaking to.'

'You're about my only friend in the universe right now,' I said. This was actually true.

'Yeah, well it'll cost you. Twenty quid a day,' he grinned.

'Very funny,' I snorted. 'I'll pay you in Twixes.'

(Twixes were his favourite. Mum always got them from the supermarket just for him.)

Ravi smiled. I felt bad for turning down his offer. Still, I couldn't face the icy stares I'd get, the bitchy comments behind my back or even to my face. Nor could I face Ava's wrath and Jackson pretending not to know me. And it wouldn't be fair to Ravi – he was too kind for his own good, being willing to take the most hated girl in school to prom night.

'So I really can't persuade you to come?' he sighed.

'Sorry. But thanks. I appreciate the offer.'

'So no prom night, no camping in Cornwall – what about Reading Festival? Is that off the cards too?'

'Guess so.'

Ravi shook his head. 'Come on, Ori – you can't hide in here forever.'

'I won't be. I'm going to France the day after you guys go to Cornwall.'

'France?' He sat up straight. 'With who? I thought your mum was going to Chicago?'

'She is.'

He looked confused.

'Mum decided to Airbnb the flat out,' I explained. 'She refused to let me stay here on my own – despite me promising I'd text her morning, noon and night. She said it's not just that she's against me being here on my own – we need the money. I said I'd get a holiday job so there was no need to Airbnb the flat out, but she said I could do that, too – when I get back.'

'So who are you going to France with?'

I wished I could lie about this, but this was probably a good opportunity for me to practise "transparency" – a word Mum had drilled into me over the last fortnight.

'What? Tell me, Oreo!' Ravi threw his screwed-up Twix wrapper at me.

I groaned. 'Believe me, you don't wanna know.'

'Spit it out, Reynolds.'

'I'm going with my grandad.' (Date of return "to be confirmed", which I wasn't sure whether to think of as a good thing or a bad thing.)

'Your grandad? I don't think you've ever mentioned your grandparents before.'

'Well I've only got the one and I never see him because A) he lives in France and B) my mum doesn't get on with him.'

'How come?'

'Long story. When my mum was little, he left my gran for another woman, and then he left that woman for another woman, and so on and so on. Bit of a ladies' man, not much of a dad. I call him Grandpa Airhead – not to his face, obviously – because he's super-forgetful and generally kind of clueless when it comes to people's feelings.'

Ravi grinned. 'So when was the last time you saw him?'

'When I was about eleven. He drops in for a cup of tea every few years.'

I had this vivid memory of Grandpa Airhead (real name Grandpa Claude), dressed like a cowboy for reasons I can't remember, handing me a belated birthday present the last time

I saw him. He'd kept it hidden behind his back, building up the suspense while rambling on about having missed my five previous birthdays and miraculously remembering to pop into WHSmith on his way over, blah blah blah, before eventually presenting me with a weighty plastic carrier bag. When I opened the bag, my excitement immediately turned to confusion. There was an unwrapped book inside – a *Lazytown* annual. I'd handed it back to him, thinking he must've given me the wrong bag by mistake. Mum had intercepted the bag, peered inside and rolled her eyes. '*Lazytown* is for pre-schoolers, Dad. Ori's *eleven*.'

'Oh right. Sorry, kiddo. Man, how time flies. I'll make it up to you next time, Scout's honour.'

'Or you could get your wallet out and make it up to her now?' Mum had suggested.

I'd ended up getting a £20 note, which had put a big smile on my face but a slightly gutted look on Grandpa Airhead's.

'So how long are you going for?' Ravi drained the last of his iced coffee and crunched on an ice cube.

'Around ten days, two weeks? It's all a bit up in the air, which pretty much sums up my grandad's entire life. He lives in a village called Frenac, near the Dordogne River in a barn that he's been converting into a music studio or something. He's a musician. Plays the guitar and produces music – or something like that? I'm not exactly sure. He's picking me up the day after you go to Cornwall and driving me over there.'

'And you're spending *two weeks* with him?' Ravi's eyes widened while he tried not to laugh.

'I don't have a choice.'

I'd argued with Mum till I was blue in the face, but she'd found a reason why every solution I'd come up with wouldn't work. Dad and Zelda had already booked a holiday so I couldn't stay with them. She couldn't (or wouldn't) change the dates of her and Chuck's holiday. And she refused to cancel renting our flat out because we'd lose money and get a bad review.

Ravi thought for a moment, then sighed. 'I'd offer you to stay at my place but my parents probably wouldn't go for it. It's a bit crowded right now what with my brothers being back from uni.'

'Don't worry, Rav. Anyway, you'll be in Cornwall in a few days' time.'

'Well if it makes you feel any better, I'd much rather go to France than spend a week in Martha's uncle's field. Remember I told you my brother went interrailing last summer? He said I could tag along with him this summer, but I turned him down to go to Cornwall – which won't be the same without you by the way.'

'Thanks.' I felt a fraction less lonely for the first time since I sabotaged my social life. 'Thanks for still being my friend.'

'It's a dirty job, but somebody's gotta do it,' he smiled.

'So, *honestly*, what do you think of my hair?' I twisted my head this way and that.

He raised his eyebrows. 'Um, yeah . . . It's great . . .'

CHAPTER FOUR

Reality Bites

'Passport?' asked Mum.

I pointed to my day bag, sitting on the gleaming kitchen floor by my feet. Our flat was literally sparkling after me and Mum had blitzed it from top to bottom. We'd de-cluttered, scrubbed, spruced and pimped to make it rental-ready. How I WISHED I was the guest.

'Wallet? Phone? Charger?'

'Mum!' I snapped. 'Enough.'

We'd been through her checklist over and over. She was clearly worried I'd be back before I'd even left, sending her Chicago plans into chaos. I noticed she was already casually glammed up in skinny jeans (so last century but she won't listen) and a floral chiffon blouse, ready to see Chuck, who was no doubt due to arrive the minute I'd vacated the premises.

'Tampons? Ibuprofen? Sun cream?' She gave her glasses a quick polish and replaced them on her nose.

I headbutted the kitchen table and stayed there, my arms folded over my head, hoping, like an ostrich, that the world would piss off. I was sixteen, and perfectly capable of packing a bag, thank you very much.

'I knew he wouldn't make it in time for breakfast. Good job I didn't go to too much trouble!' She put the kettle on and checked her phone for the millionth time that morning. 'You might as well have a cup of tea, seeing as he's not going to turn up until the last minute. Fingers crossed you can get on the next ferry if you miss this one.'

I didn't want a cup of tea. What I wanted was a reversal of reality. But three weeks had passed since The Day I Became A Social Pariah, and my life was showing no signs of improving. Apart from Ravi, who promised to keep in touch while I was away, I had zero amigos. I was Nelly No-Mates. Hilda Hermit. Mona the Loner.

Ravi had texted me on prom night to tell me I wasn't missing anything. According to him, the music was lame, Daisy was in a strop about something, Martha had got drunk, Zac had disappeared early to go and meet his new boyfriend, and Jackson had spent the whole evening trying to cheer up a grumpy Ava. Why she was grumpy, Ravi couldn't work out as neither of them would say. (I had a horrible feeling I was probably the cause.) He also sent me a selfie of him in his dinner jacket posing like James Bond, which made me laugh. Apparently hardly any of the guys had worn one, so he'd attracted loads of positive attention, some of which had come from none other than the very pretty Maya in 11R.

Ravi: She keeps looking at me. What shall I do?
Me: Jeez, Ravioli!! Ask her to dance, obvs! 💃 😵
Ravi: Maybe.

He'd gone a bit quiet since then, so I wasn't sure whether he'd made a move or not. But knowing Ravi, it was unlikely. For an otherwise confident person, he always lost his nerve when it came to girls. Selfishly, I hoped nothing had happened between them – I didn't want to lose my only friend to a new girlfriend. Anyway, he and the others had gone to Cornwall yesterday morning, so if anything *had* happened with Maya, it would be temporarily on hold. In the meantime, I'd amazingly managed to stay off social media and spare myself the FOMO.

Mum put her phone down, walked over to me and rubbed my back. I bristled. We didn't have much physical contact these days, and I was only getting it now because she was about to be rid of me.

'Oh, Piggles, I feel your pain,' she sighed.

No, Mum. You can't feel my pain. Everyone hates me – including me.

'But you know, you should go with an open mind,' she continued. 'You might end up having an *amazing* time.'

Oh pleeeease. I was going to spend two weeks with my super-doofus grandfather who I'd barely had more than a five-minute conversation with since the day I was born. I was NOT going to have an "amazing time": it was going to be the two most boring weeks of my life, *guaranteed*. The total opposite of how my post-GCSE summer was supposed to be.

'You seriously think I'm gonna have an amazing time with the man who used to leave you in the car for hours while he sat in the pub getting wasted? The man who asked to borrow money off Grandma Peggy after he'd left her for someone else?

The man who couldn't bear to give twenty quid to his granddaughter even though he hadn't spent a single penny on her in over five years?'

Mum's new, optimistic attitude towards Grandpa Airhead was baffling – not to mention hypocritical. My whole life, I'd never heard her say one positive word about him . . . until my Cornwall plans collapsed.

She returned to the kettle, twisted her hair up into a butterfly clip and took two cups out of the cupboard. 'He has many, many faults, Ori – that's indisputable. But during the conversations we've had on the phone over the last week or so, he's sounded really keen to spend some time with you. Like I've already said, he might not be around much longer. This could be your last chance to get to know him and learn a bit more about your French roots.'

'*Er, bonjour?* I'm not interested in my French roots! And neither are you – this is all just so you can go to Chicago with Chuck.'

'You're right. I didn't want you to be alone and I didn't want to cancel my trip, so I found a solution – not an ideal one admittedly, but now that we're here, I've realised this is a good thing. The clock is ticking. One day you might look back and be glad you spent some time with your grandad – even if that time wasn't a barrel of laughs. Whatever happens, you'll get something good out of this experience.' She made two cups of tea and put one in front of me. 'Besides, things could be so much worse. Life's chucked a lemon at you – or to be more precise, you've chucked a lemon at yourself – so the best thing to do in this situation is to go make lemonade.'

Make lemonade??? Pass me the spew bowl, *muchacho*.

She must've got that from one of the self-help books piled up next to her bed.

'I mean, who knows what will come your way in the next few weeks? You keep saying you don't know what career path you'd like to pursue in the future, so maybe life's about to show you the way? You know, life has a funny way of—'

'Stop! Please don't tell me to count my blessings, make lemonade or "give thanks to the universe". You've made your point – you don't need to keep repeating yourself.'

'You could go for lovely long country walks, or even take up running! God knows you could do with a bit of exercise in your life – you can't even climb up the stairs without getting out of breath.'

I gave her my most scathing look. *Running?* In your dreams, mother.

'Stop trying to organise my life!'

'I was just—'

'Uh-uh!'

'Going to say—'

'Zip! Stop! Schtum!'

'Fine.' She raised her hands in defeat and reached for her phone.

I groaned as she scrolled. 'Jeez, what's the longest you've ever gone without checking your socials? Thirty seconds?'

'God, I can't win.' She slammed her phone down and exhaled through gritted teeth. 'I'd *love* to have a conversation with you but it's a bit hard when you keep telling me to shut up. And yes, things are really taking off right now, so it's hard not to check my notifications. I'm human, too, for crying out loud!'

I got the feeling she couldn't wait to get rid of me so she could spend all day long checking how many hits her website had got and how popular her latest Instagram post had been. Since trying to launch her own vintage clothes business in her spare time outside of work, she'd become more preoccupied than ever. It was tempting to say this out loud, but it would be like holding a flame to the gas. I felt tears prick at my eyes. I so needed some love and hugs right now but I couldn't bring myself to say so. Instead I just kept doing the opposite – pushing her away, putting her down. What was wrong with me? Why couldn't I just ask for a hug? I wanted her to keep hugging me even if I tried to push her away, but how weird and messed up was that?

Instead I forced back my tears and said, 'By the way, I'm not calling him Grandpa.'

'Oh. What will you call him, then?'

'Claude. It's not like he's ever been much of a grandpa to me, is it?'

The buzzer went before she could argue. 'Fair enough. That'll be him.'

I didn't get up as she trotted onto the landing to buzz him in. While we waited for him to make his way up the communal stairs, Mum leaned back round the kitchen door and grinned at me. 'You can do this!' she whispered, clenching her fist like a football coach.

There was a thump on our front door and Mum hurried downstairs to let him in, muttering "Better late than never" under her breath.

'Hey, sweet cheeks!' I heard him say. 'Sorry I'm late, I took a wrong turning.'

'Hey, Dad. Don't worry, come in.'

'Man, I always forget how many stairs there are in this place.'

'It's good cardio.'

'I knocked on the wrong door,' he said as he plodded up the stairs to the landing. 'Your neighbours seem nice.'

'You did that last time, Dad.'

'Did I? Don't remember that. Give your old man a hug then.'

I watched out of the corner of my eye as Mum gave him a fleeting embrace.

'Well you're lookin' good, sweet cheeks,' he said as they stepped apart and looked awkwardly at each other.

'You, too,' said Mum.

She was clearly being polite. Grandpa Airhead – or Claude, as I'd decided to call him from now on – was dressed exactly the same as I remembered him: sort of like a cowboy but with the wrong style hat. He wore blue jeans, a denim shirt with embroidery on the chest, cowboy boots and a red bandana around his neck. He looked more American than Chuck, for God's sake. And then there was his dodgy baseball cap that didn't work with the cowboy shirt, pensioner sunglasses, and crime-against-fashion ponytail. He obviously hadn't changed his look in decades.

Spotting me in the kitchen, he took off his cap and flipped up the hinges of his sunglasses to reveal his normal glasses underneath. 'Hey Orinoco-pops! How's my lovely granddaughter? Blimey – you've gone pink!' He pointed to my hair as he walked wonkily towards me. His super-strange accent was coming back to me. It was part-Cockney, from having grown up in south London, with a trans-European twang, picked up from years of living abroad.

'Yup, she lopped it all off and dyed it pink in a moment of madness,' sighed Mum. (It was a moment of perfect clarity, *actually*.) 'One for the road?' She nodded towards the kettle.

'Better not. The bladder won't hold out.'

'Newhaven's only half an hour from here – and by the way, you could've stayed here last night, you know?' (Mum was so fake. She'd been so relieved when he'd said he had other plans.)

'Kind of you to offer, babes, but I was visiting an old friend. I'll pass on the tea, ta.' He stood in front of me and looked me up and down. 'Don't I get a hello then?'

'Hello,' I said, doing my best to crack a smile.

'Christ almighty, you've grown.'

'And you've shrunk.' *Oops. That just popped out.*

'Touché, kiddo. But in my defence, that's probably cos of the old hip replacements – I'm a bit wonkier an' all.' He scratched his stubbly chin. 'I like your threads – is that all the rage right now?' He gestured to my shorts, ripped black tights and red Converse boots. 'I remember your mum wearing similar clobber back in the Eighties. Anyway, I hear you've had a bit of a rough time.'

'No offence, but I'd rather not talk about it.'

'No problemo. I've made a superb playlist for the car by the way.'

'You know how to make a playlist?' I'd assumed we'd be listening to Old Man Radio for the next few days. Although I dreaded to think what was on that playlist. Other than being a ladies' man with an appetite for drink and drugs, the only other thing I knew about Claude was that he used to play guitar in a blues band. I didn't know much about "blues" other than it was what old people listened to and was unlikely to be my cup of tea.

'Don't look so surprised, kiddo. I know my Spotifys from my Facebooks.'

'I wouldn't know anything about Facebook – no one my age uses it.' I gulped down my tea. 'Shall we go then?'

'Well, if you're ready?'

'Ready as I'll ever be. I'll just use the bathroom.' I got up and brushed past him, pausing just out of sight on the landing as he and Mum began speaking in hushed tones. I strained my ears.

'Ori's highly sensitive right now,' whispered Mum, 'so just be patient with her. She's upset, really down on herself. Don't take her anti-socialness personally. Just be patient with her, OK?'

'Don't worry. It's old ground. I remember you going through the exact same thing.'

'*Really?* I find that hard to believe, given that you were never around,' snarked Mum. 'Maybe you're getting me confused with one of your much younger girlfriends?' *So much for her pledge to resist making digs at him.*

Claude took a deep breath. 'I'll look after her, don't you worry,' he said firmly.

'Good. Because I *do* worry. She's in a fragile place and you're off on Planet Lobotomy half the time, but short of cancelling all our plans and letting a lot of people down, I can't see any other option.'

'Relax, sweet cheeks. I know I weren't always around back then, but I'm a more sensible, evolved person these days – you can trust me. I'll call you regularly, keep you updated.'

I doubted this would do much to reassure her, as phone calls had never been Claude's strong point.

'Just text me,' she grumbled. 'We don't need to talk every five minutes.'

'Er . . . I'm not sure how to text on this thing. It's new. I'm a bit late to the smart-phone party – I only know how to make playlists.'

'If you can work out Spotify, you can work out how to text. Ori will show you.'

I went into the bathroom and shut the door behind me. There was no escape. In just a few minutes' time, Ori Reynolds, heinous boyfriend-snatcher and reviled social outcast, would begin a two-week sentence in Boomersville County Jail in rural France. This would no doubt be seen by many as a far too lenient punishment considering the seriousness of her crime.

I emerged from the bathroom slap-bang into Mum and Claude who'd wandered out of the kitchen onto the landing.

'All set, Piggles?' Mum ruffled my hair.

'Guess so,' I mumbled.

'Right, let's get the little lady's luggage in the boot.' Claude pointed down the stairs to where my large backpack was leaning against the wall by the door to our flat. 'This it?'

'I can do it,' I said, clomping down the stairs.

'It's all right – a bit of heavy lifting keeps the old muscles strong!' he joked, intercepting me. I climbed back up to the landing while he heaved my bag out of our door and dragged it haphazardly down the communal stairs.

I grabbed my denim jacket from the banister. Mum wrapped her arms around me. 'Keep in touch. I want regular updates.'

'OK,' I said, shrugging her off. She'd be too busy responding to all her precious notifications to worry about updates from me.

'And remember: *water off a duck's back.*' She nodded towards Claude who we could see through the landing window wrestling my bag into the boot of his car, then stretching and rubbing his back. 'If I can survive four years of living with him and six years of random weekend visits, you can survive one or two teenyweeny weeks.'

I gave her a feeble smile and plodded down the stairs to our front door.

'Ori?'

I stopped. 'Yeah?'

'Aren't you forgetting something?'

I plodded back up the stairs and dutifully kissed her on the cheek.

'No, that wasn't what I meant.' She looked at me expectantly.

I frowned. *Passport, wallet, phone, charger, tampons, sun cream . . .* No. I hadn't forgotten anything.

Oh.

I dashed back into the kitchen and grabbed my day bag.

'Well done, Einstein.'

I rolled my eyes as she followed me downstairs and out onto the pavement.

'You know what?' she said, pausing by Claude's car. 'I've got this feeling that by the time you get back, this whole thing will have blown over. Just go with the flow and make lemonade, OK?'

Jesus, woman! Stop going on about bloody lemonade. Make vodka would be better advice.

'All aboard,' said Claude, gesturing to the front passenger door. 'Oh, crapadoodledoo – left me lucky hat upstairs. I'll be back in the twinkle of a fair maiden's eye.' He lolloped back along the pavement and into the building.

'Some things don't change,' Mum muttered under her breath.

I opened the car door and climbed in.

'Have a good time in Chicago,' I mumbled, placing my day bag by my feet.

'I'll bring you back a souvenir,' she winked as I wound down the window and pulled the door closed. 'Once we've visited Chuck's rellies and done a bit of sight-seeing, I'm going to drag him round all the vintage shops. Hopefully I'll be able to bring you back something super-cool and retro!'

Claude arrived back at the car, panting and sweating. 'Cheerio, baby-cakes. Enjoy LA!' He kissed Mum on the cheek, did a few back stretches and climbed into the driver's seat.

'Ready to rock'n'roll, baby doll?' He adjusted his baseball cap, flipped down his sunglass-hinges and pressed the ignition.

Rock'n'roll? The only thing I was ready to do was cry.

CHAPTER FIVE
Cast Away

As Mum waved us off, the dashboard started beeping. I checked my door – it was shut. Then I realised Claude wasn't wearing his seat belt.

The beep grew louder and more urgent. I waited to see how long it would take before Claude took the hint, but he seemed oblivious. I noticed he was wearing hearing aids. Perhaps he couldn't hear the beeping?

'You haven't got your seat belt on,' I said, unable to stand the noise another second.

'Oops.' He strapped himself in and the torture stopped.

As we drove out of Brighton towards the A27, I could see him glancing at me out of the corner of my eye. He looked like he was building up to making conversation, so I put my aviators on and turned away to deter him.

'Check this out,' he said eventually, tapping the screen on the dashboard between us. An eye-watering screech of electric guitar made me jump out of my skin. I put my hands over my ears.

'What the hell?' I winced.

'Sorry. Bit loud. Know who B.B. King is?'

'Nope.'

Claude sighed. 'He's the most important electric guitarist that ever lived – the father of the blues. Man, I can see I've got me work cut out. But that's fine – we got plenty of time and plenty of music.'

Spare me.

'So what do you think of this sexy beast, eh?' He gestured to the slick, teched-up, brand new-smelling interior of his car. Jackson would've been impressed, for sure. Him and his dad were petrolheads – a topic I teased him about endlessly, given that Jackson was more concerned about owning the right four-wheeled status symbol than fighting rising pollution levels.

'It's a car,' I said stonily.

'Not just any car, kiddo – it's the latest hybrid, fresh from South Korea! I'm hoping we can make it all the way to Frenac on electric only – which'll mean charging up at every opportunity, but I've worked out it's doable.'

'Wait, aren't hybrids like really expensive?' I remembered Mum saying she wished she could get one but couldn't afford it. So how could my always-skint grandad afford one?

'They ain't cheap, that's for sure. I promised myself I'd get one if I won my legal case – which I did, a couple of years ago. That's how I was finally able to buy the barn I'd had my eye on for years and start doing it up.'

'A legal case?'

'Long story. Someone tried to rip me off but the judge saw it my way. Talking of pay-outs, I bet Sylvie twenty euros we could make it all the way back on electric, so if we do, don't let me forget to collect my winnings.'

'Who's Sylvie?' I asked, purely out of politeness.

'My girlfriend. My rather *lovely* girlfriend.' The way he emphasised the word "lovely" told me he meant *sexy*. 'She moved to Frenac from Balham last year. Still learning the lingo. She's got a spare set of keys, but we don't live together or nothing.' *Course not.* From what I knew, Claude didn't do serious relationships. According to Mum, he had girlfriends all over Europe, as well as loads of exes in the UK that he liked to keep in touch with.

We turned onto the A27 and Claude put his foot down. I watched as the speedometer swung up to 90mph. If Mum were here, she'd go ballistic. I gripped my seat and clenched my teeth.

'Can we slow down?' I asked.

'Yep. Just overtaking.' He eased off the pedal and caressed the steering wheel. 'Such a smooth drive. Only had her a month – ain't had a chance to see what she can really do yet.'

She?

'Are you talking about the car or have you got an inflatable doll in the boot?' No sooner had I said it I panicked I'd been too rude, but Claude just laughed.

'Boom, boom!' He slapped the wheel and whistled. 'Looks like I got me a live-wire in the passenger seat.'

I pulled out my phone. Hopefully this would signal I was done chatting for now. I considered putting my headphones on, but figured I was better off saving them for the ferry. I would need to pace my anti-social behaviour carefully in order to get away with it. My finger hovered over the Instagram icon. I hadn't opened it since before prom night – a whole week, an achievement I felt pretty proud of – but now my willpower was starting to desert me. Almost immediately Ava's name stared up at me, accompanied by a picture of them all on the train heading for Cornwall: Zac, Ravi, Martha, Daisy – arms round each other's shoulders, peace signs, devil horns, the finger. All the necessary poses to show you're having a good time with your tribe. And there in the middle, bodies pressed together, were Jackson and Ava. Still very much together. And wait – who was that, right behind Ravi? Some girl, her face obscured by Ravi's elbow, but who looked like she was hanging out with them. I read Ava's nauseating caption: *Cornwall here we come! #friendsforever*

A wave of sadness washed over me. They weren't missing me at all. Not even Ravi, judging by the grin on his face. I swiped Instagram away and swallowed hard.

'So your French must be pretty good by now?' said Claude, forcing me to abandon my gloomy thoughts. 'How did the exam go?'

'I haven't studied French since Year Seven,' I said, sliding my phone back in my pocket. 'I did Spanish for GCSE.'

Spanish oral had been one of our last exams. As we'd waited in the hall to be called one by one into the exam room, me and Ava had been trying to warm up by describing our friends and families in Spanish – giggling one minute, panicking the next. When it was my turn to go in, she'd squeezed me tight and wished me good luck. I remembered that hug: the smell of peach-scented body lotion on her skin, her ringlets getting stuck to my lips, the feel of her heart beating. I could feel that hug more intensely now than I did at the time. A pang of guilt pulled at my heart.

'*You didn't do French?*' Claude looked shocked.

'French was over-subscribed so I did Spanish instead.'

'*But you're a quarter French!*'

'No – I'm *an eighth* French.'

He cocked his head to one side while he did the (very basic) maths. 'I'm half; your Mum's a quarter; so yeah, that makes you an eighth. Oh well, be sure to keep up your Spanish then. It's just that, being half-French, you'd think I'd be a hundred per cent bilingual, but I'm not. I can understand most stuff, I just can't express myself as well as I'd like. I wish my mum had insisted we spoke French at home, but we mainly spoke in English.'

'It's not too late to improve,' I said, bored of the conversation already.

'Oh yeah, since I settled in France about ten years ago, the old vocab's been gradually coming back to me, but sometimes I'll be trying to think of a word and a Danish word pops out instead – or a German word. I've lived in too many places. And at seventy-whatever, the old brain ain't what it used to be. You learn something, then you've forgotten it five minutes later.'

I resisted the temptation to tell him that, according to Mum, he'd always been like that, which was why we called him Grandpa Airhead. Instead, we drove on without talking, listening to the racket coming out of his fancy stereo.

'So that took just under twenty-four minutes,' he announced proudly a short while later, as we pulled up behind a long row of cars at Newhaven ferry terminal.

'You were speeding.'

'Me? Never!' He tapped the settings on his screen. 'Got your passport ready?'

I fished my passport out of my bag and handed it to him.

'*Aurélie* Albertine Reynolds,' he said, opening it up to the photo page. 'Now there's a good Franglais name.'

'No one calls me *Aurélie*.'

'That's a shame. It's a lovely little nod to your French roots.'

'It's a lovely little nod to my parents' dodgy taste.'

'You could go by Albertine instead? My mother – *your* great grandmother's name.'

'I go by Ori,' I said firmly, as the car in front moved forward.

'*Yes ma'am.*' Claude saluted me, drove alongside the passport control booth and wound down his window. 'Yeah, hi there!' He flicked up his sunglass-hinges and flashed a sideways smile at the young (attractive) woman in the booth.

'Good morning, sir. Passports please.' She held out her hand.

He passed them over, still smiling. 'Nice day for it.'

'Certainly is,' she replied, studying us before typing into her keyboard.

'Haven't taken this crossing for a while. Do they still do a good fry-up breakfast on board?' He casually dangled an arm outside the window. Oh my God – *he was flirting!* She could only be about ten years older than me! I slid down in my seat.

The woman shrugged. 'I've no idea, I'm afraid.' She handed the passports back with a businessy smile. 'Have a nice journey.'

We pulled away and joined another queue of cars, lining up in front of the ferry.

'So,' said Claude, turning the engine off, 'I should probably run the itinerary by you, plus one or two other details.'

'Go for it.'

'First stop is Mont-Saint-Michel. Hopefully we can persuade Odette to leave her precious zoo and come and watch la Grande Marée, as luck is on our side and our timing couldn't be more perfect.'

'Odette?' I frowned. 'Your step sister?'

'Adopted not step, although I just think of her as my sister. Yeah, anyway, bit of a late addition to the plan, but actually, it's been something I've been meaning to do for years, but I always talk myself out of it. But when you came into the picture at the last minute, I thought to myself, *it must be a sign.*'

'A sign of what?'

'A sign that now is the time to make amends with Odette and have her come stay at my humble abode. We ain't seen each other for nearly fifteen years. And you've never even met her!'

'Actually, I met her when I was three – but I don't remember it.' According to Mum, Odette was the most interesting and eccentric apple on our family tree – an aunt she'd never really got to know and had long lost touch with. 'Apparently it was at Great Uncle Gerard's funeral, but I don't remember it at all.'

'Ah yes, course it was. In fact, that might've been the last time *I* saw her . . .' Claude gazed into the distance. 'It's all coming back to me now. You didn't take too kindly to my guitar solo.'

'What do you mean?' I had no idea what he was talking about.

'I'm not really a eulogy type of guy, so I plugged my guitar into my amp and paid Gerry a tribute in a way he'd have appreciated – he loved his blues, an' all. You was a bit young to appreciate it yourself – screamed your head off. Anyway, Odette don't like coming to England, so it would have to be something major like our brother's funeral to get her over here. I s'pose over the last few years it's been on my mind that me and her ain't getting any younger and we still have a few hatchets to bury.'

'What kind of hatchets?' I asked, mildly curious.

'Just a few niggles. Nothing that . . .' His voice trailed off as he reached below his seat and wrestled out a large road map book of France.

'You said "zoo"?' I asked. 'I remember Mum saying she had, like, five or six cats?'

'Eleven cats, two dogs, a lizard and a rat, apparently.'

Okaaay. That was a lot of pets. Some of which I didn't like the sound of.

He ran his finger down the index then flipped through the pages, passed me the book, and prodded the page. 'She lives here, this little village down the road from Mont-Saint-Michel. Her house is falling down, but you can see the mount from her front garden.'

I studied the map.

'So we're taking a detour?' This was not good news. I just wanted to get to Frenac and get this whole bloody trip over and done with ASAP. An extra stop and an extra passenger – a nutty one at that – was the last thing I needed.

'I take it you've never been to Mont-Saint-Michel?' said Claude.

I shook my head.

'Well, you can thank me later, kiddo,' he said with an exaggerated wink. 'It's incredible. A bucket list must-see.'

'Wait – are we staying the night at Odette's house?'

'Yup.'

My heart sank. I wasn't keen on staying at other people's houses – especially without a lengthy enough heads-up, and double especially if I barely knew them. Other people's houses meant toilets that didn't flush properly, doors that didn't lock properly, pillows that were too thin and the wrong kind of milk.

Claude looked at me. 'Is it the rat or the lizard? Or both? The rat lives in the garden, but I'm not sure what the deal is with the lizard . . . Presumably it ain't on the loose or the cats would get it? Guess we'll soon find out.'

Great. 'Do I get my own room?'

'Negatorai, my pinkydink co-pilot. Sofa for you, spare room for me. By the way, just to warn you: Odette can be a bit blunt sometimes. Don't take it personally – it's just the way she is. Sometimes she can say the profoundest things . . . And at other times she . . . well, she can just be Odette.'

'Can't wait,' I said, not bothering to hide my sarcasm.

'Just don't criticise her paintings. They're a bit "out there". I made that mistake once and . . .' He mimicked a knife slitting his throat. 'And don't ask about our parents either. That topic is best avoided.'

'Anything else?'

'Nope.' He started up the engine and followed the car in front of us towards the ferry.

I wondered why the subject of their parents was "best avoided". I knew virtually nothing about my grandad's siblings, other than Odette was adopted while Claude and Gerard weren't, and I was vaguely aware, from what little Mum had told me over the years, that none of them were very close. There had been fallings-out or something.

And then, from out of nowhere, a long-forgotten piece of information I'd either been told or had overheard many years ago pinged into my memory.

I turned to face Claude as we drove up the ramp onto the ferry, the sea glistening beneath us. 'Is it true that Great Grannie Albertine said "Good riddance" as they were lowering your dad's coffin into the ground?"

CHAPTER SIX

Misery

It turned out Claude's sat-nav wasn't all it was cracked up to be as it kept changing its mind about which route had the least traffic. So it took us several attempts to get out of Dieppe before we finally found the road heading southwest towards Mont-Saint-Michel.

'We could've gone Portsmouth-Cherbourg, but it's all swings and roundabouts at the end of the day,' said Claude, fiddling with his stereo to select some music.

'God – keep your eyes on the road!' I shrieked as we nearly swerved into an oncoming car. 'Just tell me what you want to listen to and I'll find it.'

'Relax, will you? I've been driving for over half a century and haven't killed anyone yet.'

'*That you know of.*'

Claude frowned. 'I think I'd know if I'd killed someone.'

'Not if they died of a heart attack ten minutes after swerving out of your way.' I sensed his irritation and decided I'd better soften my tone. 'Music choice?'

'A bit of Ry Cooder wouldn't go amiss.'

I searched through a long list of names I'd never heard of until I found it.

'Look out for Honfleur,' he said. 'We'll turn off there for a bit of lunch. It's a lovely little seaside town, I think you'll like it.'

'In the meantime, you still haven't answered my question.'

'What question?'

'About your mum saying "Good riddance" when they lowered your dad's coffin into the ground.'

Claude stiffened. 'What exactly was the question?'

God, he was annoying! He knew perfectly well what the question was. '*Is it true that she said that?*' I repeated extra slowly. Perhaps I'd offended him, although it seemed like a fair enough question to me.

'Yeah, it's true.' He kept his eyes on the road.

'Why?'

He didn't answer straight away. Just as I thought the conversation was dead in the water, he eventually spoke. 'My parents' marriage wasn't what you'd call harmonious. The old man always had another woman on the side. Every time she caught him out, he swore he'd never do it again, but he always did. She put up with it, but she lost all respect for him. So yeah, when he died, she weren't too bothered about it.'

'Why didn't she just leave him?'

'It weren't that simple in those days. She was a full-time mum. Never had a job or nothing – Leonard was old-school like that. Wanted to be man of the house, didn't like the idea of his missus bringing home any bacon. Anyway, she had me and my brother to look after and then they adopted Odey.'

'What made them decide to adopt a baby?'

'Odey weren't a baby. She was thirteen when they brought her over from France. It was Mum's idea. Dad weren't keen, but she made him do it. Before the Second World War, the old man travelled to France regularly on business – he imported French perfumes – that's how he met my mum. During the war he joined the resistance in France, helping people escape the Nazi occupation. Odey was the result of an affair between two of his contacts in France. Her dad was killed by the Nazis, after which her mum, Mathilde, ended up hitting the bottle and couldn't cope. So a few years later when Dad found out Mathilde was struggling and mentioned it to Mum, she insisted on adopting Odey. She'd always wanted a daughter and she had a big heart, your great grandmother. Anyway, we tend not to talk about all that stuff cos Odey finds it uncomfortable, so best not bring it up.' The dashboard beeped and Claude squinted at the screen behind the wheel. He pressed the windscreen spray and the wipers sprung to life. 'Remind me to fill up with washer fluid when we next stop to recharge. So, anyway, what bands are you into?'

I had lots more questions, but the way he blatantly changed the subject told me maybe Odette wasn't the only one who found it uncomfortable and I should just leave it there. And maybe that was fair enough, seeing as I had stuff I didn't want to talk about either.

'Honfleur,' I said.

'What type of music do they play?'

'No, *Honfleur!*' I pointed to a sign for the turning.

'Oh! Knackers and piss!' Claude swerved into the outer lane. 'Roger that, co-pilot.'

***

54

Mont-Saint-Michel rose up out of the sea like a mirage in the distance. We pulled over near a random campsite, got out of the car and crossed the road to take a closer look. The landscape was completely flat apart from the mount which jutted steeply out of the mud-flats like a giant walnut whip. It reminded me of the king-sized spot that had erupted on my forehead a few weeks ago in the middle of my exams. A spot so huge that Ava had named it Everest, and charted its mighty rise and decline over the next three weeks, alongside her own chin-based Vesuvius, which had come and gone in about three days (i.e. barely enough time to cause proper misery).

A warm breeze tickled my skin and I inhaled the smell of salt water. This would've been enjoyable if I'd been here under different circumstances, with my friends, with everything the way it was a few weeks ago before I screwed it all up. I felt my stomach lurch with regret. I wasn't sure which was worse – knowing how badly I'd hurt Ava, being rejected by Jackson, or being ignored by everyone else? Actually, I did know which was worse. I could survive being rejected and ignored, but nothing felt more uncomfortable than knowing I'd betrayed my best friend.

I was so grateful Ravi hadn't abandoned me. But how much longer would I be able to count on him as a friend? If he'd gotten together with Maya at the prom, would they become a couple when he got back from Cornwall?

I must've sighed out loud.

'My sentiments exactly,' grinned Claude, squinting in the sunlight. 'Pretty damn special, yeah?'

I held back the tears that were threatening to break free

and forced myself to focus.

'Yeah . . . it's like a fairytale village with a castle on top,' I said. 'Like the Disney logo.'

'Funny you should stay that,' said Claude. 'Cos rumour has it that's where Disney got their inspiration from – only that ain't a castle, it's an abbey. Parts of it are nearly a thousand years old.'

Whatever. Claude pulled his phone from his pocket, tapped the screen and held it to his ear.

'Yeah hi, Odey. We're about fifteen minutes away . . . *Oui . . . Oui . . . À tout à l'heure.*' He put his phone back in his pocket and turned to me. 'Occasionally, a higher-than-usual tide comes in and the whole thing gets cut off. It's called la Grande Marée. Although they've built this bridge now, so you can still get across at high tide. You wouldn't wanna get stuck in the quicksand. Not a good way to cark it.'

I pulled out my phone to take a photo and saw I had a message from Ava. Immediately my heart started hammering as if I was being chased by a gang of thugs. I'd got so used to her frosty silence, I didn't think I'd hear from her ever again. Did this mean she was ready to forgive me? I clicked it open, the tiniest glimmer of hope in my heart.

There's something I need to get off my chest. You keep referring to yourself as an "idiot", saying you made a "stupid mistake". But here's the thing: you're not an idiot, you're a bitch. There's a big difference. Stop trying to make out you've been anything other than calculating and manipulative. You were supposed to be my BEST friend. Trying to steal my boyfriend was bad enough, but passing it off as a "stupid mistake" is bullshit. BTW, me & Jackson are stronger than ever now, so I guess your "mistake" worked out in our favour.

I felt sick. Physically sick. I breathed in deeply a few times to steady my nerves, focusing my eyes on the horizon. She *hated* me. With good reason. I hated myself for doing something so dumb and selfish.

'Better follow doctor's orders and stretch the old spine out,' said Claude, putting his hands on his hips and twisting from side to side. 'I'm not supposed to sit for long periods of time.' He straightened up. 'Right. Shall we rock'n'rollerama?'

I followed him back to the car and climbed in.

'Everything OK? You've gone quiet – not that you were exactly chatty earlier, but–'

'I'm fine.' I was not fine. My hands were shaking. In Ava's eyes I wasn't someone who'd screwed up – I was an evil, scheming bitch and that's all there was to it. I'd never seen myself as a bitch before. Then again, does anyone?

'If you say so.' He switched on the engine and pulled away. The beeping started up.

I looked at him. This would be the *fourth time* he'd driven off without putting his seatbelt on. I'd pointed it out when we'd driven off the ferry in Dieppe, and when we'd got back on the road after lunch in Honfleur. This time I would say nothing.

The beeping grew louder. It was no good, my nerves were already on a knife-edge.

'Can you hear that?' I asked.

'Oopsie.' He grinned. 'Bad boy, Claude!' He pulled the belt

across him, shuffling around in his seat and veering the car left and right.

'*Oh dear God!*' I closed my eyes and prayed.

'No need to look so–'

A deafening honk from an oncoming car made us both jump out of our skins. Claude swerved out the way in the nick of time.

'Shit-a-brick!' he gasped, checking his rear-view mirror and waving an apology to the car behind. 'Just remind me to drive on the right, OK?'

'OK.' My heart was racing. Why didn't Mum warn me what a terrible driver he was? Perhaps she'd forgotten. She probably hadn't been in a car with him in years. Or maybe it was an old age thing? Maybe he was losing the plot? OK, so I hadn't noticed we were driving on the wrong side of the road either, but *he* was the one driving. I was going to have to watch his every move behind the wheel. Be a second pair of eyes on the road.

A few minutes later we pulled up in front of a ramshackle cottage on the edge of a village. The sound of dogs barking greeted us from within a leafy front garden. Crimson roses climbed above the front door and curled around an upstairs window, from where a black cat was peering down at us. It looked pretty idyllic to me.

'Better charge up the old motor while we're here,' said Claude, plugging a long cable into the side of the car. 'Or else we won't get very far tomorrow.'

I glanced up at the black cat in the window. He was eyeing me suspiciously, as if he already knew all about me, and had decided I hadn't quite had enough bad luck yet.

CHAPTER SEVEN

Zootopia

Inside was less idyllic than outside.

The first thing that struck me as we stepped inside the front door was the clutter – it would've made Mum's eyelid twitch. There were bookshelves overflowing with books, stacks of magazines everywhere, old moth-eaten rugs strewn with dog and cat toys. The walls in each room were covered in paintings, sketches and photos, with patches of white paint peeling off in between. Baskets, plants and hats hung randomly from the ceiling and there were cat beds everywhere – on chests of drawers, on the window seat, on the floor.

'May I?' asked Claude, pointing to a socket near the front door and holding up the other end of his cable.

'If you must,' said Odette.

'I must.'

Looking around me, I wasn't sure this crumbly old house had the kind of circuitry needed to power a hairdryer, let alone charge up a car.

We moved on. There was no corridor – each room led to the next. Opposite the front door was a bathroom *with a cat flap in the door.* Through the open door I could see a cat litter tray next to the sink. Maybe this was the cats' bathroom? *Weird.* The next room to the right was an artist's studio, with shelves rammed with paints, paintings and paintbrushes, with more paintings on the floor leaning against the wall. In the middle of the room stood an easel with a half-finished painting of a cat on it. I strained to see the name scrawled in the corner: *O. Zolaste.*

We followed Odette's hunched, skinny frame to the left, through the sitting room, the dining room, and into the kitchen, passing three more cats on the way – one on a window sill, one on a chair and one on the dining room table. Two dogs followed us: a scruffy Greyhound-like one and a smaller, shaggy Dachshund-like one. I patted the Greyhoundy one's head before recoiling at the size of his super-crusty eye bogeys. *Gross.*

'*Thé? Café? Quelque chose d'autre?*' asked Odette.

'You'll have to speak English,' said Claude. 'Ori don't speak French.'

Odette turned round, leaned on her walking stick and studied me through her narrow black spectacles. '*Pourquoi pas?*'

'Why not?' Claude translated, taking his baseball cap off and frisbeeing it onto the sofa.

I explained for the second time that day.

'Spanish?' She pulled a face and turned back towards the kitchen. '*Bof.* If you can speak Spanish, then you can learn French very easily.'

I wasn't sure what to say to that so I said nothing, while Greyhoundy kept nudging me for more head-patting.

'Sylvestre! Saucisse! *Allez dans le jardin!*' Odette pointed in the direction of the garden and shooed the dogs out of the way. 'So, tea? Coffee? Something else?'

I liked her accent – the way she pronounced "th" as "s", so that "then" was *zen* and "something" was *somesing*.

'Just water, please,' I said.

'Same,' said Claude.

'You bring me the bread?' Odette looked expectantly at Claude.

'*Oui, ma sœur.*' He bowed theatrically and handed her a paper bag with a large sesame seed-encrusted loaf in it.

'*Merci.*' She held the bread to her nose, sniffed, and let out a deep sigh. 'It is the only thing I miss from England.'

Claude and I waited outside the kitchen as it wasn't big enough to accommodate more than one person at a time – or one person and a cat, I noted, as Odette gently shooed a skinny grey moggie off the draining board. *Um, hygiene anyone?*

While Claude bored her with details of our journey, I took in the tiny kitchen. There were shelves displaying a collection of all kinds of novelty teapots in the shape of cars or animals or buildings. A variety of pots and pans hung from the wall, while the smallest of cookers slotted into the corner of the minuscule room. Between the pots and pans, cobwebs trailed from the ceiling, and there on the draining board – next to a bowl of cherry tomatoes – sat a clump of fur that threatened to take off in the breeze coming from the open window and land in the food she was preparing. *Nice.*

Odette passed a large bowl of vegetable pasta to Claude

with an instruction in French, then handed the sesame seed loaf and chopping board to me. 'Put it on the table,' she ordered, gesturing to the sunny room next door. *Please*, I wanted to say but didn't.

We placed the food on the table and sat down, just as the sausage dog decided to wee on the floor.

'Oh Saucisse, *mon pauvre!*' she gasped, getting up again. 'Saucisse is very old. He can't help it.'

She reached for a mop in a bucket that was leaning against the wall. I guessed from the convenient location of the mop that Saucisse's accidents were a regular occurrence. Good job the floor was tiled and not carpeted.

'I'll do it,' I said, taking it from her.

'Thank you.' She patted my arm and sat back down. 'You are very ... what is the word? ... Grown up.'

I felt the proud glow of a mature woman stir within me. This was the kind of compliment it would be nice to hear from my mum occasionally.

Odette continued, 'I remember you as a little child. You were three, maybe four. *Mon dieu*, you were monstrous! Screaming, shouting, stamping the foot. I felt so sorry for your mother. I looked at you and I was *so* grateful not to have children of my own.'

I froze, mop in hand. Did I just hear right?

Did she just insult three-year-old me?

Ouch. Ava's rage aside, I don't think I'd ever received such a direct burn from anyone.

Claude rolled his eyes. 'We all flung our toys out the pram

at that age, Odey. Anyway, how many animals currently in the ark?' He winked at me as she poured out glasses of water. With gritted teeth, I finished mopping up the puddle and went to wash my hands in the kitchen.

Odette shrugged. 'Twelve cat, two dog and one lizard. I can never say no to an animal in need of a home.'

I'd clocked the lizard in the sitting room as we'd passed through – in a tank, thank God.

'Claude said you had a rat as well?' I sat back down again and examined the pasta closely for fur.

'Ah yes, Salvador. He lives under the garden shed.' Odette turned to me as I speared a forkful of pasta quills. 'Tell me, why you call him Claude and not *Grandpère*?'

I paused, the fork halfway to my mouth. *Clearly this woman did not hold back.*

'Er, I guess we haven't spent a lot of time together over the years . . .' I said.

'So, just like me.' Odette gave Claude a piercing look through her glasses and gestured to help myself to a slice of sesame seed loaf. 'Personally, I tried to avoid him for as long as possible. But now it seems there's no escape.'

Talk about awkward.

Claude laughed it off. 'But we're making up for that now, aren't we, ladies?' He gave me a playful punch on the arm.

'Did you get on well when you were kids?' I asked Odette.

I sneaked a glance at Claude while she considered the question. He looked tense. 'It took some time,' she replied, inadvertently waving a slice of bread inches above Sylvestre's drooling jaws.

'I was a new arrival – but an older sister, not a younger one. It was strange for them and it was strange for me. Albertine treated us equally, but Leonard . . .' Her eyes hardened. 'Leonard struggled.'

Claude shot me a warning look. 'So, how about we all go watch la Grande Marée later?'

He really had a knack for changing the subject.

'I stay here,' said Odette. 'I can't walk far. I'm eighty years old now.'

I did a quick calculation. That meant she was born during World War Two. If her dad had been killed when she was little and her mum couldn't look after her, she must've had a pretty rough time as a kid – and then to be adopted by a couple where one person wanted you and the other one didn't? Ouch.

I watched as she ate her pasta. She had short, white hair, tied back in a little ponytail, an oval face and a bump in the middle of her nose. Her skin was wrinkled and papery around the eyes, behind her black rectangular glasses. She reminded me of that ancient fashion designer with the leather fingerless gloves.

'I guess all the animals must keep you pretty busy,' I said.

'Yes, they are my angels. I need them and they need me.'

'And her painting keeps her busy, too – right, Odey?' said Claude.

I glanced at the many paintings that hung around the room. There were lots of bold, Picasso-like paintings – of wonky boobs and wobbly butt-cheeks, mainly – plus various paintings of cats and dogs, and lots of abstract panels. There was a large square covered in what looked like lumps of soggy newspaper and splodges of red paint. Another one looked like it was covered in spiky crushed glass. And there was a colourful, sort of rubbery-looking one covered in lots of little circles, which was actually not bad. Not that I'd hang it over my mantelpiece – but maybe in the loo. I squinted my eyes to see what it was made from and shuddered. They were *condoms* – unused ones, thank God.

'Did you do all of these?' I asked.

'Yes, they are mine.'

'They're great,' I said enthusiastically, remembering Claude's warning to be polite about her art. I hoped I didn't sound like I was lying but this was one of those occasions when to be honest would've been rude – not that that had stopped *her* from calling me a monstrous toddler, but in light of my recent screw-ups, this was an opportunity to be kind.

'Sold any recently?' asked Claude.

'One or two. Enough to keep me alive another month.'

He turned to me. 'An *Odette Zolaste* painting used to fetch quite a price back in the day. She used to sell to the likes of Brigitte Bardot and Serge Gainsbourg – not that those names would mean anything to you . . .'

Rude! Of course I'd heard of Brigitte Bardot! As for the other one, fair enough.

Odette mumbled something in French that sounded like she was telling Claude to shut up. I also noticed a black and white photo pinned to the wall of a young woman wearing clown-like make-up and posing like a ballet dancer.

Claude followed my gaze. 'From her performance artist days.'

'That's *you*?' I asked Odette, pointing to the photo.

'*Oui*. A lifetime ago.'

'She was into Dada,' said Claude. 'Used to put on quite a show.'

'What's Dada?' I asked.

'*Bof*,' sighed Odette. 'The opposite of normal. We rebel against conventional, logical society and be silly, make nonsense art . . . You understand?'

'Sounds interesting . . .' *Weird.*

'These days I mainly like to paint animals, my cats in particular.'

'You on Instagram, Odey?' asked Claude. 'That's the way artists promote their work and boost sales these days.'

'Waste of time,' muttered Odette. 'I paint to protect my sanity, not to be rich.'

'It's not a waste of time!' protested Claude. 'I have an artist friend – a *lovely* lady, we went out a few times – she makes a killing thanks to Instagram.'

'An ex-girlfriend of yours?' Odette raised an eyebrow.

'As it happens, yeah.'

'What is her name?'

'It's . . . Oh crap. It's gone. Gimme a minute, yeah? The old noggin does this sometimes.'

'I suppose there are so many, you can't possibly remember them all.' She fixed him with an icy stare. 'Although I should think some are more memorable than others, *n'est-ce pas* . . . ? Some that weren't worth the heartache, maybe?'

I got the impression there was more to this conversation than was being said.

Claude shifted uncomfortably in his chair. 'Come on, sis.

Let's let bygones be bygones, yeah?' He took a sip of water. 'So, yeah, you should get yourself on the old Instagrams.'

She chewed a morsel of bread. 'I won't be around long enough to reap the rewards.'

'How do you know?' he laughed.

'Because I'm dying. One year, two maybe . . . then *bonne nuit, Odette.*'

We all fell silent.

Claude looked around the room, unable to meet her eyes. I glanced down to see Sylvestre peering up at me from under the table. He plopped his head onto my lap, asking me to stroke him, which I did, giving his gunky eyeballs a wide berth.

'Cancer?' he asked.

'*Non.* I am simply old. My body is failing. This doesn't work, that doesn't work. I have this problem, I have that problem.'

'So how do you know you've only got a couple of years left?' Claude challenged her.

'Because it is not rocket science, Claude!' snapped Odette. 'I know my body. I discuss it with my doctor friend – the only person I can trust to be *complètement* honest – and she said yes, I deteriorate slowly. I will not bore you with my long list of conditions.' Odette held out some bread to a patiently waiting cat. '*Viens, mon ange . . .*'

'Yeah, well,' said Claude, staring at his empty plate. 'Doctors get things wrong all the time, Odey. Truth is, they don't know how long you've got. They don't have a crystal ball – they just prepare you for the worst outcome. You can't give up hope. You have to-'

'Shut up, Claude. You underestimate me as always.' Odette stood up and reached for her walking stick. '*Ça va, Saucisse*? You want to make pipi again?' She gestured towards the open front door and shooed him towards it. 'Unlike you, I am not afraid of death.'

Claude looked at her doubtfully. 'You're not planning on . . . er, you know . . . doing anything silly, are you?'

'Tomorrow I get in a car with you, which I believe is very silly!'

I smirked. Clearly Odette had experienced his terrible driving before.

'I'm serious, Odey. You've got plenty left to live for is all I'm saying.'

'I quite agree!' she said indignantly, sitting back down. 'It is hard enough to leave my animals and come to your house *for a week*, let alone leave them permanently! All I'm saying is that when the time comes, I'm ready. I don't *want* to die, but we must all go some time – I accept this. So I hope my end is a good one – not that I will get to choose, but Dadaesque would be ideal.' She winked at me then looked at Claude. '*Tu comprends?*'

He nodded, clearly confused. 'Affirmative, Odey-Wan Kenobi.'

I wasn't really sure what Odette meant either, but I liked the way she spoke her truth. She didn't care whether you got her or not – a bit like her art. I liked that, I realised. Something about her kind of made sense.

I glanced at her as she chewed her pasta. 'Thank you for dinner, Odette. It's really nice.'

'*Je t'en prie, ma chérie,*' she replied with a smile.

***

Later that evening, after Claude and I returned from watching the super-tide creep up around Mont-Saint-Michel, Odette suggested we "sit" in the front garden – as if sitting in the front garden was an activity in itself. I considered excusing myself to go and watch one of the Netflix series I'd downloaded on my phone, but sensed being anti-social probably wouldn't go unnoticed – let alone uncommented on – by Odette.

As I unfolded a flimsy metal deckchair leaning against a garden table, I spotted another two cats sitting beneath a hedge bringing the total I'd spotted so far to seven – one of whom had made me jump by sauntering out of the shower while I was on the loo.

'*Du vin?*' Odette asked me as Claude and I sat down.

At last, something I understood. '*Oui, s'il vous plaît.*'

'*Pas "vous" – "tu".* We are family after all.'

Family. It was true – we were related and part of the same family, but the word didn't feel right. I barely knew this woman.

'A little rosé would go down a treat, cheers, sis,' said Claude, leaning back and untying his ponytail to unleash a mane of greasy grey hair that fell around his shoulders.

While she was inside fetching the wine, I checked my phone.

I had a message from Ravi:

Guess what? Maya's with us in Cornwall. All thanks to you, Oreo!

I stared at his message dumbfounded.

So the space I'd left in our friendship group had been filled already. I'd literally been replaced.

That girl in the picture, obscured by his elbow, that was *her*!

It felt like a kick in the teeth.

With suddenly trembling fingers I replied:

What do you mean "thanks to me"?

Ravi: You made me ask her to dance. We danced (and other stuff) and then I invited her to Cornwall and now she's here.

Me: Really happy for you, Ravioli. Yay! 🐱

Not yay. Not yay at all.

My mind started racing. Who was sharing a tent with who? How far had things gone between them? Were they in love? Arrrrgh! What kind of person was I not to be happy for him? Especially after he'd been so kind to me? Ava was right, I really was a bitch. I *was* happy for Ravi – just slightly less happy at the thought of them all welcoming Maya into the group with open arms. They'd be only too pleased to replace the evil boyfriend-snatcher with someone nice and decent. And how long before Ravi realised that this new version of the group worked way better than the old one? This was not a good development. To be out of the group was one thing, but this . . .

Claude cleared his throat as he searched for a conversation starter. I tried to stuff down my panic and focus.

'What's your drug of choice, then?' He nodded to my phone. 'Instagram? Snapplechat? Twitter?'

Snapplechat?

'Actually I was just going to look at the time-lapse video I shot of the tide coming in just now,' I said.

'Oh. Can I see?'

I selected the video and passed it to him.

'Hey, that ain't too shabby! How d'you do that?'

'Pass me your phone, I'll show you.'

He pulled his phone out of his shirt pocket. I opened up his camera and swiped along the various options.

'Well I'll be damned! So that clever little feature was there all along, right under my nose!'

'Yeah, a bit like your seat belt – just begging to be used,' I replied.

'Very funny, smart-arse.' He marvelled at the hidden powers of his new phone. 'So what does a smart-brained kid like you wanna do when you grow – er, leave school?'

God I hated that question. Why did every single adult feel the need to ask it every five minutes? I didn't have a clue. 'Don't know,' I said.

'Well, what do you *like* doing? What are your passions?'

I didn't really have any "passions" (apart from fantasising about Jackson). I liked hanging out with my friends or watching TV. I liked swimming in the sea, shopping for vintage clothes, watching films and collecting film posters. None of this was worth mentioning as he was after a "future career" type answer. 'I like reading,' I said after wracking my brains. Or at least, I *used* to like reading before school bombarded me with so many boring books for English Lit that I could no longer be arsed to read for pleasure.

'Reading? Me too. Especially sci-fi. Have you read *The Hitchhiker's Guide to the Galaxy*?'

'Nope.'

'I'll lend it to you – you'll love it.'

'OK. Um, maybe I should go help Odette,' I said before he could threaten me with any more books I had no desire to read. I got up and nearly tripped over Sylvestre, who promptly followed me inside, nose always two inches from my leg.

In the tiny, stuffy kitchen, Odette passed me three glasses from a shelf beneath the windowsill. I noticed a black and white photo on the windowsill, partially hidden by a tiger-shaped teapot. It was of a young woman in a 1950s-style dress. She had short, dark hair that curled towards her cheeks, and a confident smile.

'Who's that?' I asked.

'That is Albertine,' she replied. 'Your great grandmother. *L'ouvre-bouteille* is in the drawer. I forget what it's called in English.' She pointed to the bottle of wine she was holding and mimed unscrewing the cork. 'It's a long time since I speak English, so I'm forgetting many things.'

'Corkscrew,' I said.

'*Exactement.*' She hobbled out of the kitchen with her walking stick as I opened the drawer. 'Careful of Maurice!' she added over her shoulder. 'He's also very old, like me.'

'Maurice? Is that a cat?'

'*Non,*' she called. 'Again I forget the word – *merde!*'

'A mouse?' I edged towards the drawer and pulled it slowly open, noticing a thick hammock of cobweb billowing beneath the sideboard.

'Spider!' Odette shouted triumphantly from outside, just as a gargantuan eight-legged beast crept out of the cutlery drawer and scuttled across the sideboard.

I screamed, dropped the glasses, and staggered backwards. The floor simultaneously crunched and squidged beneath my feet and I looked down to find myself standing in a cat litter tray.

'*Ça va, Aurélie?*' Odette's voice came sailing through the window. 'Spider is what I mean. *En français* it is *araignée*. You really must learn French.'

I hoped the glasses weren't expensive ones – or worse, family heirlooms left by Great Grannie Albertine?

'Um, I'm really sorry but I may have broken some glasses,' I called out.

'*Pas de problème!*' Odette called back. She said something to Claude in French, which I hoped wasn't a criticism of me.

'Dustpan's in the cupboard under the sink,' shouted Claude.

'Dustpan – *merde!*' wailed Odette. 'It was on the tip of my tongue!'

I lifted the backs of my shoes up one by one: *bulls-eye left and bulls-eye right.* While I pondered my exit strategy from the island of soiled cat litter surrounded by a sea of broken glass, my phone buzzed in my back pocket. Seeing as I wasn't going anywhere fast, I thought I might as well check it. And if it was Ravi, to try to sound as enthusiastic as possible about his new romance.

But it was just a message from Mum and a notification from Instagram. I checked Instagram first. Ava had posted a photo of a topless Jackson grilling sausages over a firepit. Caption: **How lucky am I?** (Followed by a load of heart emojis.)

Like a swarm of wasps, lust, FOMO, shame and rejection all stung me at the same time. I closed my eyes and steeled myself. Would this ever get any easier?

Reading you loud and clear, Ava. He's *yours*. Property of Ava Etoundi. And he loves you and wants nothing to do with me, so you don't need to worry. I scrolled down to the next picture she'd posted – of Ravi and Maya with their arms round each other. Caption: **#PerfectMatch** (Plus more heart emojis.)

Another dig. She'd suggested a few times that me and Ravi should get together, that we'd make a good couple, but sometimes I got the feeling she only wanted us to get together so we could make a happy foursome with her and Jackson. It wasn't that Ravi wasn't goodlooking, he was – but having known him so long, I guess I just didn't think of him that way. And he obviously didn't think of me that way either. Something about our friendship just worked – it was special, and neither of us wanted to mess that up.

Anyway, while I knew I deserved them, I wasn't sure I could handle any more passive-aggressive Instagram posts. I licked a sesame seed stuck to my knuckle and was about to put my phone away when I spotted Sylvestre watching me from the kitchen doorway, his tail wagging like an out-of-control metronome. I glanced at his eye crusties, then at the sesame seed-covered chopping board by the sink. Wait – was that a sesame seed I'd just swallowed or . . . ?

Trying not to retch at the thought of what I'd probably just eaten – let alone what I'd just trodden in – I took a deep breath and read Mum's message.

Just boarding the plane for Chicago. Call you when I get there. Love you Piggles. Remember, when life throws you lemons, make . . . !! 🍋 xxx

But life wasn't just throwing me lemons. It was throwing me very clear messages that I was getting what I deserved. While my friends were all having a brilliant time camping in Cornwall, I was stranded in a cat litter tray, tearful and alone, with two old fossils who I had absolutely nothing in common with.

CHAPTER EIGHT

Dirty Grandpa

It was a relief to be relegated to the back seat. This way I wouldn't have to make as much conversation with Claude. On the other hand, I wouldn't be able to monitor his terrible driving either and could end up mangled to death in a car crash. If I died, I wondered, would anyone come to my funeral? Would Ava feel in the slightest bit sad, or would she be relieved that I was no longer around?

'Did you pack the brown case with my brushes and paints?' asked Odette, sounding panicked as Claude started up the engine and pulled away.

'What brown case?' He slammed on the brakes and Odette looked like she was about to have a heart attack. 'Just kidding, sis. Relax, will you? Your captain has everything under control.'

Odette gave him a scathing look and exhaled slowly.

'So how long has Osman been your deputy zoo keeper?' asked Claude, as we followed the road away from Mont-Saint-Michel, the island shrinking behind us.

'Since he arrive in the village,' replied Odette. 'He's a good friend. He takes Saucisse et Sylvestre to his place and his son will come every day to feed the other *animaux*.'

'What about Maurice the spider?' I mused.

'Maurice can look after himself. You know he has lived with me for three years?'

Three years? Did spiders even live that long? Ugh. I shivered at the memory of yesterday's gross experiences. My heart rate still hadn't returned to normal after a night spent on red alert looking out for Maurice. Meanwhile, my Converse still felt contaminated with cat poo despite scrubbing them with disinfectant. And I'd just about managed not to puke when the leftover sesame seed loaf reappeared on the table this morning at the same time as Sylvestre reappeared under it.

'I try to nurture *all* the creatures that live with me,' said Odette. 'Maurice has the right to live in peace as much as Saucisse, Sylvestre and the cats. That is why I don't touch his webs.'

'Very admirable,' said Claude, glancing at me in the rear-view mirror and trying to keep a straight face.

'You laugh at me, Claude, because you think these creatures are somehow less important than you on this planet. How very arrogant.'

'I'm not laughing at you!' protested Claude. '*Au contraire*, sis, I think it's one of your most endearing qualities.'

'Patronising fool.'

'I'm not patronising you, I'm trying to pay you a compliment!'

'So did you become close to Albertine?' I asked Odette, remembering the photo I'd spotted on the windowsill and butting in before things got any more heated in the front.

The atmosphere seemed to thicken anyway.

'Yes,' she said after a slight pause. 'We became very close. She was a good mother to me.'

'But you didn't feel close to Leonard?' I could practically feel Claude bristling.

'Let's just say I did not respect him and he did not respect me.'

Claude grumbled something in French to her to which she grumbled something unapologetic back.

'So how old were Claude and Gerard when you moved in with them?' I asked, determined not to be put off by any incomprehensible grumblings.

'*Bof* . . . Claude was eight, so Gerard was six.'

'That must've been weird, suddenly having a big sister . . . ?' I asked Claude.

'Yeah, you could say that. Right, time for some music.' He reached for the stereo.

'We are *talking*,' said Odette, batting his hand away.

From the stony look on his face, I decided to put my questions to Odette from now on.

'So did you go to the same school?' I asked.

'No. I went to a girls' school. I did not fit in.'

'How come?'

'Not British enough,' she said over her shoulder. 'I couldn't speak the language, and by the time I could . . . I still didn't fit in.'

'Odey was a bit of a character,' Claude chipped in. 'She were different. She said what she thought rather than what people wanted to hear.' He grinned at her as she narrowed her eyes back at him. 'As any self-respecting artist would,' he added quickly.

'Like what?' I asked, intrigued. 'Give me an example.'

'Well, she refused to recite the Lord's Prayer in assembly and would sing deliberately out of tune . . . What were your other offences, sis? There was no end of letters being sent home, I remember . . .'

Odette shrugged. 'I asked too many questions. It was seen as challenging authority rather than using my brain. School is not always the best environment for creative people.'

'Of course it's probably very different now,' said Claude. 'You like school, Pinkster?'

'Not really. They have dumb rules like having to wear white socks without a speck of colour on them. I mean, what's the point of that?'

'Well the point is that uniform is supposed to make you all look the same, create equality . . .' said Claude.

You don't say. 'Yes, I know that, thank you. No need to mansplain.'

'I'm not saying I agree with it!'

'What is "mansplain"?' Odette asked me.

'When a man explains something to a woman that she already knows.'

Odette cackled. '*Mansplain. J'aime ça.*'

'Lord have mercy,' mumbled Claude. 'Surrounded by flippin' feminists . . .'

'Relax, *mon frère*, we are just joking.'

'Oh, that's good to know, Odey, cos I think the last time I tried to joke with you, your sense of humour had done a runner.'

'If you're talking about Gerard's funeral, your timing was extremely bad.'

I felt like I was watching a tennis match, my head pivoting from Odette to Claude and back as the rally gathered pace.

'Well his wife's speech was an utter load of bollocks. All that rubbish about how he followed his dreams – he didn't. He did the absolute bloody opposite. She was talking crap.'

'So what? It was not the time or place to disagree. You let your jealousy get the better of you.'

'And you *weren't* jealous of him?' Claude gave her an incredulous look.

'For a long time yes, but what is the point? Nothing changes, so I let go. You embarrass yourself that day by acting like a child.'

'What did you do, Claude?' I blurted excitedly from the back seat. Other people's dramas were so much more enjoyable than having your own.

Claude spun round to look at me as if he'd completely forgotten I was there.

'Eyes on the road!' I yelled as we veered into the inside lane.

He quickly faced forward and straightened up. 'Never you mind,' he sighed wearily. 'In the meantime, we need to talk about the *Grand Opening*.'

A loud beep made us all jump as a car overtook us, the driver's middle finger extended towards Claude.

'Shove it up your anal passage, arsehole!' he shouted, returning the gesture.

'What *Grand Opening*?' I asked. 'Grand Opening of what?'

'The barn, *remember*? I told you yesterday.'

'I've no idea what you're talking about. You only told me we were picking up Odette and taking her with us to your place. You never mentioned anything about a *Grand Opening*.'

'Didn't I? Well maybe it was Odey I was telling.'

'I don't know what you're talking about either,' said Odette.

'Well I told someone!' said Claude, exasperated. '*Anyway*,' he inhaled deeply, 'I've scheduled a big party for next weekend to celebrate the opening of my barn as a public space for community events, particularly performing and recording music. The local community are all invited, and there'll be lots of live music, food, dancing, et cetera, et cetera. And you can both help me get the place ready beforehand – Odey, you can help with the food if you feel up to it, and Ori, you can just generally pitch in.' He started to sound a bit more cheerful again.

'When you say "pitch in", you mean like hanging bunting and blowing up balloons and stuff?' I asked.

'Oh possibly – didn't think of that.'

'Well, what did you mean then?'

'Painting the walls mainly, clearing the garden of rubble ... There's a wall that needs building, and some decking needs varnishing too. I've got a list somewhere.'

WHOA THERE! Rewind!

Clearing rubble ... ? Building a wall?

'I don't know how to build walls.'

'Fear not, Pinkydinks. I'll show you what to do.'

You have to be kidding.

As if "going on holiday" with two bickering Boomers wasn't depressing enough, it turned out I'd unwittingly signed myself up for the super-fun holiday activities of bricklaying and rubble-clearing. I hadn't uploaded a picture to Instagram since before "the incident" –now it looked as if my Insta-life wouldn't be returning to make anyone green with envy for quite some time. Hopefully my online absence would at least give me a sophisticated air of mystery. *For all they knew,* I could've stumbled across Timothée Chalamet's latest film set in rural France, found work as an extra, and quickly become his girlfriend – and was *so* preoccupied with all things Timothée, that I hadn't even noticed I'd lost my phone. I indulged in this fantasy as we drove, until my mind went off at a tangent designing the dress for our beach-side wedding. I didn't even believe in marriage (no one in my family had pulled off the till-death-do-us-part bit – except maybe Great Grannie Albertine, and she was only too pleased to see him go), but I felt I could probably make an exception in Timothée's case.

After stopping at a service station to charge up the car and visit the loos, I climbed back in the back seat and was about to check my phone when a twenty-something woman with bright red lipstick, cream-coloured flares and an afro climbed in next to me, making me jump out of my skin.

'*Who are you?*' I squeaked, wondering if I'd got in the wrong car.

'Céline,' she said, holding out her hand. 'You are Claude's granddaughter?'

'Er, yes?' I inhaled a lungful of sweet floral perfume and suddenly felt like a scruffy, fashionless blob in the presence of an immaculately dressed supermodel. 'Are you a friend of Claude's?' Had the dopey doofus forgotten to mention we were picking up yet another passenger?

'*Non*, I just met him in the shop,' she said in a breathy French accent. 'He asked me if I wanted a lift.'

Of course he did.

'Are you like, hitch-hiking then?'

'No – my car broke down, so I'm calling a taxi in the shop there and Claude did not have enough money for the coffee machine so I give him a Euro. Then he said he could give me a lift. He is a *very* kind man.'

And you are a *very* attractive woman. Dear God, I have the *creepiest* grandad. The *only* reason he'd offered her a lift was because she looked like she'd just walked out of a *Vogue* photo-shoot. Anyone less blessed in the looks department he wouldn't have bothered with.

'He could've been *anyone*,' I blurted. 'How did you know he wasn't trying to abduct you?'

'He told me there are two other passengers – his granddaughter with pink hair and his older sister with the walking stick. Before I got in the car, I wait and watch you go in first.'

Hmm. Fair enough. Still, how did she know I was his granddaughter? For all she knew, he could've been using me as bait to lure in other young women. God, I was starting to sound like my mother.

'I like your hair,' said Céline. 'The pink is very pretty.'

'I like yours, too,' I said. Her perfume, on the other hand, was overpowering. I wound down my window for some fresh motorway air as the Boomers heaved themselves back into the car.

'Céline, this is Odette and Ori. Everyone, this is Céline,' said Claude, putting his coffee in the built-in drinks holder and nodding at Céline. 'Flipping coffee cost me an arm and a leg and a left testicle,' he grumbled. 'Remind me not to stop here on the way back – I'd rather hang on to my right gonad.'

For the love of God, please stop referring to your man-fruits – even metaphorically.

While he was recounting the outrageous prices of everything in the shop, my phone started buzzing.

Jackson was calling me. What on earth did he want?

Had he finally worked up the courage to admit he had feelings for me? Or was he going to give me grief? I hovered my finger over the "accept call" button, wishing I had the strength to shove the phone back in my pocket unanswered, but of course I didn't.

'Can you give me a minute?' I asked Claude, getting back out of the car.

'Jackson,' I said, walking away from the car and loitering next to an overflowing bin.

Silence.

'Jackson?' I repeated a little louder.

Still silence.

Oh, I get it. *Really mature.*

'Seriously? Are you trying to freak me out? Cos that's really unoriginal, you know. It's what stalkers do, actually. Seriously uncool.' I was about to hang up when he spoke.

'*Ori?*'

'Yes, what do you want?'

'What do you mean what do *I* want? *You* called *me*.'

'No I didn't. *You* called *me*.'

Silence.

'I seriously wouldn't have the guts to call you,' I said. 'You and Ava have made it quite clear you don't want anything to do with me.'

'I must've butt-dialed you then.'

Yeah, right.

'Well now you've got me on the line, is there anything you want to say to me?' I said, anger taking me by surprise. 'Anything you'd like to add to Ava's verdict? Do you think I'm an evil, calculating bitch, too?' My voice wobbled and I felt fresh tears coming.

'No, I don't,' he replied. 'I don't think you're a bitch.'

'I know I screwed up. I hurt Ava and I put you in an awkward situation. I wish I could rewind and erase that day from ever happening. I feel so embarrassed.'

'It's fine. Let's just forget about it.'

'Really? So, can we be friends again . . . ?' A glimmer of hope lit up my heart. If Jackson could forgive me, hopefully so would Ava.

At that moment I heard Ava's voice in the background.

'I've got to go . . . *It's no one, babe – wrong number.*'

Then the line went dead.

CHAPTER NINE

Johnny English Strikes Again

I noticed Claude glance down at the smooth, bare legs of the waitress as she put our pizzas on the table in front of us.

He gave her the same side-smoulder he'd used on the woman in passport control. '*Merci* – this looks delicious!'

'*Mon dieu, stop!*' groaned Odette, as the waitress retreated back inside the restaurant. 'You are not Clint Eastwood anymore, Claude. Keep your eyes on your food.'

'What do you mean? I was just admiring this fabulous view!' he laughed, nodding towards the towering fortress on the other side of the street. 'Whatcha make of that chateau? Pretty amazing, yeah?'

We were in Amboise, a town on the River Loire. After dropping Céline off near the station, we'd driven round in circles trying to find the self-catering apartment that Claude had booked online. It turned out to be on the outskirts of town, on the ninth storey of a tower block overlooking an industrial estate. Odette had not been impressed.

'Our apartment may have a view of a warehouse loading bay, but at least we get to eat dinner looking at *that*!' Claude looked very self-satisfied. He had his dinner, his view, and a pretty waitress who was doing her best to put up with his flirting, so I guess he'd reached peak happiness.

'Anyway,' he continued, 'before we set off for Frenac tomorrow morning, I thought we could pop down the road to Chenonçeau, because the chateau there, which is built on a bridge, is even *more friggin' amazing*. Odey, whatcha reckon?'

She pulled her "*bof*" face.

'Ori?'

'I'm not that fussed about castles to be honest.'

Claude's eyes bulged. Clearly this was a difficult concept for him to get his head around. '*Not that fussed about castles? Not interested* in buildings that were built hundreds of years ago, before electricity, running water and *smartphones*? Buildings where boiling oil was poured from turrets onto enemies' heads and prisoners were tortured in dungeons?'

Buildings where ogres fought dragons and princesses were held prisoner by Lord Farquaad or an evil witch?

'If I was an eight-year-old boy, I'm sure I'd find it *fascinating*,' I snarked, taking a humongous bite of pizza and deliberately chewing with my mouth open just to wind him up.

'Chenonçeau was part of the boundary between Nazi-occupied France and the free zone during the Second World War,' Claude lectured. 'That don't interest you?'

Odette fake-coughed. *'Free zone?'*

'I beg your pardon, sister. Between Nazi-occupied France and the *so-called* free zone, controlled by the *collaborating* Vichy government. You done history, Orinoko?'

'Geography,' I replied, my mouth still full of pizza. I'd literally bitten off more than I could chew and was concentrating on not choking to death.

Claude frowned. 'So how much do you know about World War Two?'

As if I hadn't undergone enough examinations lately, Grandpa Airhead seemed to think I needed further testing.

'Hitler started it,' I said bluntly – and I was going to leave it there, but sensed I'd only be subjected to more grilling. 'We did World War Two in Year Eight, so I'm a bit rusty on it.'

'Please tell me they taught you about the rise of fascism? The Nazis? The communist revolutions in Russia and China? The Holocaust? Surely you learned about the Holocaust?'

'Of course!' I said. Why was he being so judgey towards me? I felt like I was under attack when I hadn't done anything wrong. 'We watched footage, wrote essays about it and everything.' It wasn't the kind of thing you forgot in a hurry.

'Good. Otherwise what's the point of education?'

'Of course we learnt about it,' I said defensively. 'We watched a documentary – the whole class found it shocking! Most of us were in tears.'

'*Ça va, chérie*,' said Odette, patting my arm. 'Shut up, Claude. She is not in charge of what they learn in school!'

Emboldened by Odette's support, I decided to give Claude a taste of his own medicine. 'Tell you what we *didn't* learn about, though – British colonialism. The atrocities committed by the British all over the world from Africa to Australia, or the slave trade ... So yeah, I guess there are still a few gaps in the national curriculum.'

Odette's lips crept into a smile. 'Excellent point, *chérie*.'

Claude reluctantly agreed. 'Yes, good point. I hadn't thought of that.'

Yeah, put that in your pipe and chew it, Grandpa Airhead. Or smoke it or whatever. I mean, how come old people always assumed that kids knew nothing while *they* knew everything? They didn't! They were just as ignorant as young people, but usually about totally different things – such as the fact our planet was in the middle of a sixth mass extinction. 'While we're talking about education,' I said, feeling on a roll, 'maybe you should sign up for geography GCSE and learn about how much damage Boomer capitalist lifestyles have done to the planet?'

'That's an issue I'm very aware of, as a matter of fact,' said Claude, taking a sip of his lager shandy. 'Hence the goal to only use electric to charge the car. And I haven't bought a new item of clothing in over a year. How's your relationship with fast fashion?' He narrowed his eyes at me.

'I don't have a relationship with fast fashion. I buy everything second hand from the internet, charity shops and kilo sales.' I pointed at his pepperoni pizza. 'When are you giving up meat then, Claude? A bit pointless having an electric car when you're still pumping out CO_2 by supporting the meat industry, isn't it?'

'I've already cut down my meat consumption *a lot*, actually. How much unnecessary data do you upload to social media platforms?'

What?

Claude looked triumphant. 'You could melt a solar system with the carbon emissions generated by Gen Z's addiction to social media and the data storage they use.'

'I'm not as into social media as you like to think I am,' I lied. 'God, is he always this annoying?' I asked Odette.

'Most of the time,' she sighed.

'And has anyone ever told you to eat with your gob shut?' Claude snapped.

'Nope.' I stuffed an entire wedge in my mouth and chomped away, the crust poking out for all the world to see. Claude looked away in disgust.

As we finished our food in silence, my attention drifted until I found myself looking at a boy – a *hot* boy – who was staring straight at me from a few tables away. He was sitting with an older couple – his parents I'm guessing – and while the waitress was clearing their empty plates away, Hot Boy was smiling at me and most definitely giving me the eye. I wiped my mouth with the serviette. I'm guessing he hadn't witnessed my open-mouthed chomping or he'd have had a different expression on his face.

I felt myself shiver. *Plenty more fish in the sea*, Mum had promised me. *Yeah*, I'd replied, *and most of them are sharks, eels or blobfish*. But here was someone half-decent, communicating with his eyes that if only he and I could sit together on a separate table, life would instantly become more interesting. I sat up straight, touched my hair into place and returned his smile.

'You still with us, *Aurélie*?' asked Claude.

'Mmm?' I snapped back to reality. 'It's *Ori* – not *Aurélie*.'

'So we've agreed we'll make a quick detour to Chenonçeau in the morning before setting off for Frenac.'

I gave him the thumbs up. *Whatevs.*

'And please,' begged Odette, 'No more passengers with toxic perfume.'

'She smelt all right to me,' grinned Claude.

'You only give her a lift because you want to sleep with her.'

Odette was right, but *eeugh.*

'Her car had broken down, *I was being kind.*'

'If she was fat, old, or a man, you would offer a lift?' Odette demanded.

'Of course!'

'Bah!' She batted away his protests.

'Well, I feel quite hurt by that.' Claude took out his wallet and signalled to the waitress for the bill. 'So much for random acts of kindness.'

'You could always prove us wrong and offer a lift to someone you *don't* fancy,' I suggested, stealing a crust from Claude's plate.

'*Exactement,*' agreed Odette.

Claude looked like steam was going to start billowing from his nostrils. Perhaps it was time to back down. I turned to exchange more flirtatious glances with Hot Boy, but disappointingly, he and his parents had gone.

'Oh shit-a-doodle-dandy,' blurted Claude, standing up and turning out his pockets. 'I've lost the keys to the apartment.'

Odette and I looked up at him. 'You probably left them in the car?' I said.

He crossed his fingers. 'Let's flippin' hope so.'

This was total madness.

My donut-brained grandad, who refused to wait for the owner of the apartment to return our call and tell us where to get a spare key, had decided the best plan was to break in.

'You two wait here and see if the owner calls back,' he said, handing me the car key as I helped Odette out. 'Remember to lock it.'

'But how will you break in?' I asked, imagining him wrenching the door open with a crowbar.

'Trust me,' he winked. 'I've done this before.'

'Yes, he is a professional loser of keys,' sneered Odette, as we watched him swagger towards the main entrance and press the code into the intercom. The door opened and Claude gave us a thumbs up before disappearing inside.

'His mother gave him his first door key when he was nine and he's been losing them ever since,' she explained. 'He is the Bermuda Triangle of small everyday objects and large sums of money. *Even people.*'

'People?' *Okaay* . . . That sounded ominous. 'What do you mean *people*?'

Odette bit her lip. 'It was a long time ago. It doesn't matter now.'

'Did he murder someone?'

She gave a wry smile. 'Murder? *Non.* He stole.'

Stole? What was she on about? *Stole who?*

I was about to press her for more details when I looked up and recoiled. 'Christ on a pogo stick!'

Odette followed my gaze. '*Qu'est-ce qu'il fout?*' she shrieked, stumbling backwards into the car. I slipped my hand behind her and propped her back upright.

'When he said he was going to "break in", I thought he'd meant by the front door!' I gasped.

'Me too. *Quel IMBÉCILE!*'

We stared up at the ninth floor with our jaws wide open, as Claude clung to the railings of a neighbouring apartment's balcony with one hand and strained to reach our balcony's railings with the other.

'I can't watch!' She shielded her eyes and clutched my arm. 'He is a fool but I don't want him to die!'

The owner of the neighbouring apartment stood behind him, her hands pressed to her mouth in horror as Claude's foot left her wall and dangled momentarily in the hair-raising gap between the two balconies. My heart hammered in my chest as he hung there, suspended in mid-air like a spider in a web.

I guessed the gap was a metre wide, and it was a good thirty-metre drop. Claude, who had the flexibility of a concrete lamp post, now had to twist his torso around to face our balcony, grab the railings and pull his body across. One false move and it was curtains.

'*Oh mon dieu!* He's going to die!' Odette croaked, tightening her grip on my arm as I sucked in my breath.

Finally Claude's left foot joined his right on the wall of our balcony. Now all he had to do was lower himself from the wall to the floor – an easy-peasy little jump for a sixteen-year-old parkour enthusiast, not so much when you're a seventy-five year old with two hip replacements and a dodgy back.

'He's OK,' I said, patting Odette's arm. 'He's nearly done it.'

In a move that seemed to take an eternity, Claude dropped down from the wall and safely onto the floor of our balcony, eventually letting go of the railings. When he'd got his breath back, he leaned over the balcony, gave us a heroic salute, then slid the door open and vanished inside.

Odette let out the longest sigh and leaned back against the car as if she was about to pass out.

'Are you OK?' I asked, holding on to her in case she actually did pass out.

'*Oui, ma chérie.*' She squeezed my hand. 'If I die of a heart attack tonight, do not be surprised. And do not feel sad. It would be the best gift that useless imbecile ever give me.'

She smiled and I laughed, although I sincerely hoped she was joking.

'Don't worry. If anything happens to me, Osman will take care of the animals. I have plans in place.'

I looked at her nervously. 'Plans?'

'Why do you look at me like that?' Odette looked bewildered. 'Of course I have plans! Death is inevitable for us all, so it is good to be prepared. At my age in particular, it is wise to get your affairs in order, is it not?'

'I guess so.'

'Sleepwalking is for fools.' She glanced up at the balcony. 'Time passes so quickly, *Aurélie*. Don't waste it. You must decide what is important and what is not.'

Her words prodded my conscience and I thought of Ava.

'Every day we are alive is a blessing. Of course I didn't

always feel that way, but now I try to remember this.' Odette looked at me and frowned. 'You are OK?

'Yeah, fine.'

All this talk of death was making me feel pretty nervous. Either one of the oldies could cark it at any moment – one through frailty, one through stupidity. What would I do? How would I get their bodies home? And there was a fair chance all three of us would cark it thanks to Claude's bonkers driving. Talk about stress – as if I didn't have enough of that to deal with already.

'Anyway, I guess we might as well go up and join him,' I said, checking to make sure we hadn't left anything valuable in the car. 'Is that yours?' I pointed through the rear window at a scrunched-up item of clothing in the corner of the boot. Odette shook her head.

I opened the boot and peered closer – *Claude's jacket.* As I held it up, something jingled in an inside pocket. Odette raised an eyebrow as I burrowed my hand inside and pulled out a set of keys with a castle-shaped keyring.

We exchanged looks of disbelief.

'*I thought he looked in the boot?*' I said.

'*Bof,*' said Odette. 'Not with his glasses on, evidently.'

Grandpa Airhead had lived up to his name once again.

I locked the car and guided her towards the main entrance, praying neither of them died of a heart attack before the day was over.

An hour or so later, I lay in bed staring at my phone while Odette used the ensuite bathroom. I was gutted not to have my own room, but it could've been worse – at least Claude wasn't sharing with us.

I'd written a reply to Ava's message but couldn't decide whether to send it or not. I took a deep breath and read my words again:

> You're right, I acted like a bitch. I liked Jackson and I was secretly hoping you'd break up with each other someday soon. That was selfish and dishonest of me. But how do you tell your best friend you've got feelings for her boyfriend? How do you be honest about that without causing hurt? I know I could've handled it better than I did, but I swear I never planned to kiss him that night — only to spend a bit of time on our own talking, for me to work out if maybe he liked me too or whether I was kidding myself. Turns out I WAS kidding myself, and I found out the hard way. I'm so sorry I hurt you. I know you'll never forgive me, but we all make mistakes. I've learned an important lesson. I'm genuinely glad you and Jackson are stronger than ever.

I exhaled slowly. I felt like I'd written a heartfelt apology. And apart from the very last line – which was something I hoped to feel soon – it was all true. That was the best I could do right now. I knew it wouldn't make any difference, but what more could I do? I'd ruined my friendship and broken people's trust in me. I would just have to suck it up. For the foreseeable future, I'd have to live with people judging me and thinking I was a bad person. I'd have to live with not liking myself very much.

I glanced one more time at my reply and pressed send. I was damned if I sent it, damned if I didn't, so what the hell.

Next I decided to say hi to Ravi, and to try to sound like a positive, supportive friend – happy for his new romance. Which I was. Or at least I absolutely would be – in time, once I'd got used to all the changes in my social life.

Me: Hey Ravioli. How's it going in Cornwall? Hope you're having fun. Is Maya enjoying it?

I waited for the bubbles of an instant reply but none came. I tried to push away my simmering worry that any day now he'd join the others in rejecting me.

Get a grip and have faith, Ori.

He was obviously busy. What kind of busy, I wondered? Busy hanging out with the group or busy hanging out with Maya? I pictured them all huddled round the campfire, laughing and joking, making the kind of memories you treasure forever – without me. Then I pictured Ravi disappearing into a tent with Maya. I tried to expel both images from my mind. Not helpful.

The bathroom door opened and Odette shuffled out, wearing a linen night shirt that revealed her pencil-thin legs and knobbly feet.

'Was I awful to Claude earlier?' She sat on her bed and manoeuvred herself under the covers.

I put my phone down. 'No. He's such a womaniser. You called him out on it.'

'I what?'

'You pointed it out to him. He needs to know. He left Grandma Peggy for another woman when my mum was little. He's never owned his shi—' I searched for words she was more likely to understand. 'He's never admitted he's hurt people.'

At least I'd managed to admit to my mistake. I may have got a lot of things wrong, but I'd had the balls to acknowledge my wrongdoing ... Hadn't I?

Odette stared at a framed oil painting of Amboise Castle hanging on the wall at the foot of our beds.

'Your Grandma Peggy was a nice lady.'

I had no memories of Grandma Peggy – she'd died the same year I was born. But Mum had been very close to her.

'Did you know her well?' I asked.

'*Non.* We did not have much in common. I did not make an effort to know her. Not because I did not like her, but . . . *c'est compliqué.* Claude and I were always fighting, so Peggy and I did not have much opportunity to become friends. He could never see the truth. Still doesn't want to see the truth!'

'The truth about what?'

'*Bah* – everything!' She threw her arms up in the air. 'That he has done some selfish things . . . Jacqueline and I were partners – not "friends" as he liked to call us. That he is always so frightened of relationships, that our father was not some great hero ...' She more or less spat the last few words out. 'But there's no point telling him. He doesn't listen. He doesn't join the dots...' She turned out the bedside light. '*Bonne nuit, chérie.*'

'*Bonne nuit.*'

I lay back on my pillow and took in what she'd just told me. So, Odette was gay or bi; Claude was frightened of relationships (not exactly a revelation); and Great Grandpa Leonard "was not a great hero" . . . whatever that meant? Why was he "not a great hero"? If he helped fight in the resistance, it meant he helped save people's lives, right? He *resisted* the Nazis; he chose to be on the right side of history. So, surely he must've been an OK guy?

And was she implying Claude didn't take her relationship with her girlfriend seriously? For all his faults, I hadn't heard him say anything homophobic – *yet*. I wondered how long Odette and Jacqueline had been partners for – and whether Jacqueline was still alive?

It seemed the Boomers had some skeletons in their closets. And if anything was going to make this trip less boring, it would be finding out what those skeletons were.

I turned my light off and was trying to use the rhythmic sound of Odette's gentle snoring to send me to sleep when my phone buzzed.

Ravi! I felt a surge of relief.

Ravi: All good here, Oreo. Weather's gone a bit crap. Tent nearly blew away this morning. Having great fun though – of course, would be even more fun if you were here. How's it going with Grandpa Airhead?

Me: Nightmare. He thinks he's James Bond. And now we have another passenger, his sister, Odette. She's a bit mad but I kind of like her. BTW, I've just sent another apology to Ava. Let me know if you see any signs of her hating me slightly less.

Ravi: Sure. She's not been in the best mood. Jackson spends all his time trying to cheer her up. She's paranoid he's going to dump her.

Me: God, it's all my fault. I wish I wish I WISH I hadn't made a move on him. I'M SO STUPID!!!

A few seconds went by. Was Ravi restraining himself from agreeing with me? Then:

Do you still like him?

I paused and thought for a minute. Did I? Yes. Yes and no. I don't know. Yes, I still liked him but he denied kissing me back, and that pissed me off. And not only that, but there were times in the last few months when I was sure he'd been flirting with me – or why else would I have had the nerve to kiss him? Or had I just imagined those moments? Gah! I was tired of thinking about it. I'd made a decision to forget about Jackson, to learn from my mistakes and move on, and that was what I was going to do. There's no point having feelings for someone who's made it clear they don't have feelings for you.

Me: No, I'm over him.

Ravi: Good for you. Better go, Maya's calling. Can't keep a lady waiting! x

I put my phone on airplane mode and wriggled down under the sheets as Odette's snoring suddenly advanced to turbo mode.

It was going to be a long night, with nothing but an endless supply of unwanted thoughts to keep me company.

CHAPTER TEN

Legend

The following morning, after eating breakfast at a café in Amboise, we parked up in Chenonçeau and made our way slowly towards the castle.

Claude could hardly contain his excitement as we took in the view. To be fair, as far as castles go, I suppose it *was* pretty impressive, what with it being built on a bridge over a river, and surrounded by pretty gardens brimming with brightly coloured flowers. I noticed Claude light up as I took my phone out to take a picture. Well, the castle and bridge *were* reflected pretty perfectly in the river – and even I could appreciate that.

I texted the picture to Mum with a message, keeping it sarcastic so that she didn't mistakenly think I was having a good time.

Thanks for warning me about GA's obsession with castles. If his home turns out to be full of dungeons and dragons merch then I'm on the first train home. Just saying.

'Isn't it stunning?' he said, shielding his eyes from the sun. 'The original castle was burnt down in the fifteenth century to punish the landowner for disrespecting the King – or something like that.'

'You should've been a tour guide,' I said, popping some chewing gum into my mouth.

Claude chuckled. 'Yup. Missed my calling there.'

'Have you always played guitar in a band?' I asked as me, him and Odette followed a path through the gardens.

'No, I had many different jobs before I realised the thing I did in my spare time was all I wanted to do.'

'What kind of jobs did you do?'

'Builder, waiter, delivery driver ...'

'Gigolo,' added Odette.

'I considered it – *didn't actually do it.*' Claude rolled his eyes. 'She loves to wind me up about that.'

'And what did Great Uncle Gerard do?'

'He was an accountant. Ran his own firm. He was the only one who really "made it" in the old man's opinion. Right, Odey?'

Spotting a bench, Odette sat down. 'But he was miserable,' she said. 'Apart from our father's approval, what did he gain?'

'Er, *a truck-load of money* is what he gained,' said Claude. 'You see, Ori, the old man looked down on me and Odey. He weren't impressed with our career choices. But the fact that Gerard had some proper dough rolling in, some posh clients and an actual office – now *that* he considered success. Made him look good.'

'We were the failures,' said Odette.

'But you sold art to famous people,' I said. 'How is that a failure?'

'It was the *type* of art she sold,' grinned Claude, sitting down next to her. 'Too saucy or too abstract. The old man didn't get it. Anyway, that's all in the past . . . Just imagine,' he said, pointing at the chateau, 'trying to get out of Nazi-occupied France on this side of the river and into the free zone on that side. I always think it's pretty amazing that's what our old man helped people to do.'

Odette frowned.

'What – *here?*' I asked. 'He helped people escape the Nazis across *this river?*'

'No, not here, back in Paris. He smuggled people out of Paris and sent them south to the next contact on their way to the free zone, from where they made their way onto Spain. He helped many people to escape.'

'Wow,' I said. 'That's pretty amazing.' I turned to Odette. 'Do you remember the war at all, Odette? Do you remember your dad helping people escape?'

Odette looked weary. 'I have many memories. Some of them not so nice.'

'Of course I wasn't born till after the war, but Odey lived through it – even though she was very young,' Claude said excitedly.

'My great grandfather worked for *La Résistance*,' I pondered out loud, the words sounding strange and incredible as they left my mouth. That was actually pretty cool. I couldn't wait to tell Ravi.

Odette gripped her walking stick. 'Always the same bullshit,' she muttered.

Claude patted her shoulder as if trying to soothe her. 'He wasn't always the greatest dad,' he explained to me. 'Those were intense times – and even for years afterwards, there was so much devastation and hardship to deal with, sadly being a dad wasn't his highest priority. He wasn't known for dishing out praise or cuddles. Men were different back then. Different era.'

Odette swiped his hand away.

I was about to challenge him on what he meant by that, given that he'd been a pretty rubbish dad himself, but my phone buzzed. I took it out of my pocket: a reply from Ava. My heart sped up – presumably because my heart knew what my head refused to accept, that there was no chance of forgiveness. I should've saved reading it till we were back in the car but I couldn't wait. If the verdict still stood, I needed to know.

'Excuse me a minute.' I pointed to my phone and turned away. As Claude and Odette continued their conversation in French, I walked slowly away from the bench, holding my breath while I read Ava's message:

Yeah, we all make mistakes — but like I said, what you did *wasn't* a mistake. It was planned. It was bad enough catching Jackson snogging someone else, but snogging YOU, my best friend — the one person in the world who should have my back? Do you have any idea how that made me feel? I've got nothing more to say to you. Don't text me again. You won't get a reply.

I exhaled.

'You alright, Pinkydinks?' asked Claude, getting up from the bench and coming over to me.

'Mmm, fine,' I mumbled, putting my phone back in my pocket.

'You look a bit rattled.'

'So does Odette.' Her eyes were fixed on the river, but her mind seemed somewhere else.

'Oh it's nothing. She's fine. Shall we continue our walk around the castle?'

I eyed up the chateau. I wasn't in the mood. All I could think about was how much Ava hated me. She was right. Catching your boyfriend snogging someone else was one thing, but catching them with your *best friend?* Why didn't I stop to think about how this might *really* play out – rather than how I hoped it would play out – before creating a situation where I was alone with Jackson? Once again my utter stupidity smacked me in the face. It wouldn't be surprising if the others hated me as much as she did.

Would anyone ever forgive me? I'd looked at other colleges and, finding nowhere else that offered the right courses within an easy commute, decided to stick with my original application. Would they blank me in the corridors in September? Would they badmouth me to other people – tell them what I'd done? I felt sick all over again. I guess I deserved it.

'Ori?' Claude waved a hand in front of my eyes.

'How long will it take to get from here to Frenac?' I asked.

He glanced at his watch. 'Four to five hours? We'll need to break up the journey as the old Cilla can't handle too long a stint behind the wheel.' He glanced at his watch. 'In fact, maybe we'd better shake a leg.' He gave Odette a pat on the back and helped her up off the bench.

'The old what?' I asked, confused.

'Cilla. Cilla Black: *back.* You need to brush up on your rhyming slang, me ol' China. Anyone need *les toilettes* before we hit the road?'

Odette and I shook our heads.

'OK, let's skedaddle!'

CHAPTER ELEVEN
Some Kind Of Wonderful

Jackson's gaze travels slowly from my feet up to my face. A smile spreads across his lips. 'You look beautiful,' he says, reaching for me. I take his hand and step towards him, my long satin dress swishing around my ankles. His suit makes his shoulders look even broader than usual and he smells deliciously of aftershave. 'You scrub up pretty well yourself,' I say, adjusting the collar of his tux, like they do in the movies. He brushes his fingers against my cheek and lowers his lips on mine.

'*Mork calling Orson! Come in, Orson!*' shouted Claude over his shoulder, interrupting my daydreaming in the back seat. 'Anyone home?'

'What?' I pulled my headphones out. 'I had my music on.'

'Oh. I was just asking if you like Muddy Waters?'

Weird question. 'Why would I like muddy water?' I replied.

'He's a musician! A singer – the father of the blues!' he explained.

'I thought you said that other one was the father of the blues?'

'Did I? Well they're both pioneers of modern blues. Check this out.' He turned up the music. 'What do you think?'

'Yeah, it's OK,' I conceded.

'There is hope, Odey!' he cheered. 'The rinkydink panther has some blues in her after all.'

'I prefer jazz,' mumbled Odette.

'You OK, kiddo?' said Claude. 'You've been very quiet since we left Chenonçeau.'

'I'm fine,' I said. 'Can we stop soon? I need the loo.'

'Affirmative, my rinkydink wing man. Keep your eyes peeled for facilities.'

I tried to get back into my daydream but the script kept changing. It was as if me and Jackson were two repelling magnets, our lips unable to meet thanks to some invisible force pushing us apart. Jackson goes off to find Ava, then Ravi appears in his super-smart dinner jacket, his arm around Maya. Maya narrows her eyes at me and presses herself closer to him, as if warning me to stay away from her man. She steers him away and I'm left standing on my own until Ava walks over and throws a drink in my face. Everyone bursts into applause as I stand there saturated and dripping, the school villain getting her just desserts.

'Bogs ahoy!' Claude swerved into a turn-off and followed the road towards a picnic area, at the far end of which was a small concrete toilet block and a food kiosk. We parked up and Odette took my arm as I helped her out of the car.

We queued outside the women's loos while Claude sauntered straight into the men's.

'The advantages of being a man,' sighed Odette.

Two loos eventually became free and we each went in.

Holy crap! The smell was toe-curling. I looked down at the two footholds either side of a filthy hole and gagged. I was NOT standing on that thing. I already felt like I'd contracted every germ on the planet just by inhaling the pungent stench. I unlocked the door, ran out and gulped in the fresh air.

When Odette emerged two minutes later, I asked if her cubicle had a proper loo.

'*Bof, non.*'

'I'll wait till we get to a service station then.'

'What is the problem?' she exclaimed. 'Just go pipi!'

'No way,' I said. 'It's utterly gross in there. I'll be sick.'

'Then go behind there!' She pointed to a thick clump of bushes lining the edge of the picnic area.

'You've got to be kidding! I'm not baring my arse in front of people eating their lunch. Someone might film me.'

'Up to you.' She shuffled off with her walking stick. 'You would not survive in a war, *ma chérie.*'

'We need to stop at a proper service station,' I told Claude as we got back in the car. 'Those toilets are RANK.'

'Surely you've used a hole-in-the-ground before?' he grinned.

'Nope, and I'm never setting foot in one again.'

'Well luckily, they ain't as common as they used to be. But they still exist so you might just have to.'

'You need to be more tough,' said Odette. 'I am *eighty* and *I* can piss in a hole.'

I'd be surprised if Odette made it to eighty-one after exposing herself to the bacteria in that cesspit. Then again, she'd said she wanted a "Dadaesque death", so maybe that explained her relaxed attitude.

We pulled out of the parking space, the seat belt alarm sounding immediately.

'Seat belt!' I groaned.

Claude gave me a salute, strapped himself in and turned the stereo back on.

As we crawled towards the exit, I spotted a young guy leaning against the last picnic table, holding up a paper sign that said "Sarlat". He was wearing chino shorts, a loose-fitting short sleeved shirt and a battered straw hat. He looked up as we approached and I did a double-take. *Hello Romeo!*

'STOP!' I yelled in Claude's ear.

'Changed your mind?' he said. 'Very wise. There might not be a service station for a while.'

'No,' I said, pointing to the hitchhiker. 'Aren't you going to offer him a lift?'

Claude hesitated. 'Er . . .'

'Looks like we were right, Odette,' I sighed. 'Unless you're family, you need a vagina, boobs and a millennial birth certificate to get a lift with Claude.'

Odette cackled.

'Fine,' snapped Claude, pulling up alongside the guy and winding down his window. '*Nous allons à Sarlat.*' He jerked a thumb towards the back seat.

'*Merci beaucoup!*' Hot Boy folded his sign in half, picked up his rucksack, squeezed it into the boot and climbed in next to me. 'I really appreciate it, thank you!'

'Is that a German accent I can hear?' asked Claude. 'Where are you from?

'From Berlin, but I'm travelling around France.'

'Welcome aboard. I'm Claude, and this is Odette and *Aurélie*.'

'Nice to meet you. I'm Elias,' he said, shaking each of our hands.

'It's Ori – not *Aurélie*,' I said, rolling my eyes at Claude and smiling at our guest.

'Nice to meet you, Ori.' He grinned at me and a waft of musky man-scent seeped into my nostrils. *Mmm . . .* I desperately wanted to scoop his aroma towards me and inhale hungrily. I smiled back at him and – without warning – an image of him with no shirt on, towering over me and moving in for a kiss popped into my mind. *Get a grip, Ori!* I gave my head a brisk shake. *What was wrong with me?*

'So are you guys staying in Sarlat or just passing through?' he asked us.

'Passing through,' said Claude. 'We're heading to a village just beyond Sarlat, called Frenac.'

'No way!' laughed Elias. 'That's where *I'm* going.'

'Really?' said Claude, looking at him through the rear-view mirror. 'What a coincidence. What brings you to Frenac?'

'My grandparents moved out there years ago from Berlin. I'm going to spend some time with them.'

'Hang on, you're not Rolf and Letzie's grandson, are you?' Claude craned his neck around to peer at Elias.

'Eyes on the road!' I barked at him, making Elias jump. 'Sorry,' I mouthed to Elias.

'You know my grandparents?' beamed Elias, taking his hat

off to reveal a super-cute mop of scruffy dark brown hair.

'They're good buddies of mine,' said Claude. 'I see them all the time.'

'Wow – that's crazy!' he said.

Well this was an interesting turn of events. It meant I'd almost definitely be crossing paths with this quality fitbit again. (Quality fitbit was one of mine and Ava's nicknames for a hot boy.) Finally, Lady Luck was smiling upon me!

'Guess so,' Claude chuckled. 'I'm renovating a barn in Frenac. It's a recording studio and a venue for events and gigs – a community space. Maybe they mentioned me?'

'Yes!' said Elias excitedly. 'They said a neighbour was building a community place. They're very excited about it – they *love* performing. Wait, you all perform together don't you?'

'That's right!' said Claude. 'We're not an official band or anything, but we have fun jamming together. We call ourselves The Lost Marbles – just for a laugh.'

'The Lost Marbles?' Elias frowned.

'Oh, it's an expression. When someone's lost their marbles, it means they've lost their sanity, or their memory,' explained Claude.

'Ah,' Elias smiled, joke understood. 'My grandparents will say I also lost my marbles.'

'Why's that then?' asked Claude.

'Because I just hitched a lift – they *will* be cross with me. But I didn't have a choice. The bus I was on stopped here at the toilets, so me and a few others got off. I went to buy a sandwich, and when I turned around the bus had gone without me.'

A loud snort came from the front passenger seat. Was Odette laughing at our passenger's bad luck or had she nodded off? Claude glanced at Odette and signalled to us that she was asleep. He turned the music down and whispered, 'Thirty K to the next service station, Pinkydinks – can your bladder hold on that long?'

I mean, *really?*

'I'm good, thanks,' I said with fake cheer, my cheeks burning.

'Excuse me,' said Elias, pointing to his phone. 'I'd better reply to these messages – I haven't had a signal for a while.'

'Sure,' said Claude.

I got out my phone in order to look busy too, and saw I had a reply from Mum.

Wow — cool place! The only merch you're likely to find at GA's is music merch. Can't imagine he'd have room for anything else among the hordes of vinyl he must've amassed over the years! Anyway, sounds like you're having fun! Love you xx

Fun? Er, I don't think so, *compadre*. Although – I glanced at Elias – life might be starting to look up, which is all anyone needed to know. By "anyone" obviously I did not mean Mum. She needed to know that I was *not* having fun. I texted her back.

He keeps torturing me with blues music. I'd rather listen to a newmatic drill. How can I make him stop?

Bubbles appeared.

I would've thought blues would make the perfect soundtrack for your current state of mind, Piggles. PS It's pneumatic 😄

Thanks, Mother. Sympathetic and understanding as ever. I decided to message Ravi for an update – and also to let him and the others know that I had a new "love interest".

Hey Ravioli! I think my luck may be about to change. I've met a cute guy!! How's life in Cornwall this morning?

I waited for Ravi to reply, praying it wouldn't be a long wait that would send my anxiety levels creeping up. I stared out the window, trying to look like a woman lost in her mysterious thoughts. Fortunately he texted back a few minutes later.

Ravi: Seriously? Who? Tell me more. Cornwall's not quite what I was hoping. Jackson and Ava still grumpy and Daisy and Martha keep going off by themselves. Also, the weather is just being rude. On the positive side, Zac's new boyfriend Blake joined us late last night and he's really nice.

Me: How's it going with Maya?

Ravi: Yeah cool.

I was hoping for a little more info than "yeah cool", like how the rest of the group were getting on with her, how well she was fitting in, etc, but I didn't want to sound like I was jealous or feeling insecure about being replaced. Which I obviously was.

Dammit – I needed to know.

Me: So does she get on well with everyone?

Ravi: Yeah, everyone loves her! Especially Ava. Although I think Ava would love anyone who's not you right now. Soz, Oreo.

Note to self: don't cause yourself more misery by asking a question you already know the answer to.

Me: It's OK. I get it.

Ravi: You sure you're OK? You're still my favourite biscuit 😄

Me: You're still my favourite pasta 😜

Ravi: Can't wait for you to meet Maya and get to know her!

Me: Yeah same!

Ravi: Anyway tell me about this guy. How did you meet?

Me: We gave him a lift. He's a friend of my grandad's sort of.

Obviously this was the abbreviated version. I would give him the director's cut when we next hung out in person.

Ravi: Does he like you?

While I had no reason to lie to Ravi, I wanted the rest of them to think – *to know* – that I'd moved on. Then hopefully Ava would stop seeing me as a threat, and also I would look slightly less of a loser. OK, maybe not the second part.

Me: I have a feeling he does. I'll keep you posted . . .

Ravi: Cool. Text you later.

CHAPTER TWELVE

The Castle

We passed fields scattered with hay bales that looked like giant loo rolls, brown road signs flagging places of historic interest (that got Claude peeing his pants with excitement), and towns that crept up hills, surrounding castles and church steeples.

I felt tense being in such close proximity to a hot-looking male. I could literally feel the heat coming from Elias's body, and I was all too aware of his light brown, muscly thigh being just a few inches from my wobbly white one. He was manspreading, but it wasn't his fault as Claude's seat was pushed so far back, there was nowhere else for his legs to go.

Despite the two oldies sitting in the front cramping my style, I decided I'd be an utter moron if I didn't make the most of this opportunity and attempt some polite chitchat with Elias and hopefully pave the way towards "getting to know each other". I broke the ice by asking him how long his grandparents had lived in France for (twelve years) and conversation was flowing quite smoothly until he wound down the window a fraction and I suddenly remembered with horror that I hadn't put any deodorant on that morning. I froze. How bad did I smell?

I couldn't smell anything – surely I'd be able to smell my own BO? But what if I was nose-blind? And so I clammed up and turned back to my phone to mask my embarrassment.

At least I'd been able to gather the following intel:

• He'd just done the German equivalent to A-levels.

• His mum was Turkish, his dad was German, and he had two sisters, one older (twenty-three) and one younger (fourteen).

• He was taking a gap year before going to university in Munich to study Environmental Science and planned to backpack his way around Europe, working and travelling, starting off at his grandparents' place in Frenac. (Obviously I passed all this on to Ravi and was looking forward to his feedback.)

Most crucially of all: he didn't seem to have a girlfriend. Or boyfriend. I couldn't be certain of his sexual orientation, but I got the feeling he was straight. Or possibly bi. In other words, if I hadn't already blown it by smelling like a mouldy egg sandwich then I was in with a chance.

We dropped Elias off at his grandparents' front door – a fifteen minute walk from Claude's barn. I had a feeling I'd be taking a lot of "strolls" for "fresh air" over the coming days.

Odette opened her eyes. 'We are here?' she croaked.

'Not yet, sis. Just dropping off our passenger.' Claude pressed a button and the boot popped open.

'Thank you for the lift,' said Elias, climbing out of the car and fetching his rucksack. 'Nice chatting to you, Ori. I'm sure I'll see you around.'

'Well your folks are coming over to celebrate the opening of my barn next weekend, so why don't you come along too?' said Claude. 'I'm having a big party.'

For once I could've fist-bumped him. This rare display of genius from Claude redeemed him from drawing attention to my bursting bladder earlier. (Which I miraculously managed to hold for another forty-five minutes before we found a service station with a decent loo.)

'Sure, that would be great. See you then, if not sooner.'

Dear God, let it be sooner.

He patted the side of the car, swung his rucksack over his back and headed up the drive to a pretty looking house with navy blue shutters and a leafy garden where a wooden windchime hung from a willow tree.

'*Il semble très charmant,*' said Odette, as we drove off.

'Very charming indeed,' agreed Claude. 'Charming, polite, *and rather handsome,* wouldn't you say, Ori?' He glanced in the rear-view mirror and waggled his eyebrows at me.

I pulled an unamused face and he laughed as a ringtone blasted out of the car door speakers.

'Claude Marchand,' he said in a fake-casual telephone voice.

'Hi sweetie!' a voice called out. I guessed this must be the "lovely" Sylvie.

'Hey sugarbun! Can you hear me?'

'Just about. Where are you?'

'Nearly back at the ranch, honeybunch. I'll call you in half an hour, yeah? Are you at yours or mine?'

'I'm back at mine. I put a casserole in your fridge earlier.

And I've bought a little surprise just for you – some new sexy underwear.'

'Whoa! I lost my earphone thingamajig so you're on loud-speaker, babe. Keep it clean!'

Odette sniggered.

'Oh lord! Excuse me, everyone. Er . . . Looking forward to meeting you all tomorrow evening. See you then!' An embarrassed Sylvie hung up, while Claude grinned from ear to ear.

'Looking forward to *that*,' he muttered.

A question suddenly occurred to me: 'Why is your surname Marchand when Great Uncle Gerard's was Lambrook?'

'Lambrook was our old man's surname,' said Claude. 'Marchand was our mum's maiden name. I preferred Marchand, so I changed it. Worked better as a stage name.'

'Stage name?'

'Back in the day. Touring. Playing the old *gee-tar.*'

'Right. And so *your* mum's surname was "Zolaste?"' I asked Odette.

'Non,' sighed Odette. 'Her name was Mathilde Lubin. I created Zolaste when I became an artist.'

Three siblings, three different surnames. Kind of weird . . .

'So you both changed your surnames?'

'Why suffer a name that doesn't fit you?' sniffed Odette. 'You can reinvent yourself whenever you want. Don't let the past define you.'

Her words took a few seconds to register. I sat up straight and was about to ask her what she meant by that exactly but Claude butted in.

'*Anyway*,' he said with exaggerated cheer, 'we're here! *AND* we made it the whole way on electric, so Sylvie owes me twenty euros!'

We turned down a narrow tree-lined lane and pulled up in front of a large, white, modern building that looked more like a newly-built dental practice than a country barn.

'That's it?' Odette snorted. '*Quelle horreur!*'

'It looks a lot more appealing on the other side,' said Claude. 'It was riddled with woodworm, so I had to rebuild most of it.'

Claude parked up under a tree in his driveway, and I helped ease Odette out of the front passenger's seat, while Claude stretched his back and shook out his legs. Together we unloaded the boot. It was late afternoon and our shadows were long and willowy on the ground, but it was still stinking hot.

'This way, clan!' beamed Claude. 'Come see *my* castle.'

Inside the barn was a vast open-plan space with a high ceiling supported by old wooden beams. At one end of the room was a low stage with a microphone on a stand. To the right of the stage stood a couple of trestle tables holding several computers and a load of expensive-looking recording equipment. At the other end of the barn was a woodburning stove surrounded by sofas and a coffee table. And in the middle was a cluster of dining tables and an actual bar, although it didn't have any beer pumps or optics. And just about everywhere you looked, there were guitars on stands, large potted plants – and, as Mum had guessed, stacks of records.

Claude waved us over to him and pointed to the stage. 'That's the creative, music-making party zone.' He then turned and pointed towards the sofas at the opposite end. 'And over there is the chill-out zone. We only use the woodburner in the winter, of course.' He then swept his arm majestically towards the back wall that overlooked the garden. The wall was lined with multiple floor-to-ceiling windows and sliding doors, through which the sun was beaming, casting impressive rays of light across the inside of the barn.

'This way, ladies! Just dump your stuff here and follow me.'

I let go of Odette's suitcase and it toppled over, knocking a guitar off its stand. I caught it in the nick of time.

Claude sucked in his breath. 'Ooof, that was lucky. That's Stevie. I don't use her much these days but we share fond memories.'

'Stevie?' I frowned.

'Yeah, got a few more slung around the place. That's Patti over there.' He pointed to a shiny red electric guitar on a stand next to a giant cactus. 'And at the back you've got Layla, Grace, Janis and Tina. *Never touch Layla*,' Claude whispered in my ear. 'She – sorry – *it's* my most precious one. We go back a long way, me'n'Layla. Anyway, this way.'

I rolled my eyes. *Gimme a friggin' break.*

We followed him through the sliding doors and stepped out onto a patio where there was an outdoor dining table and parasol. The garden was enormous, and backed on to shady woods, fenced off by a half-built wall. A rusty old caravan sat lonely and neglected in the far left corner that bordered the next door neighbour's garden. Beside it stood a revolving pole washing line, with several pairs of Y-fronts and a T-shirt pegged to it.

'If you go through the woods at the end of the garden,' said Claude, pointing into the distance, 'it's just a five minute walk to the river, where I often go for a dip – I'll show you later. In the meantime, let's go back in and grab a cuppa.' He ushered us back inside.

'We are sleeping in here?' asked Odette, peering up at a corkscrew staircase that led to a mezzanine level above.

'Yeah,' said Claude. 'Your room's over there, Odey.' He pointed to a couple of doors at the side of the stage. 'You get the private guest suite.'

'So where do *you* sleep – up there?' I pointed upstairs.

'Nope. *Out there,*' he replied, disappearing into the kitchen and flicking the kettle on.

Odette and I followed him.

'Out there *where*?' asked Odette.

He pointed out the window at the old caravan in the back of the garden.

'*There*? Why?' I asked, drifting back towards the corkscrew staircase and climbing a few steps. Craning my neck, I could see a pile of mattresses next to a heap of sleeping bags.

'Because,' said Claude, 'I was living in there while the barn was uninhabitable and I haven't got round to moving in yet. When you two have slung your hooks, I'll be moving into Odey's room. But if business takes off, I'll probably build an extension. Anyway, I *like* sleeping in the caravan. I've lived in many a caravan in my time and I'm *très* fond of them.'

'Who sleeps up there then?' I climbed back down the corkscrew staircase.

'The bands,' said Claude, leaning out of the kitchen doorway to see where I was. 'It's all included in the price. They do a gig, we film and record it, they camp upstairs. It ain't The Ritz but it's perfectly comfortable. Had about three bands and two solo artists stay so far – although I'm not officially open for business yet, so mum's the word.'

'Where am I sleeping then?' I asked.

He pointed to the mezzanine.

'Or bag yourself a sofa next to the woodburner. Go wherever takes your fancy, sweet cheeks. *Mi casa es su casa.* Sleep on the stage if you like.'

Er, no thank you. The mezzanine was pretty much a stage in its own right – there was zero privacy. There was a railing to stop you toppling over the edge, but no wall, no door, nothing to shield me from prying eyes while getting dressed and undressed. What did the bands make of that? Or didn't they care?

'Hot beverage? Cold beverage? *Summink a bit stronger?*' asked Claude, as the kettle boiled.

Yes – something a lot stronger sounded good to me!

'Do you have mint tea?' Odette asked doubtfully.

'Morroccan mint, organic fennel, calming chamomile, redbush, raspberry or nettle . . .' He pointed to a shelf lined with every type of herbal tea under the sun. Some were in packets, others were in large glass jars with loose leaves inside. The shelf below was rammed with tubs of vitamins, Bach Remedies, small bottles of essential oils, scented candles and incense. Neither shelf looked like it belonged in the kitchen of a drug-loving blues guitarist.

Claude pointed to the large jars. 'These are the business if you wanna detox. Cost a bloody fortune, but man do they flush out your pipes. I'm in the habit of looking after myself these days. Body is a temple an' all that.'

Odette sniffed. 'Mint is fine, thank you.'

'Pinkletinx?' Claude raised his eyebrows at me.

I didn't have the courage to ask for "something a bit stronger". 'Normal tea, please.'

As he opened the fridge to fetch the milk, he paused: 'Still can't believe we picked up Rolf and Letzie's grandkid. You'll love Rolf and Letz. They're salt of the earth. Rolf's an architect – retired now – and Letzie teaches yoga. They live just around the corner from Sylvie – and they both play a mean guitar. You'll meet them all before the party anyway.'

This was good news – I would get to see Elias for sure! A glimmer of positivity to make my time here more bearable.

Claude handed us each a cup of tea.

'Anyway, as of tomorrow, I'll need your help, Pinkster. Like I said before, there's a lot to do so we'd better get an early start.

'How early?' I asked. Summer holiday lie-ins were a basic human right.

'Not that early – seven? Eight?'

I tried not to choke on my tea. This "holiday" just kept getting more and more fun.

Claude hooted with laughter. 'Cop the mug on that!' he said to Odette, nodding towards my stony expression. 'I thought you could start by doing the pastry run. The earlier you get down the *boulangerie*, the less of a bunfight it is, if you'll pardon the pun.

The pains au chocolat are all gone by 8.30.'

A trip to the boulangerie *could mean a chance meeting with Elias . . .*

I took a deep breath and gave Claude the thumbs up. 'Fine.'

He raised his cup of tea and clinked it against mine. 'Right, let's go relax in the yard for a bit and then I'll stick that casserole on.'

I quickly snapped my new surroundings to send to Ravi, who hadn't yet responded to my cute guy intel update.

'What's the wifi password?' I called to Claude as he pulled out a chair for Odette on the patio.

'*Ishotthesheriff*, with a number one for the I. Wifi's a bit dodgy here.'

He wasn't wrong. But after a few patient breaths, I managed to WhatsApp Ravi a few pictures of Studio Marchand, AKA Boomersville County Jail.

'Come on kiddo!' shouted Claude. 'I'll introduce you to one of my birds.'

I stepped warily onto the patio. 'How many girlfriends have you actually got?' I asked dryly.

'Oh, like that is it?' Claude gave a terse smile and gestured towards the trees at the end of his garden. 'I was talking about my *birds of prey*. They're not *mine* obviously, they're just regular visitors to *chez Claude*.'

I followed his outstretched arm to where a large, predatory-looking bird was perching high up in a tree at the end of the garden.

'Oh, right. Sorry,' I mumbled.

'No problemo,' said Claude. 'I think that's Monty. He's a red kite.'

Odette gazed admiringly at Monty and cooed something in French.

'Knew you'd be impressed, sis,' said Claude. 'Whatcha reckon, Pinkster? He's a beauty, ain't he?'

I nodded. 'Yeah. He's pretty cool.'

'There's some binoculars knocking around somewhere. I'll find 'em for you later. They're pretty powerful so you can get a closer look.'

'OK.'

I checked my phone – Ravi hadn't even seen my message yet. I nibbled a fingernail. Shame those binoculars couldn't see all the way to Cornwall, to Martha's uncle's field, so I could see what was going on. Although, how would that help me get on with my life?

Maybe I'd be better off pointing them in the direction of Elias's grandparents' house instead?

CHAPTER THIRTEEN
The Breakfast Club

The following morning I woke up to the sound of my alarm at a barbaric 7.00 a.m.. I sat up in bed, grabbed my phone and turned the alarm off.

No messages or notifications. Not a single response to my intel or my photos from Ravi, who *had* seen them. *Man, I hated those little blue ticks!*

Summoning every ounce of willpower in my being, I resisted the urge to do a full social media scan to see what they'd all been up to, and tossed my phone out of reach before I could change my mind. I had to trust that Ravi would respond soon. He wasn't someone who used silence as a punishment and he wouldn't deliberately ignore me.

Although, he might unintentionally ignore me if he was having a really good time . . . ? *Gaaah – shut up, brain!*

Trying not to let the silence panic me, I peeled back my sleeping bag and got up. (I'd decided the mezzanine was in fact the best place to sleep after finding a folding privacy screen tucked around the corner.) I looked over the railings. The sun was streaming through the windows and Odette was already up and sipping a cup of tea outside under the parasol, her hunched, scrawny back to me.

I was going to say good morning but it was too early for awkward small talk so I sneaked past and headed for the bathroom, only to find someone was already in there. The door flung open and Claude appeared in a cloud of steam, his hair in a bun, a bath towel wrapped around his hairy old man belly.

'Morning, Pinkeroo. I'd give it a minute if I were you – there's no window and the fan's buggered.'

'You shower *here*?' I asked.

'I do indeed.'

'Isn't there a shower in your caravan?'

'There is, but I use it to store me clobber in. Still up for a pastry run?'

'Yeah, I'll just have a quick shower.'

'FYI, the water temperature goes from arctic to inferno and back sixty times a minute. So *achtung*, yeah?'

I flapped the door back and forth to disperse the steam cloud and lingering smell from the loo (which Claude didn't seem at all embarrassed about) before going in and locking the door behind me. The sink was coated in mini man-hairs (suspected origin: nostrils – *ugh*), there was an empty bottle of man-shampoo lying in the bottom of the shower, and the loo had about three sheets of bog roll left. I wondered what the "bands and solo artists" made of this place? Having watched Mum pimp and polish our flat into an unrecognisable Airbnb, I reckoned Claude could do with a few tips. Then again, maybe roughing it was all part of the gigging lifestyle?

I showered and dressed quickly, eager to get out of the stuffy, stinky bathroom.

'Odette, what pastries would you like?' I called, grabbing the breakfast cash Claude had left out on the side last night.

She didn't answer. I went outside to where she was sitting and touched her lightly on the shoulder. 'Odette?'

She turned her head towards me, a faraway look in her eyes. 'I was in another place, another time . . .' she said.

'Would you like some pastries?' I asked, eager to get going and not miss my chance of bumping into Elias.

'*Non merci, ma chérie.* I found some muesli. I will have that.'

'OK, back in a bit.'

I hurried out the door, tugging my crop top into place and checking the flies on my shorts were done up. I didn't even know where I was going but it couldn't be too hard to find in a village this size.

I walked down the lane that led from Claude's barn back into Frenac, noticing the perfect rows of trees on either side of me and how pretty they looked, the sunshine filtering through the leaves. There were a few other houses along the lane, all very idyllic looking – the kind of thing Mum salivated over when she was bored and scouring the internet for her dream house. As I turned the corner onto the main road that led into Frenac, the houses became closer together and started to feel much older, like they belonged to another century. The heat bounced off the cobbled pavement and I felt as if the sun was hugging me, telling me I was going to be all right. For the first time in weeks, I felt my spirits lift. Maybe this was all down to the hot, sunny weather. Had it been grey, windy and drizzly, I doubt I would've felt this cheery.

Eventually I saw a sign saying 'Place de Victor Hugo' pointing towards an alleyway. The narrow passageway meandered between crumbly old buildings with windowsills draped with hanging plants and multicoloured flowers. I half-expected Cinderella to step out of a front door and shake out a rug in front of me – that's how oldie-worldie this place felt. Eventually the alleyway spat me out in a sweet little square – an open space that stretched between a church on one side, and a couple of cafés, a *boulangerie* and a small supermarket on the other.

Pretending I had the confidence of Billie Eilish and Dua Lipa combined, I adjusted my sunglasses and strutted gracefully across the square towards the *boulangerie*.

'*Bonjour mademoiselle!*' chimed the old man behind the counter as I walked in and joined the back of a short queue.

'*Bonjour,*' I replied. How did he know I was a "*mademoiselle*" and not a "*madame*"? I narrowed my eyes at him.

This was something me and Ava could really go to town on: Men were referred to as "*monsieur*" no matter what their age or marital status, so why weren't women? At least in English you had "Ms", which was better than nothing. I wondered what Odette made of it.

Sadly there was no sign of Elias anywhere – but luckily being stuck in a queue meant there was still time for our paths to cross. In the meantime, there was a dizzying choice of pastries to choose from and the smell was turning my taste buds into water fountains. I realised, as I neared the front of the queue, that something miraculous had happened that morning – I'd been up nearly an hour and *still* hadn't looked at any of my socials! I felt proud and strong, as if I'd managed to go a whole week without chocolate (which would, obviously, never happen.)

Five minutes later, having agonised long enough over my choices, I left with a bag full of goodies and reluctantly made my way back across the square. The optimism I'd felt twenty minutes earlier was starting to drain away. Maybe I wouldn't see Elias at all? If he was spending time hanging out with his grandparents, he might not go out that much. He'd been polite and friendly in the car, but not flirty. Not super-chatty. He hadn't given me the impression that he was keen to see me again. Maybe he *did* have a girlfriend or boyfriend and it just hadn't come up in conversation?

As I walked back across the square, I suddenly remembered it was Martha's birthday. I stopped and WhatsApped her a happy birthday message. In the blink of an eye, I crumbled and broke my social-detox to see if she'd posted a birthday picture yet. She had, at one o'clock in the morning: a photo of her opening a present, surrounded by our friendship group in front of their tents. I liked the picture and commented that I hoped she had a great day. Hopefully I'd get a reply or, at the very least, she might "like" my comment?

Apart from Ravi, I'd had little contact with any of them since the week after I committed the crime. And now, even Ravi had gone quiet. I thought about texting him again but decided against it. We were an hour ahead in France. He was probably still asleep in his tent. With Maya? I felt an uncomfortable pang of something I couldn't quite put my finger on. Loneliness? Jealousy? *Loser*dom? As if I didn't know it already, it was now pretty clear I was no longer a member of the group. I'd been kicked out. Permanently.

I was in a social abyss.

A free-floating spirit, in between lives.

To not have any friends was one thing. But to *have had* friends who no longer wanted anything to do with you, was far worse.

And if I'd lost Ravi's friendship, too? That would be more painful than anything.

When I got back to the barn, both the oldies were sitting outside on the patio beneath the parasol with cups of coffee.

I grabbed some plates from the kitchen and took them outside.

'Good job, Captain Pinkster,' said Claude. 'Find the *boulangerie* OK?'

'Yup, easy.' I put his change on the table.

'Great,' he said, opening the paper bag and inspecting its contents. 'Would you grab us another plate, babes? We've got a guest coming any minute.'

While I was fetching another plate from the kitchen, there was a knock at the front door. I went to answer it.

When I looked through the double-glazed door, my heart leapt into my mouth. It was Elias!

'Hiya. Didn't expect to see you so soon,' I said, stepping aside to let him in and trying not to let my euphoria show.

'Same,' he smiled. 'My grandfather said Claude might need some help getting his barn ready for opening night.'

'Oh right,' I said. 'You'd better come this way.'

I led him out onto the patio, where Claude stood up to shake his hand.

'Well, small flipping world,' he laughed, ushering him into a seat next to me. 'It's very kind of Rolf and Letzie to lend your services, so I thought the least I could do was give you breakfast.' Claude offered him a pastry. 'Coffee?'

'Thank you.' Elias took a pain aux raisins and put it on his plate while Claude poured him a coffee from the cafetière. 'Nice to see you all again,' he grinned at each of us. 'So how can I help you?'

Claude cleared his throat, took his list out of his jeans back pocket and smoothed it out on the table. 'Well, if we're all sitting comfortably, I shall begin . . .'

Elias and I waited for Claude by the half-built part of the wall that marked the boundary of the very large garden. I wondered how long it would take us to finish it. It wasn't a high wall (it came up to my waist) but as I followed the line markers around the back corners of the garden, I was guessing there was a good twelve or so metres in length left to build. In the thirty degree heat, this was going to be very sweaty work.

Elias held out a bottle of sun cream. 'Want some?'

'No thanks, I'm good. My moisturiser is SPF 30.' I'd be fine.

'I got sunburnt last summer,' he said, unfolding a floppy hat and patting it onto his head. 'It was horrible I felt sick for days.'

'Ouch,' I said. 'Sounds nasty.'

Even wearing a majorly uncool hat, he still looked drop-dead gorgeous.

'My mum won't believe I'm putting sun cream on *or* wearing this stupid hat, so can you take a photo for me?' He passed me his phone. 'If I send evidence, she won't bother me so much.'

I laughed. Mum had left me a voicemail earlier, reeling off a long list of things to be careful about from avoiding sunstroke to not losing my passport. *Parents.* I took the phone from him and stood back while he pulled a silly grin, holding the sun cream in one hand and pointing to his dodgy old man's hat with the other. I literally felt weak at the knees.

'Say cheese,' I instructed.

'Cheeeese. You English have some strange customs!' I handed it back to him and he examined the picture. 'Good. Now she can't complain.'

Neither could I. Although, it wasn't exactly ideal having my body turn to jelly every time Elias opened his mouth to speak or combed his fingers through his hair. It was like being in the presence of a god. Christ, this was worse than being attracted to Jackson. At least with Jackson I *knew* him, I'd grown up with him. He'd made my heart beat faster but he hadn't reduced my legs to jelly. This losing control of my mind and body had to stop. I needed to have a word with myself to remember that I was no longer some pathetic, lovestruck little girl craving attention from some ordinary, totally-my-equal-in-every-way guy.

'Everybody ready?' shouted Claude over the rumble of the cement mixer.

'Did you say you used to be a builder?' I asked him.

'Affirmative, Leader One. One of my first jobs, many moons ago, was working on a construction site – by the way, you got a sun hat?' He frowned at me.

'Yeah, I'll go grab it in a minute.' My new look sadly didn't work with hats and I refused to look like a helmet-head in front of Elias.

'OK, I'll go check on the cement while you two use the wheelbarrows to ship that pile of bricks over here – in sensible amounts so you don't do your backs in. Then I'll give you a trowel each and show you how to build a wall.'

We each took a wheelbarrow and headed for the stack of bricks. Elias spotted a pair of gloves in the bottom of his wheelbarrow and handed them to me. 'You should protect your hands,' he said.

'Thanks,' I said, looking around for another pair. 'I'll ask Claude if he's got any more.'

'Don't worry.' He started to load up. 'I'll go find some in a minute.'

He gave me the gloves! Could that have been the first true act of chivalry I'd ever experienced? Would Jackson have given me the gloves in the same situation? I doubted it. Back in the middle of exams, on a baking hot day, Jackson had asked for a swig from my water bottle and glugged the entire lot. I'd laughed it off, but now it struck me how selfish that was, as I wouldn't have done that to him.

Maybe it made sense that Elias would be more mature, seeing as he was older? Either way, he'd just earned five gold stars from the Gold Bullion Vault of Ori Reynolds. Plus, he'd earned another five yesterday for being polite and chatty to the Boomers in the car. Again, chit-chat with adults was not one of Jackson's strong points. On the few occasions he'd met my mum, she'd barely got a hello or goodbye out of him. Once I'd had to defend him after we'd given him and Ava a lift home, and he'd mumbled "Cheers" over his shoulder as he leapt out of the car and reached for his vape pen. For Mum, if it wasn't audible, it didn't count.

I carefully unloaded my barrow-load of bricks next to the wall and went back to get more. I was starting to sweat, but at least I'd remembered to put deodorant on this time.

'Are you going travelling on your own or with friends?' I asked Elias, hoping to get an idea of his relationship status as we filled up our wheelbarrows again. (If he was seeing someone, then hopefully that would put an end to my brain's uncontrollable habit of indulging in cringey romantic daydreams.)

'On my own most of the time, but I plan to meet a friend in Italy soon and another one in Poland, and I will visit my cousins in Turkey.'

It still didn't sound like he had a girl/boyfriend, but I'd have to fish further to be sure.

'So how long will you be travelling for in total?' I asked as Claude walked past and threw a pair of gloves to Elias.

He wiped his dusty hands on his shorts and put them on. 'Eight to ten months, I hope. It depends how long my money lasts and where I can find work. What about you? How long are you staying here with your grandfather?'

'Just a week or so. I'd love to go travelling but I start sixth form college in September.'

'You are seventeen?'

'Sixteen.' I felt myself shrink. Although – why should I feel ashamed of my age? It wasn't like he was an adult and I was a kid! *Hold your head high, Ori.*

We wheeled our barrows wonkily back across the garden.

'Are you going to visit England on your travels?' I asked.

'I don't think so. I was there last year. I went to London, Oxford and Bath.'

'Not Brighton? *Rude,*' I joked.

He laughed. 'It wasn't up to me. My parents wanted to visit Oxford and Bath. I heard Brighton's great though – I'll go one day, for sure. I'd like to go to Pride. You have been?'

'I've been to the parade. It's great – lots of dancing in the street and amazing colourful costumes. You should definitely go one year.'

'Sounds cool. I will definitely go.'

We concentrated on unloading the bricks. He still hadn't revealed whether or not he was in a relationship and I couldn't think of a subtle way of finding out. I wracked my brains for a way to re-boot the conversation, but nothing was coming.

'So . . . what will you do at college?' he said eventually, wiping sweat from his forehead.

'Psychology, art and philosophy. Not sure I've made the right choices, but I'm looking forward to a clean, fresh start,' I said a little more seriously than I'd intended.

'Yeah?' he smiled at me.

I got the feeling I'd accidentally let him see inside my head. A wave of emotion swept over me from out of nowhere and I had to look away as my eyes misted up. *Keep it together, Ori. Keep it together. Burst into tears right now and he'll think you're unhinged.*

I focused hard on unloading the bricks and managed to smooth my emotions back into place.

'You OK?' he asked.

'Yeah, good.' I fake-beamed.

'I really think you should put this on.' He passed me his sun cream. 'Your skin is nearly the same colour as your hair.'

'OK, fine.' I took it from him, squirted some onto my fingers and massaged it into my face. 'Is it all blended in?'

He gave a thumbs up. 'Perfect.'

For a second or two I felt tempted to tell him everything – there was something about him that made me feel I could trust him, but I wasn't sure why. Until I could work it out, I needed to remember to keep my mouth shut. If he knew how I'd kissed my best friend's boyfriend, he'd probably think I was a snake. I picked up the gloves and put them back on.

Anyway, being older than me, would Elias even be interested in someone fresh out of Year Eleven? Probably not. I had to play it super-cool – not something I'd excelled at so far in my life. On the other hand, when it came to betraying friends, pouncing on someone who wasn't interested in me and looking like a total loser, that was something I'd nailed fairly effortlessly.

I'd learned my lesson. I wasn't going to make the same mistakes again.

CHAPTER FOURTEEN
A River Runs Through It

Latest update: Daisy's pissed off cos Martha still owes her £20 from before prom. Martha keeps making excuses even though she's got the money. She also owes Zac £10, so he's annoyed too. Jackson and Ava keep fighting — he's getting fed up with her paranoia. (So is everyone else.) Maya threw up on her sleeping bag in the middle of the night so no one got a good night's sleep. I get the feeling we won't last a whole week here. Anyway sorry for late reply. Your grandad's place looks awesome! Got yourself a German bf yet?

Lying in the hammock later that day in the evening sun, I stared at Ravi's message and felt a strange feeling of calm wash over me. When my phone had buzzed a few hours earlier, I'd been in the middle of cementing a brick into place, so I hadn't been able to check it immediately. In fact, I'd been so busy bricklaying and chatting to Elias, that I'd actually managed to forget about my phone and had temporarily let go of why Ravi hadn't replied. That I'd managed to ignore my phone from the moment it had buzzed till now, *almost five hours later*, was nothing short of a miracle.

While it was a relief to hear from Ravi and feel reassured that we were still friends, it was almost annoying to get an update on the others. I no longer wanted to know what or how they were doing. On the other hand, the fact that they were all getting annoyed with each other in the middle of their camping holiday made me feel a fraction better – not that I meant to feel smug that they weren't having the greatest time, but hey, I was only human. I was still the only one who'd been ghosted. They might all be getting grouchy with each other, but at least they were all still friends.

I replied to Ravi.

Sorry I didn't reply sooner – I've been bricklaying! And sorry to hear things are a bit awks in Cornwall. Hope Maya's OK now. I don't have a German bf yet, but it's looking promising – he's helping me build a wall! We're getting to know each other over the cement mixer! 😆 #wonderwall #buildingarelationship Sorry, can't stop the puns! 😜

I pressed send and opened Instagram. Martha hadn't replied to either my WhatsApp message or my comment on her photo. In fact, she'd responded to everyone else's comments *except* mine. *OK, thanks for the burn, Martha. Good to know where I stand.*

My phone pinged with a new message. *From Ava.*

I seriously hope you're satisfied.

What the hell did that mean?

I immediately reported it to Ravi in the hope he could shed

some light on what on earth she was going on about. I held my breath while I watched the bubbles and waited for his reply.

They broke up earlier. Not sure who dumped who. A lot's happened in the last few days. Can't speak right now, I'll fill you in later.

I looked at Ava's message again.

What happened to them being "stronger than ever"? Was this all my fault? I realised then that what I wanted more than anything – more than Jackson – was Ava's forgiveness, and everyone's forgiveness – even if our friendships were over. My throat tightened. And if they'd just split up, I was never going to get it. Them staying together and becoming "stronger than ever" was my only hope of ever being given a second chance. And now that was gone.

What else could I do to put things right? I'd apologised to them both. Dropped out of prom night. Dropped out of Cornwall. Lost all my friends. Had a reputation as a bitch that was likely to follow me into sixth form college. Just when it felt like life was starting to improve just a teeny weeny bit since That Fateful Day – just when I was starting to hate myself a little bit less, now it was all flaring up again. Would this ever end?

My phone started ringing and I nearly fell out of the hammock. It was Mum. I supposed I ought to answer it seeing as I'd missed her call earlier.

'Piggles! Caught you at last! How's it going with Grandpa Airhead?' Mum's voice echoed down the phone from Chicago.

'Fine.'

'I hear you've been getting acquainted with Odette?'

'Yeah.'

'Does she still tell it like it is?'

'Yup.'

'And are she and your grandad getting on OK with each other?'

'Yup.'

'Ori, from your monosyllabic answers, it's clear you're not happy. What's wrong?'

I let out a long, deep sigh, hoping I sounded so depressed it'd fill her with unbearable guilt for abandoning me in my hour of need. 'Jackson and Ava have split up, which means she'll *never* forgive me now.'

'Oh Piggles. Give her time. You've got to remember, finding out your partner's cheated on you is a really hideous experience – not least when it's with your best friend of all people.'

God, shut up Mum! Like I didn't know this already.

'It's properly traumatising when the two people you trust most in the world have–'

'OK, yeah I get it. Thanks, Mum. Look, I've got to go.'

'It'll blow over, Ori. Give her some time and then ask if you can meet to talk it through.'

'Sure, gotta go.'

'I love you, Piggles! Something good will come out of this, you'll see.'

'What, like lemonade? Maybe I'll start my own brand?'

'*Stay strong, Ori.* Remember, this too shall pass. Bye now.'

'Bye,' I said in my sulkiest, most miserable voice.

How wrong she was! Things were *not* passing. They were

getting *worse* – not better. I needed to go for a walk and clear my head before it exploded with uncomfortable feelings. Then I remembered the river.

I jumped out of the hammock, headed to the back of the garden, leapt over the cement board and climbed over the half-built wall.

'Hey pink cheeks, where ya goin'?' Claude shouted from the patio. He was wearing an apron and waving a spatula.

'Just going to check out the river.'

'OK, well don't be long, Sylvie's on her way over – she's dying to meet you! And nosh will be ready in half an hour.'

'I'll be back soon.'

I walked swiftly through the woods till I came to the river bank. Standing on the pebbly shore, the water lapping at my feet, I felt a sudden overwhelming urge to rush in to the water and swim. Could I? Should I? Claude had said it was a safe spot, so why not? I looked around to see if the coast was clear. There were people downstream but they were far away enough for me not to care, so I kicked off my flipflops, stripped off my shorts and top and waded into the water in my bra and knickers.

As the cool water enveloped my waist, I stifled a shriek and lowered myself in, swimming towards the centre of the river. Within seconds I no longer felt cold, but *free*. The fresh river smell filled my lungs and hit my bloodstream – like an injection of nature, a natural high.

I let the current take me twenty yards or so down river, then swam towards the edge and paddled my way back to my starting point. I decided to try swimming against the current, but it was so strong it took a lot of effort just to stay in the same spot and not get pulled along. Feeling my muscles start to ache, I swam back to where my feet could touch the bottom.

I looked around me. Woods lined the river bank on either side, but in the distance sheer cliffs dropped straight into the water, craggy shadows on their walls signalling hidden caves and ledges. There was nothing but nature here – wild, beautiful, soothing nature. I closed my eyes and tilted my head back, allowing my skin to soak up the last of the sun's rays. When I looked up again I glimpsed a flash of blue in the distance. Was that a Kingfisher? I strained my eyes, hoping to see it again.

I drifted a little, my feet brushing along the riverbed, all the while tracing the craggs in the cliff-face, hoping to spot the Kingfisher again. Unable to find it, I looked down into the water where I could see my feet, pale and magnified against the sand and stones beneath. A shoal of fish flitted by just a few metres away. I held my breath – it was magical. It was like swimming in an aquarium. My desperation started to fade a little.

As the sun disappeared from the river, I decided it was time to get out. I pulled my clothes on over my wet underwear and headed back to the barn, dripping as I walked. *Note to self: bring a towel next time, doofus.*

'Finally!' sighed Claude, as I walked in to find him, Odette and Sylvie all sitting on the sofas. 'We were about to send out a search party. Dinner's ready – we've been waiting for you.' His cheery tone was laced with annoyance.

'Sorry, I lost track of time. I went for a swim,' I said, water trickling from my hair down the back of my neck.

'Yeah, I can see that,' he said. 'This is Sylvie, by the way.'

'Hi. Nice to meet you.' I mustered a smile.

'Nice to meet you, too, Ori.' She shone warmly back at me. 'Come and have a glass of wine!'

I could see why Claude fancied her. She was attractive, slim and smiley, with wavy, grey-blonde hair that managed to make her look younger without looking like she was trying to hide her age. Relaxing on the sofa in a floaty blouse, white capri pants and silver Birkies – she was obviously one of those people who knew how to be fashionable without trying too hard. I guessed she was in her mid-sixties – younger than Claude at any rate.

'I'm a bit wet,' I replied. 'I forgot to take a towel.'

'A spontaneous swim in the river? Good for you!' she gushed. 'Why don't we all go tomorrow night? Make it a date?'

Claude and Odette glanced at each other.

'I'll watch,' said Odette.

'If *I'm* going in, *you're* going in,' Claude said to her.

'We'll see . . .' Odette sipped her wine.

'Can I just have a super-quick shower?' I asked.

'Yeah, hurry up. We're all bloody starving,' Claude rolled his eyes. 'By the way, you look a bit sunburnt. I've got some stuff you can put on it.'

I zipped up to the mezzanine, grabbed a change of clothing and hurried back down to the bathroom where I was confronted by a human tomato in the mirror above the sink. My skin felt hot to touch. *Great.* Still, fingers crossed it would settle into a radiant, sun-kissed glow by morning that would make Elias do a double-take. While I showered I wondered what was going down in Cornwall. Maybe it was all just a storm in a tea cup, as Mum would say. Ava and Jackson had probably made up by now. *Whatever.* It wasn't really any of my business anymore. I was well out of it.

When I turned the shower off I could hear raised voices coming from the main room. I pressed my ear to the door.

'You never once apologised!' (Odette.) 'You never acknowledge what you did!'

'I did apologise!' (Claude.) 'I never meant to hurt you. But I also did you a favour – you went on to meet someone who worshipped you.'

'*A favour?* We were happy. We were *in love.* Then you came along and destroyed our relationship.'

'I couldn't help my feelings for Jacqueline. And you're sort of forgetting she couldn't help her feelings for me. I'm sorry, Odey – she wasn't as in love with you as she led you to believe.'

'You did what you always do – *charm, seduce, abandon.*'

'Er, maybe I should give you guys some privacy . . .' (Sylvie.)

'No stay, Sylvie!' (Odette.) 'You must know what kind of man my brother is. He had an affair with my partner! For over a year they lied and cheated, until I found out.'

'It was four bloody decades ago!' (Claude.) 'We've been over this again and again. I'm much more mindful of how I handle things these days.'

'Pah!' (Odette.) 'But the damage you did, Claude! I was *broken.*'

'I'll go and check on the dinner.' (Sylvie.)

'*Non!* Stay where you are, please!' (Odette.) 'I suffered depression, I took pills . . . I wanted to die! It took me years to recover from your affair. The fact that I eventually fall in love again is not relevant to this argument. You did so much damage and you have never sincerely apologise to me for what you did.'

Silence.

'Well I'm sincerely apologising now. I'm sorry. I was a total dick.'

'You *still are* a total dick!'

I quickly pulled on my clothes, yanked open the door and strutted towards them as if I hadn't heard a word.

Sylvie put her glass of wine down on the coffee table and stood up. 'Look, I think you guys need some time to talk things over. I'll catch up with you tomorrow.'

'But we haven't eaten yet!' said Claude, grabbing her arm.

'See you tomorrow, everyone!' Sylvie hurried to the front door. Claude ran after her and stepped outside, closing the door behind them.

'Are you OK?' I asked Odette as I threw my towel up the corkscrew staircase and sat down on the sofa.

That was some revelation. I imagined a younger Odette, feeling crushed, alone, beyond hope. I reached out and touched her gently on the arm.

'Odette?'

'I'm not feeling my best.' She got up and reached for her walking stick.

'What was all that about?'

'Claude . . .' She shook her head, unable to find the words. 'He does not change.'

CHAPTER FIFTEEN
Sense and Sensibility

The following morning, I was in the kitchen, hunting high and low for the normal tea bags when Claude walked in and flung a bag of pastries at me. 'Dish 'em up, babes!'

'Where are the normal tea bags?' I asked. I had a headache and needed urgent hydration.

'Tea bags, fleabags! Try this coffee. It's amazing. You won't be disappointed.'

I poured the pastries onto a plate while Claude rinsed out the cafetière and dolloped two scoops of fresh coffee in it. A heady smell hit me the second he opened the packet.

'Odette seemed pretty upset last night,' I said pointedly, filling a large glass with water from the tap and glugging it down thirstily. 'Is everything OK between you?'

He bustled around me, gathering plates and cutlery. 'Oh, it's all ancient stuff. We have a little bicker about it every ten years or so.'

'A *little bicker*? She wanted to die! She took pills!' I glared at him, the adrenaline picking up the pace in my body.

How could he brush it off like that? Where was his remorse?

Claude filled up the cafetière with hot water from the kettle. 'Look, I've tried to make amends many times over the years but she's never let it go – even when she married Cyril, she continued to shut me out.'

'Wait, she got married after that?' I hadn't expected to hear that. Odette didn't seem the marrying kind any more than Claude did. 'And Cyril is – *was* – a man?'

'Yeah. She married Cyril in the late Eighties, then he died ten or fifteen years later. I got the impression they were happy together, not that we saw much of each other. So I think there's a lot more to Odey's demons than just my affair with Jacqueline.'

Whatever – *a year-long affair with your sibling's partner* was just plain cruel. I'd fallen asleep last night thinking about it. It made my crime seem like small fry by comparison. Not that it made me feel any better about what I did, but it helped to hear a real example of something far, far worse.

'How long were you and Jacqueline together for after Odette found out?'

'A little while – eighteen months or so?'

'What happened to her? Jacqueline, I mean?'

'We went our separate ways. Didn't keep in touch.'

'Did she try to get back together with Odette?'

He shrugged. 'Not as far as I know. The damage was already done. Look, I'm not proud of what I did, but there you are. It happened. Can't undo it, but can't spend the rest of my life begging her forgiveness either.'

'How *hard* did you try to make amends?' I asked accusingly. Knowing him, not very.

'*Really* hard!' He looked a bit put out. 'She wouldn't have it. Refused to talk to me while me and Jacq were together. Then when we split up, each time I tried to put things right it was like – *BOOM*!' He mimed an explosion. 'I weren't in the best place myself. Career going nowhere. Not looking after myself. I couldn't face Odey's rage any more so I gave up. Kept my distance.'

He concentrated on pressing down the cafetière plunger.

'Time's running out,' I said. 'You two need to sort things out, like, once and for all.'

Claude sighed. 'Yes, I'm aware of that, thank you. We've managed to be mostly civil to each other on the rare occasions we've met over the last twenty years. And when I sent her an email last year, I was surprised to get an almost friendly reply – which is why, after some thought, I invited her to come and stay. And here we are. So you see, things are progressing.'

I thought about Odette's announcement that she didn't have long to live. Maybe she was ready to finally put the past behind her.

'I know she cares about you.'

'What makes you think that?'

'When you were dangling between those two balconies the other night, she didn't want you to die.'

Claude's lips twitched. 'Well that's good to know. And I care about her too, Pinkster. Which is something I intend to let her know, don't you worry.' He nodded towards the garden. 'Shall we?'

I carried the pastries outside to the patio where Odette was sitting while Claude followed me with the cafetière. I was starting to like this breakfast: pain au chocolat, coffee and sunshine. It beat Coco Pops, TikTok and being nagged by Mum to hurry up any day. And Claude was right about one thing – the coffee was good.

'Odey, I'm sorry we argued last night,' said Claude, filling her cup. 'Can we talk later?'

Odette gazed into the distance. '*Si tu veux.*'

'I think it's important we talk it through. Just the two of us, in private.'

She avoided eye contact. 'My schedule is clear.'

'Great. Thanks.' He cut his pain aux raisins in half and turned to me. 'So you and Elias made good progress on the Great Wall of China yesterday. I reckon you'll have it finished by late afternoon at this rate.' He slurped his coffee and squinted at our handiwork in the sunshine. 'Nice lad, isn't he?' said Claude. 'You get on with him OK?'

'Yeah, fine,' I said casually, shifting my chair so it was more in the shade of the parasol.

'Your mum said you'd had some, er . . . "boy trouble"?'

I felt my cheeks colour up. (As if they weren't red enough already. My sunburn hadn't calmed down as much as I'd hoped.)

'What did she tell you?' I narrowed my eyes.

'Nothing really – just that you'd had some heartache.'

If I were to tell them how I'd snogged my best friend's boyfriend, Odette would think I'd inherited my grandad's genes. In fact, what if I actually *had* inherited his genes? Maybe my dumbass mistake was all down to biology? *God no, don't let me be like him.*

'Ori?' Claude prodded my arm with his knife. 'You OK, kiddo?'

'I'm fine. She was exaggerating. It's no big deal.'

'Hellooo!' A voice called out from inside the barn. 'I hope you don't mind I came in. I knock but no one could hear me.' Elias strode towards us, his floppy hat shielding his eyes from the sun.

'Elias, my good man,' said Claude. 'Come and grab a pain au naughtiness!'

'I eat already, thanks. I'm ready for work. Oh, this is for you from my grandma.' He undid his bag and took out a jar of strawberry jam.

'Oh beautiful. Thank you. I'll call her in a bit.' Claude admired the handwritten label. 'Nectar of the gods, this stuff.' He passed it to me so I could admire it, too, crammed the rest of his pastry in his mouth and got up from the table. 'Excellent. Let's crack on.'

Before grabbing a wheelbarrow, I slathered myself in sun cream and put a pale blue bucket hat on to prevent my cheeks getting any redder than they already were. Surprisingly, there was something weirdly liberating about accepting I looked ridiculous. With no chance in hell of Elias being likely to fancy me, the pressure was off and I could relax.

'Very wise!' called Claude from across the garden as he used his trowel to toss cement around on the cement board as if it were pizza dough. 'I almost can't tell where your hair ends and your face begins.'

Ha ha.

Elias laughed. 'You definitely got burnt yesterday.'

'Yes, OK, I admit I was an idiot. I over-trusted my moisturiser. But today I'm fully prepared.' I pulled out my water bottle to show him. 'See? Like you, I'm going to send a photo to my mum. Can you do the honours?' I handed him my phone and posed, swigging from my bottle. Today I was on a mission to stay shaded and hydrated.

Elias pointed to my hat. 'Pull it down more so it shades your face. Otherwise she'll see you already got burnt.'

'Good thinking.' I adjusted my hat and Elias snapped away.

My phone started ringing while he was holding it. 'Incoming!' he announced, glancing at it before passing it back to me.

Jackson. Whether it was another so-called "butt dial" or a dose of abuse, I wasn't in the mood. I declined the call and thrust it in my back pocket. For two people who wanted nothing more to do with me, him and Ava couldn't seem to leave me alone.

'Everything OK?' he asked, pulling on some gloves.

'Yeah, just someone being annoying.'

'These little devices . . .' He patted his shirt pocket where I could see the outline of his phone. 'Notice how you are feeling fine one minute and then your phone beeps and in seconds you're in a not-so-good mood? I had to turn off my phone for a while because of my ex-girlfriend. Actually, I'm grateful to her, because now I turn my phone off a lot. It's my new normal.'

I pressed a brick into place and smoothed away the excess cement with my trowel. 'Why did you need to turn it off?'

'It's a long story. We split up. We were together for a year but I began to realise we didn't have much in common, so I finish it. I tried to tell her as kindly as possible, but she refused to accept we were finished. So then I had to be really clear, but that made her angry.'

'What did she do?' I asked, picking up another brick and buttering one end like a slice of toast. It was a strangely satisfying process.

'She sent me lots of messages, calling me bad names. Saying negative things about me in group chats, on social media . . . Some of her friends also took her side. Our exams were getting close so I just decide to turn off my phone, stop using social media. I needed to concentrate on my studies. We both applied to the same university, so I changed my application to a different place and deferred a year.'

'Wow.' I wanted to tell him I'd also come close to changing my college application in order to avoid someone. But it was different. He hadn't done anything wrong, whereas I had. 'She sounds pretty unreasonable.'

'I hope she'll see things differently one day, but I don't know.'

'I'm in a similar situation,' I said. 'Well, similar but different.'

'You have an angry ex-boyfriend?' He took off his hat and used it to fan his face.

'No, I have an angry ex-*best* friend.'

Ugh. It was too cringeworthy to share my dramas with someone I barely knew – especially someone I had a crush on.

'What happened?' he asked. 'Why are they angry with you?'

Could I trust him? Would I regret telling him?

I paused while Claude approached with his spirit level and lined it up with the brickwork. 'Coming along nicely. Good job. As you were.' He sauntered off again.

I wanted to talk about it. It needed to come out. Apart from Mum and Ravi, I hadn't opened up to anyone about it.

A fresh perspective, from someone who didn't know me, might be helpful.

Here went nothing.

'Her name is Ava. I made a mistake.' I hadn't realised how much I'd been holding my breath until I exhaled.

'You don't have to talk about it if it makes you feel uncomfortable.' He carried on smoothing out the excess cement, his trowel scraping against the brick.

'I just don't want to be judged any more. I've been judged a lot lately – not least by myself.'

'I promise I won't judge you.'

'Impossible. I did something I shouldn't have done. You're going to like me a lot less when I tell you.'

'Maybe I don't like you anyway?' He punched me playfully on the arm. 'I'm just kidding. Seriously, what did you do? Murder her dog? Copy her exam thesis?'

'I kissed her boyfriend, Jackson.'

He grinned and raised his eyebrows. '*Okaaay*, I can understand why she might be angry.'

'I was wrong. There are no excuses. I don't know what I was thinking but I should never have done it. I've apologised but she won't speak to me – she totally hates me.'

'And her boyfriend? Was he happy to kiss you?'

'I got the impression he was – until she walked in and saw us.'

'Oh man.' Elias laughed, his perfect white teeth making me melt with lust. 'And they are still together?'

'They might have just broken up, according to my friend Ravi.'

'So maybe now is your chance . . . ?'

I shook my head vigorously. 'No, I don't think so. It's not worth it.'

'You don't like him anymore?'

I didn't know what to say. I liked Jackson a little bit less as a person, but I was still attracted to him – which didn't even make sense. My head was in a complete jumble. What did it matter anyway? He was probably trying to win Ava back right that minute.

'I just don't want people to hate me. I've never felt so crap my entire life.'

Elias patted me sympathetically on the shoulder. 'Look, we are young and we make stupid mistakes. Don't beat yourself up so much. If you murdered her dog, that would be much worse.'

'Keep up the pace, you two!' shouted Claude, tipping another bag of sand into the cement mixer. 'I'll need some help painting inside later. We mustn't fall behind schedule. By the way, Elias, we're all going for a splash in the river later, if you fancy joining us?'

'Sure, it will be a good way to cool down,' he replied. 'We better get back to work.'

I felt lighter all of a sudden. Someone knew about my crime and didn't hate me for it. Thank God for Elias. Thanks to him I felt happy for the first time in weeks. It was nice to know there was more to him than just a fit body and a snoggable face. I can't believe I'd told him all the gory details but he was just so easy to talk to, funny, and listened without judgement. He was someone you could have serious conversations with *and* have a laugh with – "boyfriend material", as Mum would say.

I suppressed the urge to sigh out loud. I had to be smart this time and keep things real: this was a friendship. A friendship that would probably last the next week or so until we both went our separate ways. Maybe we'd stay in touch, maybe we wouldn't. If he wasn't on social media, I wasn't even sure *how* we'd stay in touch?

Extremely Important Memo to Self: Elias wasn't flirting with me, he was just being friendly. He was two years older, about to go off travelling, then to uni – there's no way he'd be interested in starting something up with a sixteen year old who was about to start sixth form college in another country. Besides, I got the feeling he definitely didn't fancy me, so that made things simple: I knew where I stood. (And *I liked* knowing where I stood.) I just had to make sure I didn't start flirting with him – I'd already embarrassed myself enough for one year.

As I cemented another brick into place, Elias peeled off his T-shirt and threw it to one side. I immediately looked the other way so that I didn't start drooling at the sight of his bare torso.

'Ori?'

I turned back round. He was waving the sun cream at me.

'Would you put it on my back for me? I can't reach.'

Oh God. I was doomed.

'Sorry, maybe I shouldn't ask this?' He looked a bit embarrassed. 'It's OK, I can do it.'

'No, it's fine!' I said in an unexpectedly high-pitched voice. 'It's just greasy, yucky stuff. I hate it. Bleurgh! But it's fine, give it here. Don't want you to burn.'

'Thank you,' he grinned. 'I appreciate it.'

I took the tube, instructed him to lean forward and squirted a large dollop onto the centre of his back.

'Aargh – it's cold!'

'Don't be a wuss.' I massaged it into his skin and tried to keep my mind on the job.

'That feels good. You can massage my shoulders at the same time if you like! They're pretty sore from yesterday.' He grinned at me over his shoulder, eyes twinkling.

Wait – was he *flirting*? I gave him a sarcastic grin back, even though my heart was doing high-speed acrobatics.

'I'm joking of course,' he laughed. 'Not about my shoulders though – they ache like crazy. Don't yours?'

'Yeah, they do.' I passed the sun cream back. 'All done.'

'Thanks,' he said. 'Let me know if I can return the favour.'

'Wokay.' *Wokay? What the hell was that?* 'I mean, OK. Will do.' *Kill me now.*

CHAPTER SIXTEEN

As Good As It Gets

Ravi: So . . . I'm back in Brighton.

Me: What? Why?!

Ravi: Ava and Jackson split up and couldn't be anywhere near each other. Daisy and Martha weren't getting on and Maya had to leave anyway for a family thing. So we all packed up and came home yesterday — except Zac and Blake who were happy to stay on their own.

Me: That sucks. Sorry to hear that. You could always come and hang out here at Studio Marchand!

Ravi: My dad wants me to help out at the garden centre. Seriously, I cannot spend the rest of the summer shifting potted plants and answering old people's questions about geraniums. I'll DIE of boredom. 🥴

Me: At least it'll look good on your CV . . . ?

Ravi: Woohoo.

Odette gripped my elbow as we made our way slowly through the woods to the river. The evening sun filtered through the trees, the warm breeze tickling my skin. Once again, I became aware of my spirits lifting as the woods swallowed us up.

Learning from Ravi earlier that the Cornwall camping trip had come to a premature end after just four nights didn't bring me any satisfaction. I actually felt nothing – apart from some anxiety at how deeply Ava must hate me by now.

I'd deleted Jackson's voicemail without listening to it. No doubt he blamed me as much as she did. I kind of got what Claude had said earlier about not being able to face Odette's rage any more – I couldn't deal with any more rage from Ava, Jackson or anyone else right now. I was just glad to be far away. This wasn't my dream holiday by any means, but given that I'd been having a laugh with a cute German guy while building a wall (my new skill), it had already beaten my lower-than-low expectations. Not that I'd dared to admit that to Mum when I spoke to her earlier – I couldn't face her smugly pointing out that maybe I was having a good time after all. I didn't even mention Elias to her, but I had a feeling Claude had, as she'd asked if I'd met "anyone interesting" yet?

'Did you and Claude have a talk earlier?' I asked Odette as we weaved our way through the trees, her walking stick tapping the ground with each step.

'Yes, we talked.'

'Did he apologise for everything that happened with Jacqueline?'

'Yes, he did. And I have forgiven him.'

'Really? You're completely cool with each other now?' I wasn't sure whether to believe her. Surely forty years of resentment couldn't just disappear like that?

'This afternoon he apologise very sincerely to me. I am finished being angry. I carry anger in my heart for too long – and I am miserable. I should have forgiven him many years ago but I could not. I liked being right, it made me feel superior – which was a nice change from feeling inferior. But enough. I am not perfect either. I love my brother and I know he loves me. This story is finished now.' She knocked a fallen branch out the way with her walking stick.

Inferior was how I'd been feeling ever since committing my crime. Small. Low. Grimy. By comparison, Ava seemed tall, strong, shining bright. Untouchable.

'*Mon dieu*, it's hot,' muttered Odette.

'The river will cool you down,' I assured her. 'When I went for a swim last night, it was amazing. It was just so soothing . . . I can't really describe what I mean. I just felt so much better afterwards.'

'You connect with nature,' she said knowingly. 'In the water, with fish beneath you, birds above you, and trees all around you.'

'It's called green-bathing,' said Claude, catching up with us as we arrived on the pebbly bank. 'Scientists say it's the best type of medicine there is.'

He yanked off his T-shirt and did a few stretches before strutting unevenly into the water in his skin-tight trunks. It wasn't a good look, but Claude didn't seem to care.

I settled Odette down carefully on a large log, dumped my towel on the ground and stripped off my shorts. This time I was properly prepared and wearing a bikini.

'Ah, fantastic!' gasped Claude as he waded in. 'There's

no place better than Mother Nature's bath tub. Going to join me, ladies?'

'Come on, Odette,' I said. 'I'll hold on to you.'

She was wearing jeans cut off at the knee, a loose T-shirt and a pair of wet shoes that Claude had handed to each of us from a random collection in a plastic storage box kept beneath his caravan.

'*Bon, d'accord.*' She stood up and took my arm. 'Just to my knees. That is enough.'

I slowly inched forward, holding her securely as she looked where to step, her balance often wobbling on the stony ground.

'Look!' She squeezed my arm and pointed to the opposite bank with her stick. 'The bird! Claude – look! I forget the name!'

'Kingfisher,' said Claude, treading water in the middle of the river. 'You see them a lot round here. It's one of the many reasons I fell in love with this place.'

'I can see why you like it so much,' I said, easing Odette forward until we were up to our knees. I noticed how she seemed to breathe in the calmness of the river.

'Hey everyone!' Elias emerged from the woods in a pair of baggy trunks, his towel draped over one shoulder.

'*Guten Abend!* So pleased you could join us,' said Claude.

'Is it cold?' asked Elias, dropping his towel on the pebbles and walking in up to his ankles.

'A bit of a shock to begin with,' said Claude, 'and then it's fan-bloody-tastic!'

'*Tiens, ma chérie.*' Odette patted my arm. 'I will return to the log now.'

I helped her back to the shore and eased her onto the log, while

Elias rocketed into the water and plunged beneath the surface.

'Go swim,' ordered Odette. 'I'm happy here.' She patted the log beneath her.

I eased myself in pretty quickly compared to my first attempt the day before, as I now knew it wouldn't take long to warm up.

'Look!' called Elias.

I watched as he swam against the current, then relaxed, letting the river take him downstream. I trod water for what felt like ages, hoping to see a fish. The feeling of weightlessness and the soothing gurgling of water washed all my thoughts and worries away. I thought about what Odette had said about connecting with nature. It was true – in that moment, I felt fully blissed out, like I was part of the river.

When I looked up, Claude was sitting on the log next to Odette, throwing stones into the river and saying "plop!" every time one kerplunked into the water.

Elias burst out of the water next to me, making me jump.

'God!' I splashed him in the face. 'You gave me a fright!'

He laughed and followed my gaze towards Claude and Odette. It was as if they were both in a trance, Odette turning a stone over in her hands and staring into space, Claude hypnotised by the concentric circles his "plops" were making in the water.

'I think Claude discover a new type of meditation,' whispered Elias. 'With sound effects.'

I started to laugh. Claude's "plops" were super-cringey and yet somehow I totally got the satisfaction it was giving him just saying it out loud. I cracked up.

'What's so funny?' grinned Elias.

'Plop!' I hooted, falling backwards into the water.

Elias started to laugh too.

Claude looked up. 'This is very therapeutic, I'll have you know. Haven't you kids ever heard of *plopotherapy?*'

He stood up. 'Shall we head back to the ranch, Odey? I'd better get the dinner on – it's nearly seven already.'

She offered him her arm and he heaved her off the log.

'You guys take your time. Dinner will be ready by eight – Elias, you're welcome to join us.'

'Thank you but Oma is cooking dinner tonight.'

'No worries, mate. Hey, ask your folks if they wanna come over for a jam tomorrow night,' he said. 'We could do with a little warm-up before the launch party.'

Elias gave him a thumbs up as they turned and disappeared into the woods.

'You have a nice family,' he said.

'They're a pair of fruit-baskets,' I replied.

He frowned at me. 'Fruit-baskets?'

'Banana-brains, slightly nuts?' I searched for an internationally understood word. 'A bit crazy? I barely know them and yet just from the last few days I feel like I've known them all my life.'

'Well, I like them. Come on, I'll race you to the other side.'

We pegged it towards the far shore, both drifting diagonally as the current slowed our progress. Elias slapped his hand on the rocky bank first and waited for me to catch up.

'I'm not a strong swimmer,' I said.

'Me neither. Ready, steady, go!'

We raced back again, then swam around for a bit, debating whether we could handle living in a place as wild and countrysidey as this full-time.

'Ori!' Elias hissed, pointing at the water and signalling to be quiet.

I paddled slowly towards him. 'What?'

'There!' he whispered.

I followed his gaze but still couldn't see. 'Where?'

He took my arm and pulled me gently towards him, letting go when we were standing side by side, our bodies touching. Again he pointed. 'Right there. See them?'

I gasped as I saw a giant fish, about a foot long – and another, and another. An actual group of them, like a fleet of ghostly submarines. 'Wow!' I exhaled.

I would have liked to have put my goosebumps down to the fact I was standing just a few feet from a large shoal of enormous fish, but I was also leaning against Elias's bare flesh and my heart was thudding so loudly I'm surprised the fish couldn't feel it pulsing through the water.

'Pretty amazing, huh?' he said, not moving away, even though he could've done, now that the fish had glided away.

'Yeah. Incredible.'

I wondered what would happen if I were to turn around and face him? I swear I could feel an energy crackling between us, but no doubt it was just my overactive imagination up to no good again, desperate to see things that weren't there. And yet he still wasn't moving away. I could even feel his warm breath on my shoulder . . . If a guy doesn't mind standing this close to you, it means he likes you, doesn't it? Otherwise he'd move away – right? So, could this be a sign that he liked me? He'd pulled me towards him and now that he'd shown me what he wanted to show me, he wasn't rushing to have his personal space back.

I imagined what it would be like to kiss him, then banished the thought from my head and drifted gently away before I got it all wrong and embarrassed myself again.

'I should head back,' I said. *Bravo, Ori.*

'Sure,' he said, a flicker of disappointment morphing quickly into a smile. 'Me too.'

CHAPTER SEVENTEEN
The Pursuit of Happyness

The following day, the smell of fried onions and garlic wafted out of the kitchen and up to the mezzanine as Claude prepared food for the evening's dinner party with Elias and his grandparents. The smell seeped into my nostrils and made my stomach growl. It had been another long, hot day and I was sitting crossed-legged on my mattress in front of the floor-to-ceiling window, clutching Claude's binoculars, and trying to focus on an impressive-looking bird in the early evening shadows. Was it Monty? I couldn't tell one bird of prey from another. Living in an upstairs flat in the middle of Brighton, the only birds I ever saw were seagulls, who liked to screech from the roof above my bedroom.

Downstairs Claude swore loudly as he tripped over something while doing the hoovering – my shoes, probably. I hadn't even noticed the noise of the hoover, I'd been so engrossed in looking through the binoculars.

I stretched my aching back and reached for my phone to google birds of prey. As I scrolled through images of kites and buzzards, it started ringing.

Jackson.

Again? *WTF?* I leapt up and stared at my phone.

Answer or ignore? Answer or ignore? Answer or ignore?

What the hell did he want? To give me more grief now that he and Ava had split up? Or to let me know that whatever I may have heard on the grapevine, they were still very much together, so not to get any ideas?

'Jackson?' Nervous energy kicked my heart into gear like a shot of caffeine.

'Ori! I didn't think you'd pick up.'

'What do you want?' I tried to keep my voice as casual as possible, while scurrying around trying to pick up a stronger signal. Mobile phone reception wasn't the greatest at Claude's place.

'I wanted to say sorry.'

'*You* wanted to say sorry to *me*? Sorry for what exactly?'

'For freezing you out.' I could hear a loud beeping in the background, like a lorry reversing or train doors closing.

'Oh, right . . .' What was I supposed to say to that? Was I now *unfrozen*? Should I ask about him and Ava? Or should I pretend I didn't know they'd split up?

'Me . . . Ava have . . . up.' The line was breaking up.

'What?' I opened an upper window and leaned out – as if that would make any difference to the signal.

'Me and Ava have broken up,' he repeated a bit louder. 'Sorry, it's a bit noisy in here.'

'Oh. I thought you guys had worked things out and were . . . doing fine?' I resisted the temptation to say "stronger than ever".

'I feel awful. It's all my fault.'

'It's not all your fault. It's more complicated than that.'

'You don't blame me?'

'No. I did before – but not any more. I've been doing some thinking...' His voice trailed off.

'Well I'm sorry anyway. I really regret what I did and I wish you and Ava could get back to normal again.'

'That's not going to–' The signal kept coming and going and a loud speaker in the background wasn't helping either. '... heads up ... me thinking and ...... you ...... to talk things through – if that's OK with you?'

'What? I can't hear you very well. Where are you?'

'Ori, can you hear me?'

'Yeah, but I've got to go.' The sound of the vacuum cleaner was getting louder and louder. Claude's head appeared at the top of the corkscrew staircase.

'OK, I'll call you later,' he said.

'OK, bye.' Wait – why would he call me later? What more was there to say? But he'd already hung up. I flopped back down on the mattress.

I wasn't sure I wanted to talk again later. Maybe by the time we started college in September it would feel OK for us to talk, but until then, I didn't want anyone accusing me of jumping in there the minute it was over between him and Ava. Not that I intended to "jump in there", but there was no doubt that's what I'd be accused of. If he called again later – and who knew whether he would or not – I would tell him it was best for us not to contact each other until everything had one-hundred-per-cent blown over.

Besides, what was there to talk about? He'd said sorry for freezing me out, and I was grateful for that. One less person hated me, and that felt like a major leap forwards. Although, as Ravi was being super-slow in responding to my last message (along with a picture of the wall I'd helped to build), I was once again wondering if our friendship was starting to matter less to him, now that he and Maya were "a thing".

'Aha!' said Claude, switching off the hoover and pulling a hairball out of the hose attachment. 'There you are! Fancy lending us a hand?'

I was already knackered from painting walls all day. Elias had only joined us for a few hours earlier that afternoon, to help paint the windowsills, but he was returning later with his grandparents for dinner and "a jam" – a word that implied I'd be doing a lot of cringing later. In the meantime, I decided I'd better show I was willing to take on another task, even though all I wanted to do was lie on my bed and stare at the ceiling.

'Sure,' I said, feigning enthusiasm. 'Want me to hoover up here?'

'No, I'll do that,' he said. 'How about you help Odette in the kitchen? She's an amazing cook. She could teach you some age-old family recipes, handed down through the generations to Great Grannie Albertine to her, and now to you.'

While I hated cooking with a passion, the thought of learning a secret family recipe passed down through the generations of my ancestors was quite appealing, although I wasn't sure why. Maybe it was something to do with exploring a part of my identity that I hadn't given much thought to before. I heaved my heavy limbs up off the floor and headed downstairs, while Claude began hoovering the mezzanine.

'What are you making?' I asked, peering under the lid of a bubbling pan and letting a cloud of steam escape.

'Coq au vin,' said Odette, dipping a spoon in and blowing on it. 'Chicken in wine stew. The recipe of your Great Grannie Albertine.' She held the spoon out towards me. '*Tiens.*'

'No chicken for me,' I reminded her.

'Not for me either. I make for the others. Just try the sauce.'

I stepped closer and allowed her to slip the spoon in my mouth. '*C'est bon?*'

'Yes, *c'est* very *bon*,' I replied, licking my lips.

'Claude said it needed more salt!' she tutted. '*Mon dieu*, English people have terrible tastebuds.'

'What, every single one of us?' I teased.

'Yes, every single one of you!' she laughed. 'You are nation of tinned spam lovers.'

'I've never eaten tinned spam in my life!' I protested. 'Anyway, can I help you?'

'*Oui, ma chérie.* You can make the *tarte aux pommes*. Please, peel the *pommes* and slice into thin wedges.' She pointed to a bowl of cooking apples on the counter. 'I am also making a cheese and onion quiche for us vegetarians.'

I opened the cutlery drawer and rummaged until I found a peeler. We stood in silence for a few minutes, peeling, chopping, stirring, until Claude clattered past, wrestling the hoover back into a cupboard. He reappeared in the kitchen and grabbed a large knife.

'So, Pinkydinks, ready for some jamming tonight?' he asked, attacking a large onion.

'Guess so.'

If Elias hadn't been joining us, I'd have probably invented a headache and gone to bed early to zone out on TikTok. Watching a bunch of pensioners crooning and strumming guitars wasn't exactly my idea of entertainment.

'There are plenty of instruments to go round. Some of them more amusing than others,' he said with a mischievous smile.

'What do you mean, "plenty of instruments to go round"?' I asked.

'Everyone joins in, kiddo. Odey, you'll shake some maracas, won't you?'

Odette rolled her eyes and ignored him.

'Shame Gerry can't be with us. *He'd* have joined in.' Claude's eyes were watering from the onion. He rubbed them with the back of his wrist. 'He used to tinker around on the guitar,' he explained to me. 'Gave up too soon, though. He was so under the old man's thumb – he never stood a chance.'

'I don't understand. Why did he quit?' I asked.

'Wanted the old man's approval more than he wanted to learn guitar. Our dad was determined that one of his kids would get a *real* job, so he turned all his attention to Gerry and piled the guilt on thick as cement. The result was that Gerry became an accountant, started his own business, wore a shirt and tie to work and had "clients" who drove fancy cars. The day he took the old man out for a spin in his own brand new Porsche ... That was Dad's proudest moment. He'd given up with me and Odey.'

'He did not *give up* with me!' Odette snorted, taking a large, pointy knife from the drawer and slicing through the middle of a large round lettuce.

Claude looked confused.

'He never cared about me in the first place!' she scoffed. 'Even if I was the next Monet or Van Gogh, with my paintings hanging in prestigious galleries, he would never have been proud of me.'

'Come on, now, Odey. He was a stuffy old fart for sure – no doubt about that. He was conservative, conventional – and there weren't a creative bone in his body. But stubborn old prick though he was, he wanted the best for each of us in his own way. He loved us equally deep down.'

Odette spun round, waving the chopping knife. 'What planet do you live on, Claude? He wanted the best for *you* and *Gerry*. He did not want *me* at all. I was an embarrassment. He did not love us *equally* – Albertine yes, but Leonard? You are joking!'

Claude's face fell. 'Don't say that, Odey. It's not true. He just didn't know how to relate to a thirteen-year-old girl – especially one that came from so much hardship. He never knew how to express his emotions – even with me and Gerry, so it's not surprising he didn't know how to be around you.'

Odette looked up at the ceiling despairingly. 'He is not the man you think he was!'

'What does that mean?' asked Claude, alarmed. 'What are you implying?'

She took a deep breath. 'Now is not the time. Your guests will be here soon.'

'Don't leave me flipping dangling, Odey. I need to know!'

'He never lay a finger on me, if that's what you're thinking.'

Claude's shoulders sank with relief. 'You're sure? Please tell me the truth.'

'The truth was he never touch me *at all*. Not once. Not a hug, not a kiss on the forehead, not a pat on the shoulder. Nothing. I was invisible to him. He tried to pretend I wasn't there. He was ashamed of me. Do you know how that made me feel?'

Odette plunged the knife into the chopping board and hobbled out of the kitchen. I ran after her.

'Odette, are you OK?' Lame question – of course she wasn't OK. I followed her to her bedroom door and reached for her arm before she disappeared inside.

'I will be fine,' she said, brushing me gently away.

I moved aside so she could close her door and returned to the kitchen where Claude and I stared at the lethal weapon, standing upright on its tip, until he cleared his throat and pulled it out of the chopping board. 'Don't worry, kiddo. She'll be all right.' He felt its pointy tip with his finger. 'She's a tough old egg – her shell is solid titanium. Nothing can break her. She's a survivor.'

'Jesus – really? You think just cos she's strong on the outside she isn't hurting inside?'

'What I mean is–'

'Her dad was killed, her mum was an alcoholic and her adopted dad didn't want her – she must've been through hell! And then you pinched her girlfriend! I mean, do you ever think of anyone except yourself? And talking of rubbish dads, you weren't exactly World's Best Dad yourself – let alone

World's Best Grandad! Mum's been going to therapy cos of you for years – bet you didn't know that, did you?'

I was about to storm out of the kitchen but he caught my arm.

'Ori, I admit I've not been a great father to your mum, and a bit of a useless grandad to you–'

'*A bit?*'

'*A lot.* But I'm trying to make up for things now – with you, with your mum and with Odey.'

'Really? I don't see how.'

'Please give me a chance. I'm trying. Tell you what, I'll cancel the jam tonight so the three of us can sit down and talk. Talk *properly.* Clear the air once and for all. Everyone can say their bit and be heard. A *family summit*, if you will.'

Hmm . . . Which was more appealing? An awkward, probably heated discussion with the Boomers or an evening with hot, tasty food and hot, tasty Elias?

'Where's me flipping phone?' said Claude, rummaging around the kitchen. 'I'll call Rolf and make up some excuse.'

The doorbell rang. We looked at each other.

'*Guten Abend*, Claudie-Claudie!' a woman's voice sang from outside.

He sighed. 'Too late. Sorry, kiddo.'

CHAPTER EIGHTEEN
Pitch Perfect

'You're early!' Claude beamed as he welcomed Elias and his grandparents inside.

Elias smiled and passed me a large bowl of fruit salad, his fingers brushing mine as I took it from him.

'No Claudie, we are actually ten minutes *late*,' said Letzie, as she slipped a guitar case from her shoulder and put it next to the stage. 'You said six o'clock, yes?'

'I thought I said seven?' Claude scratched his head.

Letzie threw her long, grey plait over one shoulder and took her phone out of her handbag. She showed him the screen. '*Sechs, mein Liebling.*'

'Steady on, saucy!' joked Claude, as she gave him a playful slap. 'Well I meant seven. Pressed the wrong flipping key.'

'Darling, you really must wear your glasses when you text.' She kissed him on the cheek and swept towards me, her long, swishy dress billowing around her ankles, an assortment of bangles jangling on her wrists. The smell of lavender wafted towards my nostrils. 'You must be the lovely Ori. So nice to meet you!' She enveloped me in a tight hug and stood back to observe me. 'So is the Great Wall finished?'

'Yeah, finally,' I said.

Elias's grandfather put a bottle of wine down on the dining table and held out his hand. His index finger was wrapped in a bandage. 'I'm Rolf. Sorry my English is not so good as my wife's.'

'Ori.' I shook his hand. 'And I'm sorry I don't speak a word of German. What happened to your finger?'

'I am chopping potato. Finger get in the way.'

Rolf's mane of straight white hair was almost as long as Letzie's. He wore tapered pin-stripe trousers, a shirt and waistcoat and pointy ankle boots (which his feet must've been melting in). A neatly groomed long, white beard, tied in a ponytail, grew from his chin while a shiny shell hung from a leather cord around his neck. If Gandalf were to turn himself into a Rolling Stone, this would be the result.

'Elias, let's show your folks the fruits of your labour,' said Claude, guiding them outside. 'I'll just grab a few glasses and open this.' He picked up Rolf's bottle of wine and leaned towards my ear. 'Can you entertain our guests while I go check on Odey?'

I nodded.

'We'll have our family summit tomorrow – Scout's honour.' He did some weird three fingered salute and scurried off towards the kitchen.

I stepped outside the back door.

'A masterpiece!' declared Rolf, admiring our work. 'But I feel guilty – our grandson comes to stay with us and we condemn him to hard labour.'

Elias slapped his back. 'It's OK, Opa – I need the money.'

What? Claude was paying him while I was working for free? I clenched my jaws together. I'd be adding this topic to the agenda for tomorrow's family summit, *for sure.*

Letzie slid an arm around my shoulder. 'So nice to finally meet a member of Claude's family. How are you liking his barn? He's very proud of it, you know.'

'I love it,' I said, surprised to find myself genuinely meaning it. 'It's not what I was expecting at all.'

'It's the first time you stay with your grandfather, yes?'

'Yes.'

'Do you think you'll come again?'

I gave a cheery shrug. 'Maybe?' I hadn't given it any thought. But now that I was thinking about it, it wasn't a dead-set "no", which, again, took me by surprise. But then, maybe the whole reason my stay so far hadn't been a complete nightmare was because of Elias.

'Maybe you can come again next summer and work behind the bar?' she grinned. 'He's so determined to make this venue a success, you know? The whole village is behind him. A music venue in Frenac – it's the most exciting thing to happen here in years!'

'Evening everyone!'

We all turned around as Sylvie stepped out of the back door clutching a bottle of wine, wearing an oyster pink jumpsuit with her silver Birkies.

'Hi,' we chorused. Letzie dropped her arm from my shoulder and threw her arms around her. 'That outfit looks so *pridd-eee!*' she gushed.

'Hi Ori,' Sylvie kissed me on the cheek. 'Sorry for my early departure last time.'

'Oh, no worries. I understand.'

'Are things better between those two now?' she asked in a hushed tone.

'Up and down. I'm sure it'll all get sorted.'

As Sylvie turned to hug Rolf, Elias tapped my shoulder.

'Is it true we all have to play instruments?' he asked, a worried look on his face.

'Uh-huh,' I sympathised.

'I was thinking,' he lowered his voice and leaned closer to my ear, 'we join in for two or three songs, then we make an excuse and go for a swim in the river.' His breath in my ear and his suggestion to go to the river again made my body tingle all over. I swallowed and tried to focus. 'What do you think?' he whispered.

Yes please thank you with chocolate sprinkles on top! The thought of how we'd brushed against each other in the river yesterday was definitely something I wanted to repeat.

'Could do, possibly . . .' I said as if I wasn't bothered either way.

He touched my arm and I broke out in goosebumps. 'When Oma and Opa play guitar they go into another zone, like a parallel universe or something. We can sneak away . . .'

I tried to look casually, *mildly* tempted, while my body decided to do its own thing and shiver uncontrollably with excitement.

'Are you *cold*?' He glanced at my goosepimpled arms, amused.

I shook my head and inched discreetly away from him. If he breathed in my ear one more time I was going to pass out.

'Anyway, they'll be so drunk, they won't even notice we're gone . . .' he said out of the corner of his mouth. 'Trust me!'

'OK fine,' I sighed as if I was doing him a favour.

He grinned, gave me a fist-bump and went to get himself a drink.

He was probably right about the oldies – although so far I'd only witnessed Claude *sipping* wine, rather than necking it. Still, he wouldn't care if we disappeared for a bit. I looked over my shoulder: Odette was back in the kitchen again, spooning coq au vin into Claude's mouth. I couldn't keep up. Talk about a love/hate relationship.

We ate dinner outside on the patio, with everyone raving about the coq au vin and asking Odette what ingredients were in it. After dessert (my *tarte aux pommes* was a storming success), Odette retired to her room, claiming too many screechy guitars gave her a headache. Sylvie and I helped clear up while Claude went to fetch his dreaded bag of instruments. He returned five minutes later, plonking what looked like a large, heavy potato sack onto the table.

'Anyone without a guitar, grab something from Santa's sack,' he instructed, reaching for the guitar leaning against the wall behind him (*Layla*, I believe).

Sylvie grabbed the sack and pulled the drawstrings apart. 'Take your pick.' She held it open towards me and Elias.

We eyed it suspiciously.

'Come on, guys, it won't bite.' She shook the bag. 'Rolf, how about you? You're guitarless tonight.'

'Goddamn potato,' he moaned, plunging his bandaged hand into the bag and pulling out a harmonica.

'Come on, you two. Live a little!' She pushed the bag towards Elias.

He reached in and pulled out something that looked like a wooden log. He gave it a shake and the sound of hundreds of tiny beads rattled inside it. Rolf guffawed and patted him reassuringly on the shoulder. 'Don't look so scared, Elias – you used to love playing with your rain-stick when you were little.'

Elias shook the rain-stick in Rolf's face, making him flinch. 'Opa, please stop the terrible jokes.'

'*Nein, mein Junge* – I'm just getting started!'

The oldies all snorted with laughter.

'The sooner we escape, the better!' Elias whispered in my ear, his hot breath flaring up my goosepimples again.

I was starting to get the feeling that the spark I'd felt between us yesterday in the river wasn't just my imagination. But still, I didn't dare trust my instincts. They were too unreliable.

'Your turn, Ori.' Sylvie pushed the bag towards me.

I pulled out a tambourine and pushed the bag back to her, watching as she pulled out a triangle and searched for the stick to go with it.

'I need a ding-dong,' she said, rummaging through the bag.

Claude smirked and was about to make a joke when he caught my eye. I glared at him. *Just don't.*

Sylvie cleared her throat and trilled out a *doe, ray, me*, holding her voice steady on a long note. Immediately Rolf raised the harmonica to his lips and together with Claude and Letzie, they all played the same note.

'I'm on fire!' declared Letzie, looking very serious.

At first I thought she meant she wasn't feeling well, but then they all broke into song. I was pretty taken aback – *they could actually play*. Letzie closed her eyes as she sang, as if she were standing in front of a packed stadium, channelling the music to thousands of devoted fans. While me and Elias felt awkward just holding an instrument on our laps and listening, Letzie gave no hint of self-consciousness whatsoever. She was lost in the moment, feeling the music, making shivers run up and down my spine. I felt an unexpected sense of envy that I couldn't explain. I wanted a piece of that – whatever it was – that contented, happy magic. Claude and Sylvie smiled at each other as they strummed, hummed and dinged on either side of her. After the chorus (which included the words *"I'm on fire"*) Rolf lifted the harmonica to his lips and blasted it like Mick Jagger.

When the song finished, Letzie fixed me and Elias with a stern look. 'Guys! Could you look just a little more enthusiastic, please? You need to join in! If you don't know the words, just shake your instruments, OK? That's what they're for!'

'Don't you know any Springsteen?' Rolf asked incredulously.

'Er . . . Not really,' I said.

'A few songs,' said Elias. 'But not that one.'

Rolf sighed. 'I worry about the young people, Letzie. They don't know the Boss! What is the world coming to?'

Letzie rubbed his back. 'They'll find their way eventually, my love. Have faith.'

'OK,' said Sylvie. 'Let's try something everyone will know. The Beatles: *Ticket to Ride*. You know it?'

'Sort of,' I mumbled.

'Yes!' said Elias confidently.

She counted to three. This time me and Elias joined in and I was surprised to realise I actually knew some of the words.

If you'd told me four weeks ago that I'd be banging on a tambourine with a group of guitar-strumming septuagenarians, I would've laughed in your face. But there I was, doing just that and having a surprisingly good time (despite regular cringey jokes about instruments that looked or sounded like body parts). We went on to sing another three songs before Elias nudged me and whispered, 'Come on, it's now or never!'

While the oldies were topping up their drinks, Elias sprang up. 'Me and Ori are going for a walk down by the river to see the bats and maybe have a swim,' he announced as I stood up to join him.

Bats? I hoped he was making that part up.

'But we do Roxy Music next!' Letzie protested. 'Let's stick together?'

'You guys stick together,' said Elias. 'We'll be back in an hour.'

Letzie pulled a face. 'You see, Claudie? I told you. They don't want to hang with us. We are not cool enough for them.'

Claude squeezed her shoulder. 'No, Letz. We're *too* cool for them. *So* cool, they can't handle it.'

Elias snorted. 'We won't be long, Oma.'

'Careful of them bats!' Claude called after us. 'They prey on teenagers with undeveloped taste in music.'

'Ha ha, very funny,' I shot back over my shoulder as I grabbed my towel from the washing line by Claude's caravan.

I held my breath as I sank into the cold river and resisted squealing from the shock – not wanting to look like a wimp in front of Elias, who had already swum to the other side and back.

I stared down through the water, looking at the smooth, round stones beneath my feet.

'What are you doing?' asked Elias, emerging at my side.

'Looking for fish.'

We stood side by side, still as statues, staring into the rippling water.

'There!' He pointed to his left, where a small shadow flitted past, just a few yards away.

I looked for the rest of the shoal and spotted them a little further away, a shudder of excitement travelling through me. What *was* this? Had I spent so much time with old people that I'd suddenly developed a passion for fish-spotting? How far away was I from buying a rod, a pair of waders and posting selfies on Instagram of me cradling a ten-kilo trout?

It wasn't about identifying fish though. And I certainly had no interest in catching them. Or even touching them. I just liked being close to them in the water. And I liked watching the birds too. Hearing their chirping, feeling their presence. Was I having some kind of spiritual experience? Was Elias feeling it, too? He was standing as still as I was in the water, just watching and listening.

'I could stay here for ever,' I said softly as a bat skittered across the sky in front of us and disappeared into the cliff-face.

'You mean here in Frenac, or here in the river?'

'Here in the river. It feels like . . . heaven.'

'I know what you mean.'

'You do? I can't put it into words. I don't know how to explain it.'

'You feel like you're at one with the river. You're not thinking about anything else right now. You're here in this moment.'

'That's it!' I gasped. 'How did you put it so perfectly?'

'Oma's a real hippie. She tries to tell me these things for years. She used to bring me here as a kid. It's only now, standing here with you, that I finally understand what she means. I think all the times I've been here before, I've been too busy swimming, playing in the water . . . I never just stopped and stood still. I think I understand now. Oma says you must switch off your mind and open up your heart, then you can feel a connection to life around you.'

'That's exactly it! I would never have found the words to explain it, but that's it.'

'She practises connecting every day. Not just in nature, but at home, in the supermarket, anywhere.'

'I can't imagine feeling like this in the middle of a supermarket.'

'She says you can, but it takes practice. She's been doing it for years.'

'Wow, you've got a cool grandma.'

'Your grandfather is cool too.'

I laughed. 'He's SO not cool.'

'My grandfather says Claude is not only one of the nicest

people he knows, he's also the most talented blues guitarist he's ever met. He says Claude should have been famous – *would have been famous*, if he hadn't had problems with drugs.'

'Really?'

'He admires Claude for beating his addiction.'

'Claude was never very interested in me or my mum.'

'So maybe now he starts to realise what he has missed?'

'I like you,' I said, taking myself by surprise. *Aargh – Ori! Stop thinking out loud!* 'What I mean is, I *like* your company. I feel like I can be myself around you.'

A big grin spread across Elias's face. 'Thank you.'

I waited for him to return the compliment but an awkward silence hung between us. Great. This was total proof that my instincts weren't to be trusted. How did I always manage to get things wrong and embarrass myself so expertly? Why didn't I think before I spoke or acted? And yet that was the most brave and honest thing I'd ever said – he had to give me something more than just *thank you*, surely? Then again, he didn't *have* to do or say anything. OK, deep breaths. I didn't regret what I'd just said. I would not shrink into a hole for having the courage to be myself.

I was fine. I didn't need approval. I didn't need confirmation that I was an OK person. I just needed to keep my chin up. Keep my head held high. My dignity had my full permission to stay exactly where it was.

'Ori.' Elias turned towards me, interrupting my silent meltdown. Beneath the water, he slipped his hand into mine. 'Can I kiss you?'

Stunned, I nodded lamely as he pulled me towards him, his arms sliding around my waist. I couldn't quite believe this was happening. I'd just convinced myself he wasn't interested and now here I was, standing waist-deep in a river, kissing someone I liked who liked me. I prayed he couldn't feel my heart galloping at a million miles an hour as our lips touched. I hadn't imagined the electricity – it was real. As the sun set behind the woods and we merged into the shadows, I melted into the moment.

I don't know how many seconds or minutes slipped past as we stood there kissing, but all the while I couldn't quite believe this was actually happening. If I wasn't already in heaven before, I totally was now.

When we got back to the barn, the Boomers were packing up their instruments. Elias discreetly dropped my hand as we walked up the garden towards them.

'But it's still early!' protested a drunken Rolf. 'We haven't done Al Green yet.'

'Yes, but it's only two days till the Grand Opening and there's still a lot to do,' Sylvie reminded him.

'I can help,' said Rolf.

'Cheers, Rolf, but we don't want you having any more injuries,' said Claude, escorting them to the front door. 'I know what you're like with a hangover.'

'I didn't drink enough to have a hangover,' moaned Rolf.

'Come on, old man!' Letzie steered him out of the door. 'Thank you for a lovely evening, Claudie. Please tell Odette her cooking was fantastic and we look forward to seeing her again at the party.'

'Will do,' said Claude.

'You need me tomorrow?' asked Elias.

'If you're available?' said Claude.

'OK, see you in the morning.'

'Cheers, mate. Really appreciate it. No rush, we'll see you when we see you.'

Elias waved and gave me a lingering look as he left with his grandparents. I waved back.

Claude patted me on the back. 'We've got a lot to do tomorrow, so get a good night's kip, Rinkydinks.'

'Good night, Ori,' said Sylvie. 'Hope the bats didn't disappoint!' She gave me a knowing wink.

Claude put his arm around her and as they headed outside to the caravan, he pinched her bum. Normally this would have grossed me out, but luckily, I was too dazed from snogging Elias to care.

With the barn all to myself (except for the sound of Odette's muffled snoring coming from her room) I couldn't contain my joy any longer, and leapt onto the stage to do a happy dance. With the spotlight shining down in the middle and all that space, I twirled backwards and forwards, shimmied, twerked, bounced, jumped, shook invisible pompoms and did the running man. I then got a bit ahead of myself and attempted a very clumsy cartwheel, staggered on landing, and would've toppled off the stage if I hadn't windmilled myself back upright.

When I looked up, two faces were peering at me through the front door.

I screamed.

'WHAT THE HELL?' I panted and glanced at Odette's bedroom door, fully expecting her to emerge in a state of panic. Miraculously, she didn't. Heart pounding and legs trembling, I climbed down off the stage and approached the front door.

'Somebody help me! I'm being spontaneous!' wailed Ravi as I yanked the door open, my cheeks feeling hotter by the second.

I blinked in confusion.

'*The Truman Show*,' he explained. 'The bit when –' he stopped, clocking my impression of a rabbit frozen in the headlights. 'Never mind.'

'Whoa!' gasped Jackson. 'What did you do to your hair?'

I stared at them both in disbelief. Was I hallucinating?

'Um . . .' Ravi frowned. 'Can we come in?'

CHAPTER NINETEEN

Arrival

'What the hell are you doing here?' I asked as they stumbled inside, all sweaty and dishevelled, and dumped bulging rucksacks on the floor. 'Why didn't you let me know you were coming?'

They glanced at each other awkwardly as my heart rate gradually returned to normal.

'Jackson was worried you wouldn't want to see him,' explained Ravi, taking off his trainers. 'We reckoned it would be easier to just turn up, then if you didn't want us here, there's a campsite we can go to. We've got all our camping stuff.'

'It's nearly eleven o'clock,' I said, glancing at the clock on the wall. 'How did you get here?'

'Train to Paris,' said Ravi. 'Then another train, then a cab. It's been a long day.'

'And how on earth did you find my grandad's place?'

'We asked the cabbie if he'd heard of Studio Marchand and he said yeah and asked if we were performing at the opening party,' said Jackson, looking pretty pleased with himself.

I blinked and rubbed my forehead. I was still reeling from the fright they'd given me – let alone the surprise of the century that they'd come all this way without telling me.

'Sorry,' said Jackson. 'We should've warned you.' He held my gaze, his eyes twinkling, as if testing out his trusty magic to see if it still worked on me. The fact that I even noticed was hopefully a sign that it didn't – at least, not like before. 'I like it, by the way!' He nodded towards my hair. 'Pink suits you.'

'D'you think it'd be OK to stay just for tonight?' asked Ravi. 'Would your grandad mind? We can check in to the campsite in the morning.'

I glanced up at the pile of mattresses and sleeping bags on the mezzanine.

'I doubt he'll mind,' I said. 'Although I should probably warn him you're here in case you run into him in the morning and freak him out.'

'Don't suppose you've got any food?' said Jackson. 'I'm flipping ravs.'

I led them into the kitchen and opened the fridge. 'But aren't you supposed to be working in your dad's garden centre?' I asked Ravi, taking out the orange juice and the cheese.

'We struck a deal. I persuaded him that as our Cornwall trip had been cut short, I hadn't yet had a proper break since studying for my GCSEs.' He grinned at me. 'Plus I paid for my ticket myself out of money I'd already earned working Saturdays.'

'Does Ava know you're here?' I asked Jackson.

'Not yet,' he replied. 'All the others know is that we decided to go on a last-minute interrailing trip. We never said we were coming to see you.'

I wondered how long it would be before the others figured

it out – if they hadn't already. I made them a couple of cheese sandwiches and led them back into the main barn to sit by the empty log burner.

'And what about Maya?' I asked Ravi.

'She's away visiting family for the next week . . .' he replied.

That wasn't exactly what I meant, but Ravi was too busy running his eyes along a shelf of records.

'Man, this place is awesome!' said Jackson, putting his (still-in-trainers) feet up on the coffee table and looking all around him. 'Check out all those guitars!'

'Yeah, don't touch them,' I said bluntly, pushing his feet off the table. 'It won't go down well.' I think my tone took him back.

'Can't I just have a little go?' He stuck his bottom lip out.

'Not if you want to make it to your seventeenth birthday,' I said.

'I can't believe your grandad lives in such a cool place,' said Ravi, tucking into his sandwich. 'Has he gone to bed? We don't wanna disturb him.'

'Technically he lives outside in that caravan.' I pointed out the window. 'Although, really that's just his bedroom and the barn is his front room, bathroom, kitchen and work space – as well as a performing and recording venue.'

'*Cooool*,' said Jackson, eyeing up the stage. 'He sounds like a dude.'

'Yeah, this isn't what I expected when you talked about your Grandpa Airhead!' grinned Ravi.

'*Grandpa Airhead?*' Jackson hooted. 'You call him *Grandpa Airhead?*'

'Sssh!' I hissed. 'My great aunt Odette's asleep in that room over there.'

'Your great aunt?' Ravi frowned.

'I told you already, Ravioli – remember? We picked her up on the way.'

'Oh yeah. Forgot. There's been a lot going on.'

Fair enough.

'Anyway, it's a long story. I didn't know she was coming too. You'll meet her in the morning. Don't be fooled into thinking she's some fragile little old lady. She's so sharp she'll make minced meat of you in seconds.'

'Right . . . So, um, how's the German boyfriend, Oreo?' Ravi looked away and sipped his orange juice.

I noticed the micro-muscles in Jackson's face tense just a little. He carried on trailing his eyes around the barn, pretending to be deeply distracted by all the guitars and vinyl.

I smiled nervously. 'Well he's not exactly my boyfriend . . .'

'But you like him?' grinned Ravi, picking at a loose thread on his T-shirt.

'Well, kind of . . . yeah . . .'

'How d'you meet him?' Jackson avoided my eyes.

'God, is this an interrogation or what? He's the grandson of one of Claude's friends.'

'He's not a Nazi is he?' he snorted.

I rolled my eyes. '*Seriously?* Please don't say anything like that in front of him – it's totally NOT cool.'

'Sorry – just kidding. So where are we sleeping?' he asked, glancing up at the mezzanine and then looking directly at me.

His lips twitched mischievously.

Why did I get the impression he thought he was going to be sleeping in a bed *with* or *next to* me? I felt annoyance bubble up inside me. That *so* wasn't going to happen. Who did he think he was, turning up here out of the blue after treating me the way he did?

I stood up. 'I'd better let Claude know you're here. That room over there is the bathroom. The one next door to that is Odette's room so don't go in there, and I'll be moving into the one next door to that.' It was the laundry-slash-storage room, and having only poked my head round the door briefly, I wasn't even sure I could fit a mattress inside. But if that didn't work, I'd sleep on the sofa. 'I'll be back in a minute.'

'Ori.' Ravi stood up. 'I'm sorry we turned up without warning you.'

'It's fine,' I reassured him. I didn't mean to sound annoyed – at least not with him. He wasn't the one I felt annoyed with. The question was, *why were they here?*

I opened the back door, marched across the garden and rapped my knuckles on the caravan door.

'Hello?' Claude's voice sounded muffled from within.

'It's me, Ori.'

'Now's not the best time, kiddo. I'm otherwise engaged!'

UGH! Too much information.

'I just wanted to let you know that two of my friends just showed up. I'm really sorry – they'll leave in the morning.'

'No problemo, sweet cheeks. If they wanna lend a hand, they can stay as long as they like!'

'OK, thanks. Night . . .' I'd had a feeling he'd say that.

I walked slowly back towards the barn. I wasn't even sure I wanted them to stay. If Ravi and Jackson were here any longer than one night, it wouldn't be so easy to spend time on my own with Elias. And right now, that was all I wanted to do.

'Ori?' Jackson stepped out of the shadows by the patio making me jump. 'Can we talk?'

Guess I didn't have a choice. 'OK . . . ?'

He looked behind him to make sure Ravi was out of ear shot.

'Basically my head's been a mess ever since the day we, er . . . *kissed* . . .'

'So it's "we" now?' I nearly choked with surprise. 'Cos I was starting to think I must've imagined the part where you were kissing me back.'

'You didn't imagine it. I'm sorry. It's just . . .'

'Go on.' I folded my arms. *Fess up, big boy.*

'The whole thing just, like, took me by surprise and when Ava walked in on us, I didn't know what to do. I didn't handle things very well and I'm sorry.'

Fair enough. We could lay this to rest now.

'I know I put you in an awkward situation. And I'm the one who should be sorry about that, and I still am. But thanks for admitting it ended up being a two-way thing. I appreciate it.' I gave him a friendly pat on the shoulder and went to go inside.

'Wait!' He stepped in front of me, blocking my way. 'That's not all I wanted to say.'

I had a feeling I no longer wanted him to say what he was about to say.

'There's nothing more *to* say,' I said cheerfully. 'I apologised. You apologised. We're good now. We can be friends again. Sort of. Not in front of Ava, maybe.'

'That's just it. I don't want to be "just friends".' His eyes fixed on mine.

I swallowed as he stepped towards me, taking my hand in his.

'Hey, Ori?' The back door opened and Ravi appeared. I pulled my hand from Jackson's. 'Sorry to interrupt, but do we just help ourselves to a mattress?'

'Yeah, I'll show you.' I followed him inside, holding the door open for Jackson who sighed and reluctantly followed.

I helped them set up their beds, showed them where everything was and used the excuse of a morning pastry run as a reason I needed to be up early – that and the full day's labour that lay ahead in which we needed to get the barn finished. Once they'd helped me drag a mattress down the corkscrew staircase and into the laundry room, I said good night and closed the door.

Ever since Elias and I had waved each other good night, all I'd wanted was to be alone so I could replay our kiss over and over again. The way he looked at me, the way he touched me . . . I hadn't wanted that moment to end. I'd never experienced anything so magical. I just wanted to go back and relive it again and again.

Was I falling in love? Was he falling in love with me? He was going travelling. Then he was going to university in Germany. And I'd be going home in less than a week. Unless . . . ? Unless we *both* changed our plans?

I could feel my mind getting sucked into Fantasyland again. But this time it wasn't completely unrealistic because I had proof that Elias liked me. But *how much* did he like me? It felt like I was holding the string of a heart-shaped helium balloon in my hand. I knew I should tighten my grip on it before it slipped up, up and away, out of reach, taking my daydreamy mind with it . . .

CHAPTER TWENTY
The Half Of It

Jackson lay on his side curled up in a ball. His nose was making a whistling sound as he breathed. Lying there fast asleep, the unzipped sleeping bag exposing his bare chest, I felt a familiar flame flicker within me. Perhaps I wasn't as over him as I'd thought I was.

Ravi nudged him with his foot and he flopped over to face the other way, still deep in slumber.

'He can sleep for England,' said Ravi. 'In Cornwall he was always the last one up. Come on, let's go without him.'

'OK,' I agreed. It would give us a chance to catch up properly.

We climbed down the corkscrew staircase and ran straight into Odette coming out of her bedroom.

'Hi Odette. This is Ravi. Ravi, this is my great aunt Odette.'

'*Bonjour*,' said Odette. 'I did not know more guests were coming?'

'Neither did I,' I said.

'We didn't even know ourselves,' said Ravi apologetically. 'It was all a bit of a last minute decision.'

'*We?*' said Odette.

'Our friend Jackson is upstairs,' I explained. 'He's fast asleep.

We're just going to the *boulangerie*. Do you want anything?'

Odette shook her head. I signalled to Ravi to give us a minute and followed her into the kitchen.

'Are you OK?' I asked her.

'*Oui, ma chérie.*' She took the muesli out of the cupboard and last night's fruit salad out of the fridge. There was still loads left.

'Claude said we should have a family summit, to, like, clear the air and make sure everything is cool?'

'Perhaps that is a good idea,' she said wearily, pouring muesli into a bowl and adding a ladle of fruit salad. 'There is more to say and I must find the courage to say it.'

'But the whole Jacqueline thing – that's cool now?'

Odette reached for the jar of mint tea. 'Yes, that chapter is closed. *Fermé.*'

I opened my mouth to speak but paused. Was Claude including me in the summit just to be polite? It was *their* stuff, *their* problems. It wasn't really any of my business. And yet the reason I felt it *was* sort of my business was because Claude's past had had an effect on Mum, and Mum's past had had an effect on me. Hadn't it?

I opened my mouth again. 'But . . .'

'*Vas-y!*' She shooed me out of the kitchen to where Ravi was waiting by the front door. 'It is too early for talking. Don't worry, Claude and I will talk later. Sixty-seven years of misunderstanding cannot be solved in one conversation.'

I nodded and nudged Ravi out the front door. I put my sunhat on as we walked out of the driveway.

'Nice hat, Betty Bucket-head!' he laughed.

I shot him a warning look and tried to think of a witty retort, but since he'd got rid of his bird's nest, there was nothing to make fun of, so I elbowed him instead.

'I've already been sunburnt once,' I said, 'and I'm not gonna lie, I'd rather be Betty Bucket-head.'

He pulled the hat over my eyes and dodged out the way before I could retaliate.

For a moment, as Ravi and I walked along the tree-lined lane, I wondered if I was dreaming.

'I can't believe you're actually *here*, Ravioli!' I said, shaking my head in disbelief. When I'd woken up earlier, it had taken a few minutes before I remembered him and Jackson were here, *sleeping upstairs*. And then – bam! The surprise sent me reeling all over again.

'Neither can I, Oreo,' he laughed. 'Beats wet and windy Cornwall!'

'So it sounds like it's going well with Maya, then?' I probed.

'Yeah, but it's not serious between us,' he shrugged, sticking his hands in his shorts pockets.

'But I thought you really liked her?'

'I *do* like her. She's really nice. I'm just not sure if she's what I'm looking for.'

OK. Interesting . . .

'What *are* you looking for?' I asked, curious. I mean, Maya was *very* pretty and popular.

He raised his eyebrows. 'Someone I can talk to, have a laugh with. Someone I can be myself with.' He caught my eye.

'And you didn't have that with her?'

'I didn't *not* have it with her – it's hard to explain. I'm not sure we're the right fit. Maybe some time apart will help me work it out.'

I got the feeling I shouldn't press further.

'So how did you and Jackson end up as interrailing partners? I mean, I know you're mates, but you're not exactly besties.'

'We were on the train coming back from Cornwall when he just sat bolt upright and said he needed to see you.' He rolled his eyes.

I tried to picture the scene as we turned into the medieval alleyway. So, what? Jackson had some kind of out-of-the-blue realisation on the train? Like in the movies? Ravi looked up at the balconies with their potted plants and trailing flowers above our heads. He sighed happily. 'Can't believe I'm here!' he said for the millionth time.

'Where were Ava and the others when Jackson said he needed to see me?' I asked.

'The girls travelled back separately. It was just me and him on the train. He basically just announced that it was *you* he was supposed to be with, not Ava, and that he was going to take the train down to Frenac and find you.'

'How did he know I was in Frenac?'

'I'd already told him you were staying with your grandad. The night before we packed up and left Cornwall, it was chucking it down and I said I wished I was in France with you in thirty degree sunshine. Maybe I sewed the seed in his mind?'

'So maybe he's here for the weather rather than for me?' I joked.

He grinned. 'Well *I'm* here for you, Oreo, *whatever the weather.*'

I never knew whether he was pulling my leg or not. Ravi always had this way of joking and sounding serious at the same time. He was hard to read. Just when I started to think that the others were right – that he *did* like me – he'd say something to convince me I was wrong.

'You're so cheesy,' I sighed. 'So, anyway, he roped you into coming too? Didn't he think he could find it by himself?'

'Something like that,' he mumbled. 'But I was only too happy to put working in my dad's garden centre off for as long as possible. Anyway, tell me about the German guy. What's his name?'

'Elias.'

'So, does Jackson stand a chance against Elias?' he teased.

'Look!' I swept my arm theatrically towards the main square. 'You're not admiring this pretty village with its *olde* buildings and chic café culture.'

'It's amazing. I'm loving it!' Ravi glanced around him, shielding his eyes from the sun. 'So does he?'

'Stop winding me up, Ravioli. Nothing seems real right now.'

'Can't help winding you up. It's a lifelong habit.'

I punched him. 'Yeah, an annoying lifelong habit.'

'You haven't answered my question!' He gave me a playful nudge.

'I'm not going to either.' I nudged him back and railroaded him into a lamp post.

'Watch it Oreo, or I'll drop you on your head again!'

'Don't even think about it.'

We were about to enter the *boulangerie* when we ran slap bang into Elias, coming out with a baguette in one hand and a bag of pastries in the other. I caught my breath as I replayed our kiss for the hundredth time.

'Hey!' he greeted me cheerfully, tucked the baguette under his arm and held out his hand to Ravi, looking slightly confused. 'Hi, I'm Elias.'

I introduced them and explained about the unexpected arrival of my two friends.

'I'm sure Claude is very happy to have more helpers,' he smiled.

'True,' I agreed.

'I will see you later. I must take Oma and Opa their breakfast. Nice to meet you, Ravi.'

I waved him off.

'Nice guy,' said Ravi, as we entered the *boulangerie*. 'Looks like Jackson's got some serious competition.'

I elbowed him hard in the ribs.

Claude stood in the middle of the garden, surveying his expanded army of helpers while shielding his eyes from the scorching sun. Elias and I were on ladders, yards apart, doing the fourth and final coat of the walls inside the barn. Jackson was mowing the vast lawn and Ravi and Sylvie were sorting through a jumble of poles that formed the framework for a marquee.

Beneath a tree in the far corner of the garden, Odette sat in the shade wearing a straw hat, her easel in front of her, a portable box of paints and brushes at her feet.

I observed the satisfied expression on Claude's face. Two extra helpers working for their board and lodging was pretty much the answer to his prayers. Elias noticed it too.

'He seems very happy about your friends being here,' he said, pressing his roller into the tray of paint.

'You can say that again.'

'So the one with the muscles, that's the one you kissed?' asked Elias.

I felt my cheeks burning. 'Correct . . .'

'So he broke up with your best friend?'

'Also correct . . .'

'So now you can be together?' He said it cheerfully, as if the idea didn't bother him at all.

'I don't think so,' I replied, concentrating on my brush strokes.

'Why not?'

I shrugged. 'It doesn't feel right anymore.'

'Listen, Ori.' He put down his roller and looked at me. 'He came all this way to be with you. You don't owe me anything – I'm not going to get in the way.' He seemed sincere. A little *too* sincere. The fact that I couldn't detect any signs of jealousy in his voice whatsoever was disappointing. A little jealousy would've been really OK with me. Did last night not feel as magical to him as it had to me?

'There's nothing for you to get in the way *of*,' I said.

'I'm just saying, you are free to do as you like,' he smiled.

I wanted to ask what exactly he meant by that but Claude came over.

'Nice work, guys. It looks bloody amazing what you've

done. I'm very grateful to you both. We are so nearly there! Just forty-eight hours to go!'

'What else is there to do?' asked Elias.

Claude pressed his fingers to his temples and tried to recall his list. 'Clean the bogs, unpack all the glasses, go to the supermarché, buy lots of nosh and make lots of nosh. All of which can be done tomorrow – I swear this is our last day of DIY and decorating or so help me baby Jesus.'

'What about balloons and bunting?' I asked. 'You know, *the fun part?*'

'Sylvie's balloons and bunting manager. Ask her. Oh, and I thought that tomorrow, once we're done with all the food prep, we could all go and have a celebratory swim in the river.'

'All of us?'

'Yeah, everyone, man!'

'I'm not sure if Ravi and Jackson are staying . . .'

'Well tell 'em they can stay as long as they like, Pinkydinks – so long as they pitch in.'

He was about to walk off when I climbed down the ladder and stopped him. 'What about our family summit?'

'I haven't forgotten about it – it's just all got a bit manic today.' He glanced around him. 'Might be best to reschedule for after the Grand Opening?'

'Odette said there were things she needed to tell you. It sounded kind of important.'

Claude nodded. 'Right, OK . . . Well if I see a window, we'll squeeze it in before, and if not, then the day after the party for sure. OK?'

I wanted to make him promise to have our summit today, but looking around me at the amount of activity going on and the number of people around, there didn't seem any point. Instead I nodded my agreement and headed off outside to check on Odette.

She was so engrossed in her painting, she didn't notice me approaching. I stood behind her and looked at how she moved her brush gently across the canvas. She was painting a watercolour of the hills in the background, the wheat fields with their bales of hay, a town that snaked up a hill, with its church spire piercing the sky.

'Can I get you a drink, Odette?' I asked, moving into her line of vision so I didn't make her jump.

'*Oui, ma chérie*, a glass of water, *s'il te plaît*.' Her eyes never left the canvas.

'I like your painting.'

'It is a present for Claude. Don't tell him. It's a surprise. I just pretend I do it for my own pleasure.'

I guessed if she was making him a present, she couldn't be *too* angry with him.

'It looks very ordinary – I mean, not as in boring, as in, you know ... *not quirky?*'

'It isn't finished yet.'

'Oh. By the way, our family summit has been postponed.'

'But of course.'

Was she being sarcastic?

'He *promised* we'd all talk so I'll make sure he keeps his word,' I said firmly.

'*Ça va, ma chérie. Ça va.*' She dipped her brush in her jar of water and swilled it around. 'So which one is your boyfriend?' She gestured vaguely in every direction where there was a young, topless male hard at work. 'No buses for ages, then three arrive together, *non*?'

I laughed nervously. She beckoned for me to come closer and bend down so she could whisper in my ear.

'*Écoute*: The Asian one, he likes you. The white one, he likes himself. The German one, he lives too far away.'

'Thanks. That's, um, helpful advice.' Wait – *what?* 'What makes you think Ravi likes me?' I asked out loud.

'He is Ravi?' She nodded towards him.

'Yes.'

Odette gave me a withering look. 'Are you blind? It's the way he looks at you.' She pointed to her eyes. 'I tell it how I see it.'

'I noticed.'

She cackled.

I sneaked a look at Ravi grappling with the marquee poles as I made my way back into the barn. Ava had always seemed sure Ravi liked me, too. How could other people be so certain when it wasn't obvious to me at all? For every incident where zhe was *possibly* flirting with me, there were at least two incidents where he absolutely, one hundred per cent, wasn't. If Ravi liked me, he did a really good job of hiding it. Anyway, if he really *did* like me, why didn't he just say so? It wasn't like I was a stranger or someone from a different class at school – unlike Maya, who he most definitely *did* like. Or up until very recently, at any rate.

While I was in the kitchen filling a glass from the tap, I felt a presence behind me. Without even turning round, I knew it was Jackson.

'So, like, how serious is it . . . between you and the German guy?' he asked.

'The *German guy* has a name,' I said, turning off the tap and turning round. 'But to answer your question, it's none of your business.'

'Look I can't blame you for, like, meeting someone else. I know it's taken me a while to sort out where my head's at but when I realised it's you I wanted to be with . . . Well, I came all this way, didn't I?'

He was standing a bit too close. I stepped back and leaned against the sideboard.

'I didn't ask you to come,' I said.

He held his hands up. 'I know, I know, but doesn't me being here *prove* how serious I am about you?' He looked me in the eye and I felt my heart start to beat a decibel louder. His cheeks were pink from the sun, he had a cigarette tucked behind his ear, and he smelt of deodorant and aftershave. I wondered if he'd put sun cream on.

'How are things between you and Ava?' I asked.

'We're over. She's not talking to me.'

'Did you break up with her to be with me, or did she break up with you and then you thought you might as well give me a try now that you're free?'

Jackson looked down at his feet and then up again. Hah! It was satisfying to watch him squirm. Those deep green eyes had lost their power.

'Is that how little you think of me?' he asked.

'Who broke up with who, Jackson?'

'She broke up with me because she believed I had feelings for you. Turns out she was right.' He looked directly at me.

Okaay . . . That could be true, but I wasn't sure whether to believe him or not. This was what I'd always wanted to hear, and now that I was hearing it, it made me feel nervous, uneasy. Like a responsibility I wasn't ready for.

'Things weren't exactly going brilliantly before that anyway,' he continued, running his fingers through his quiff. 'We argued a lot. She'd get annoyed at me for stupid little things like not texting back straight away, or buying her a latte instead of a flat white. I was always having to prove how much she meant to me and whatever I did, it was never enough. It was starting to make me like her less and less. So . . .' He exhaled, his shoulders sinking. 'Anyway, if you're with the German guy – *Elias* – I'll back off. Just say the word.'

'I'm not *with* anyone,' I said, walking around him and out of the kitchen.

I didn't mean to be frosty to him. I was just starting to feel majorly confused. Just as I'd long suspected, it wasn't all love hearts and roses between him and Ava. She'd made no secret to me, Daisy and Martha of how much it annoyed her when he'd spend a load of money in the vape store and then ask if she could pay for his Big Mac. Or how it did her head in when he'd cancel their plans at the last minute, just as she'd put the finishing touches to her makeup, ready to go and meet him in town. What I didn't know was how much *she* also irritated *him*.

But instead of feeling any satisfaction, I just felt like a balloon that had been blown up and let go of. I no longer cared.

I thought I'd done pretty well to move on from my Big Mistake. I'd dealt with the fall-out, put the past behind me, and sucked up the booby prize – a "holiday" with Grandpa Airhead. Now I was making the best of things and was just starting to feel OK when Jackson rocked up, turning my world on its head again.

I should've been over the moon that the guy I'd dreamed of being with for so long had travelled thousands of kilometres to declare his feelings for me. And yet I wasn't. Instead I felt a slow, bubbling dread that Ava and the others would blame me even more than they did already. Sixteen hours ago I'd been standing in a river, kissing a beautiful boy, all my troubles forgotten. Now I had problems to solve again. I had to figure out A) what I wanted and B) what I wanted aside, what was the *right* thing to do?

CHAPTER TWENTY ONE
That Awkward Moment

Later that evening, the pizza was going down faster than the setting sun.

While Odette had retired to her room to rest, Claude and Sylvie had driven into town to pick up some takeaway pizzas to feed our team of hungry workers. I didn't think I'd ever seen anyone eat as fast as Elias, Ravi and Jackson. If that stack of pizzas had been the last source of food on the planet, I wouldn't have stood a chance.

Ravi took a slice from the last remaining box and handed it to me. 'You're not fast enough, Oreo.'

'I didn't realise it was a race!'

Elias stood up. 'I better get back and spend some time with my grandparents. Thanks for the pizza.'

'You're welcome,' said Sylvie.

'Appreciate your help, mate,' said Claude. 'Coming for a swim tomorrow?'

Elias frowned. 'I'm not sure yet – I will let you know.'

I'd noticed he'd been texting a lot in the last few hours. He seemed distracted, and I was reminded that he had a life in a faraway place that I knew very little about.

He said his goodbyes, fist-bumped Ravi and Jackson while climbing over their sprawled-out legs, and made his way to the door. I got up and followed him, closing the front door behind us.

We walked until we were safely out of earshot of the barn. I had no idea what I was going to say – I just needed to know what was going on in his head. We'd kissed, so what happened next?

'Yesterday . . .' I began. 'That was . . . Er, I um . . .' Nope. Words weren't happening. And his intense stare was making it even harder to find a way of asking *do you want to be with me?*

I took a deep breath. Change tactic. 'When are you planning on leaving Frenac?'

'Not sure. Maybe the day after tomorrow? My friend has found work for me in Italy but I need to start in the next few days or they'll have to find someone else.'

I guessed that's what all the texting was about.

'The day after tomorrow?' I hadn't expected that. I'd either expected a vague "I'm not sure yet" or "I think I might stay longer than I originally planned". I tried not to let the shock show. 'You're going to miss the Grand Opening party then?'

He shrugged. 'Maybe. I haven't checked out train times yet.'

I felt floored. His voice was so casual, it was as if nothing had happened between us. Fine. I could handle endings. But I *despised* it when people denied beginnings.

'So that's it?' I said.

I mean, had I just experienced the World's Shortest Romance?

Why did guys always have someone else they'd rather be with or something else they'd rather be doing or somewhere else they'd rather be? Or was it "just me"?

'Ori . . .' He lifted my chin.

I ducked backwards out of reach. Having your chin tipped upwards for a kiss was one thing, but having it tipped upwards to be given some pity-filled bullshit on why you're being dumped was another. Not that I was being "dumped" technically-speaking, but I was about to be told why I wasn't going to be "taken on" in the first place, which basically amounted to the same thing. He opened his mouth to speak but I interrupted him.

'It's fine,' I said confidently. 'I wasn't really sure how long you'd be here for anyway. Well, I'm glad we met. You've made my working holiday way more fun than I expected.'

I held out my hand for a friendly shake.

He gave me a bemused look. 'Can we at least hug?'

'Sure, sure!' I gave him a matey squeeze followed by a cheerful salute and turned back towards the barn. Onwards and upwards. You win some, you lose some. Knackers and piss (as Claude would say).

'Ori, if I stay here with you any longer, it will get harder and harder to leave. Part of me wants to stay, believe me – but we both know it would only end with us having to go our separate ways. Better to say goodbye now, don't you think? Like, quit while we're ahead?'

'Yeah, sure, great!' I replied super-merrily. 'Totally get it.'

'I'm sorry, Ori,' he said sincerely, then smiled. 'Ha, *sorry*

Ori rhymes!' He quickly straightened his face when I didn't crack up laughing. 'Seriously, I *am* sorry.'

'No worries,' I shrugged and turned to go back inside. 'See you later.'

'We can keep in touch!' he called after me. 'Anyway, this isn't even goodbye – I'll see you again before I go.'

'OK!'

Yeah, whatever.

I made a beeline for the loo. I locked the bathroom door, sat down on the toilet lid and took a deep breath to keep the tears from coming out. I just needed a minute to process the abrupt ending of my holiday romance and reset my mental satnav.

OK, Ori. This hasn't gone the way you'd hoped, but a week ago you didn't even know of Elias's existence, so . . . ? So you can't be too upset. Your holiday with Grandpa Airhead has already been way better than you ever would've imagined, has it not? You had a romantic moment with a good-looking guy in a beautiful setting. You've felt better about yourself for the first time in weeks – maybe months or years even. You've actually been having a good time. So it hasn't all been bad. And would you really want a long-distance relationship with someone you'd hardly ever get to see? No, Dodo, you wouldn't. You want a relationship with someone who you can spend lots of time with. Someone like Elias but who preferably lives in the same country.

I took another deep breath, stood up and flushed the loo. Maybe Elias had done me a favour?

Back in the barn, Sylvie was sounding out Ravi and Jackson's opinions on the best party food.

'I'm going to do a chicken curry and a veggie one,' said Sylvie, tapping her pen on her bottom teeth. 'Letzie is doing a cheese board and a pasta salad, and Rolf is doing a potato salad, if he can manage not to chop any more fingers off. But I need some more ideas.'

'Dips?' said Ravi. 'Personally I love guacamole, with lots of garlic and coriander.'

'Great idea,' said Sylvie, jotting it down in her notebook.

'Garlic bread?' suggested Jackson, his eyes on his phone. 'I love garlic bread.'

'This is helpful. Keep them coming, boys.' She scrawled again, while Claude leaned back on the sofa, yawned loudly and closed his eyes.

Sylvie nudged him in the ribs. 'Maybe you should go to bed, hon? You don't want to burn yourself out before the big day.'

'Too tired to move.' He yawned again.

'Claude!' Sylvie elbowed him and stifled a yawn herself. 'Go to bed because you're making *me* yawn.'

'Yes, ma'am!' He sat up, his eyeballs swimming round in circles, and heaved himself stiffly off the sofa. A snapping sound like a log crackling in the woodburner made us all look up.

'Relax, it was just me knees.' He arched his back, making his spine click loudly. Ravi and Jackson exchanged glances. Their lips twitched. 'It all works, just got a bit of wear and tear, that's all. Right, *bonne nuit*, kids! Thanks for all your help today. See you in the morning.' He gave his hips a wiggle and walked crookedly towards the back door.

'I suppose I should turn in as well,' said Sylvie, closing

her notebook. 'Ori, will you check on Odey before you go to bed?'

'Sure,' I said. 'I'll clear up. You go to bed.'

'Thanks, sweetie. Good night, all!' She blew us each a kiss and followed Claude outside.

And then there were three of us. An awkward silence filled the room.

'How about a game of cards?' said Jackson, pushing the tower of pizza boxes to one side and reaching for a deck of playing cards that was sitting on the coffee table.

'Let's clear all this up first,' said Ravi, getting to his feet, gathering up the boxes and taking them into the kitchen.

I picked up a few empty glasses and followed him.

'Those can go in the recycling bin outside,' I said.

'Right.' He went to change direction. 'Um, so Elias told me earlier he might not be here for the party, which, er, seems a shame seeing as he's done so much work around here.'

'Yeah, I know . . .' I tried to arrange my face so that it contained no trace of my guttedness at Elias's imminent departure, or my embarrassment that the Hot German BF I'd bragged about to Ravi was about to vanish into thin air after just one snog.

'He's a really nice guy. I can see why you like him so much.'

'Oh, it's not serious or anything. Just a bit of fun, that's all.' I took the pizza boxes out of his hands to distract him from the water pooling in my eyes. Despite having a very rational and grown-up word with myself, emotion was welling up inside me and threatening to burst out of my tear ducts any second.

Ravi put his hand on my arm. 'I don't like seeing you upset.'

'I'm not upset!' A tear trickled out of my eye. 'OK, I am. But it's not what you think.'

'What is it then?'

'It doesn't matter. I'd better go and check on Odette.'

I darted out of the kitchen and took the pizza boxes outside to the recycling bin.

What was wrong with me? Why was I crying? I couldn't really be in love with Elias after such a short period of time. He was gorgeous, our kiss in the river was a moment I'd never forget and, while I was gutted he was leaving, I couldn't have developed feelings *that* deep for someone I'd only known a week, surely?

I tried to think. What was *really* bugging me?

I'd made a massive fool of myself with Jackson. Had I gone and made a fool of myself all over again with Elias? It seemed the minute I let my feelings for someone show, they rejected me. I burst into angry, silent tears and gulped hungrily at the air as they came gushing out. I just wanted someone to love me. Was that too much to ask? I had this horrible aching loneliness inside me. No boy seemed to want to be with me for longer than five seconds. My best friend hated me. My dad wasn't interested in me. My mum couldn't wait to be rid of me and I'd been literally dumped on my grandad because no one else wanted me around. Was I so unlovable?

I heard the door open behind me.

'Ori, what's up?'

Jackson slid a hand onto my shoulder and turned me towards him. I so badly needed a hug I was in no state to resist. I buried my head in his chest and carried on crying while he hugged me and rubbed his hands up and down my back.

'It's OK,' he murmured, his lips close to my ear. 'I've got you.'

For one brief moment it actually felt like someone genuinely cared about me – until . . . His lips moved down towards mine and the next thing I knew his tongue was in my mouth. I reeled backwards, shoving him off.

'*Not now*, you dick!'

'But I thought . . . ?' He threw his hands in the air. 'I was just trying to comfort you!'

'Comfort? Or snog? Two different things.' I shoved past him and went back inside, heading straight for the bathroom so I could splash cold water on my face and rinse my mouth out – his nicotine breath was disgusting. I took a moment to compose myself before emerging and going into the kitchen to finish the clearing up. But it had already been done. The kettle was boiling and Ravi was scanning the jars of herbal teas.

'What *is* all this stuff?' he asked as I walked in.

'Posh herbal tea,' I replied.

'Um, are you OK?' He clocked my bloodshot eyes.

'Fine.'

'And what about Odette?'

I slapped my forehead. 'Back in a minute.'

I scurried out of the kitchen and round the corner where I stopped outside Odette's door and knocked. There was no answer so I opened the door and peered inside. Her room was dark, except for the rectangle of light coming from behind me through the open door. She was lying on the bed, propped up against the pillows, her eyes closed, her body as still as . . .

I froze and searched for the rise and fall of her chest. It was too dark to see properly so I crept forwards, not wanting to switch on the light in case I woke her up.

I leaned over the bed. 'Odette?'

Silence. I touched her arm and her eyes flew open, making me jump back.

'Oh thank God,' I exhaled. 'For a minute there I thought you were . . . um . . .'

'Dead? Well if this is heaven, I will complain to the manager. This bed is bouncy, that chair is ugly and this socket doesn't work.' She squinted at me. 'I would prefer to die in action, in some interesting, memorable way, not in bed. But if fate insists on taking me while in bed, it better not be on this cheap trampoline in this ugly room.'

'I came to see if you were OK?' She clearly was.

'*Oui, ma chérie.* I'm fine. Forgive me if I don't socialise so much. I find it very tiring. Besides, I don't understand those two English boys. They mumble too much. The German one speaks better English than them. But enough of them. I worry for Sylvie. She is an attractive, intelligent woman – what does she see in Claude?' She sighed.

'I think they make a good couple,' I said, realising it was true. 'And they seem to really like each other.'

'They *do* make a good couple! But does *he* see that? I'm not so sure!' snapped Odette. 'Bah . . . Ignore me. I wake up in a bad mood.'

I smiled. 'That's OK. Can I get you anything to eat or drink?'

'*Non, ma chérie.* You are very kind. So mature. Are *you* OK?'

I was about to say that I was fine but I hesitated.

'Talk!' instructed Odette, gesturing to the "ugly" chair.

I sat down and told Odette all about how I'd been stupid enough to try and steal my best friend's boyfriend without stopping to think what I was doing.

'I still can't believe I did it,' I said, shuddering at the memory. 'It's like my brain just deserted me.'

Odette smiled. 'Everyone makes mistakes. *Everyone,* without exception.'

'Well no one I know has made a mistake quite as bad as mine.'

'*Yet.* Give them time, *chérie.* They will.'

'How can you be so sure?'

'Because they are human! And when they fuck up – excuse my English – they will hopefully learn from their mistake just like you have. Just like Claude has. After his affair with Jacqueline, he never had another affair ever again! He make many other mistakes, sure, but not that. But *unlike me,* you will hopefully find forgiveness in your heart much sooner. And in the meantime, you need to forgive yourself.'

I felt a lump in my throat and dropped my eyes to the floor.

'I put myself on a very high pedestal so I could enjoy giving Claude neck-ache. And I still do . . . my poor brother. *Tiens . . .*' She pointed to the desk where the canvas she'd been painting earlier was propped up against the wall, its back to the room. 'If anything happens to me, make sure Claude gets my painting.'

'Can I take a look?'

'*Mais oui.*'

I switched the light on and picked up the small canvas from the desk. Against the backdrop of a pleasant, rural landscape, were the addition of three people sitting in deckchairs with their legs casually crossed – one with a donkey head, one with a chicken head and one with an elephant head.

'Who are they?' I asked pointing to the people. 'And why have they got animal heads instead of human ones?'

'The donkey is Claude, the chicken is Gerry, and the elephant is me.'

I waited for her to explain but she didn't.

'He will understand.'

'If you say so.' I put the painting back on the desk. 'But why are you an elephant?'

'It will all make sense. But first I need to speak to Claude. Tomorrow I will tell him.'

'OK . . .'

Tell him what exactly?

'*Bonne nuit, chérie.*' She waved me out of the room.

I said good night and closed the door gently behind me.

CHAPTER TWENTY TWO
Life As We Know It

I woke up early to the sound of bird song.

Annoyingly, now that I was sleeping in the utility room, I couldn't just sit up in bed and look out the window onto the back garden. The utility room window looked out onto the driveway – where my bird of prey friend was less likely to make an appearance. I stared vacantly at the ceiling and wondered how long Ravi and Jackson planned on staying. And how long would Claude be cool with them staying? And most importantly, how long did I *want* them to stay?

Hopefully Jackson had got the message that nothing was going to happen between us. I was 95% sure I no longer fancied him. OK, maybe 80% sure. When he was wandering around with his top off, it was still pretty distracting, but all the hurt caused by my Big Mistake had cooled my feelings for him. Plus he could be a little immature – something I'd been blind to before. The good news was that I was no longer a trembling blob of jelly in his presence. I guess I had Elias to thank for that. He made me feel good about myself – even if only for a short while. And it felt good to fancy someone other than Jackson for a change – someone I actually connected with.

I hoped Jackson and Ravi would leave the day after the Grand Opening. It had already been decided they were staying for the party – Claude had invited them. They'd helped with a lot of the preparation, so it was fair enough. And I didn't mind if Ravi wanted to stay on. I could see us having a laugh, hanging out together. But Jackson and I didn't have the same kind of friendship. Anyway, I wasn't even sure what day I'd be going home myself. Mum and Claude had been vague about that right from the start. I didn't even know if Claude was driving me and Odette back, or whether I'd be taking the train, coach or flying. I'd stopped thinking about it when Elias had first come round to help, funnily enough.

Voices came from the other side of my bedroom door. Claude and Sylvie were rattling about. I got up, put my flip flops on and went to make myself a coffee.

'Morning Pinksteroo. You're up early!' Claude pointed to the cup he was filling from the coffee machine. I gave him a thumbs up and he handed me the coffee he'd poured for himself before pouring himself another one.

'Last day of party prep today,' said Sylvie, cutting up a melon on the chopping board and adding it into a large glass bowl filled with fruit, nuts and yoghurt. She sprinkled some seeds on top. 'Want some of this, Ori? It's my special muesli.'

'Er, maybe later.'

'I'm having some,' said Claude. 'It's bloody good for you. If you're bunged up, it'll have you shitting through the eye of a needle in no time.'

Sylvie winced. 'That's not really selling it, hon.'

'Anyway, I believe Captain Party-Sparkles here has ordered a bonkers amount of bunting at your bequest.' Claude took a loud slurp of coffee.

'That's right,' sang Sylvie. 'I thought we're probably gonna use it over and over again, so might as well get some proper fabric bunting.'

'Cool,' I said. 'What about balloons?'

They both pulled a face. 'Well, sweet cheeks, as the world's running out of helium and we need that stuff for making heavy duty medical equipment and shit, I'd say wazzing it away on balloons might be a tad uncool, yeah?'

'*The world's running out of helium?*' That was a new one on me.

'I know, right?' laughed Sylvie. 'Who knew?'

'Well I was actually referring to normal balloons anyway,' I said.

'I'm surprised at you, Pink Panther,' said Claude. 'All that latex and polycrapoline or whatever it's made of – basically crap that ends up in landfill for several millennia or tangled in a tree annoying our feathered friends. We can let our *inner joy and sparkle* be the balloons of this party.'

'Oh nicely put, hon!' Sylvie pecked him on the cheek and Claude spanked her on the bum.

I resisted rolling my eyes. 'Shall I go on a pastry run?'

'Negatorai, my rinkydink party-panther. Well, not on my behalf anyway. I'm being a healthy boy today and sticking to Sylvie's fibre-fest muesli. She's made enough for everyone, so help yourselves. Meanwhile, Sylvie's about to head off to the *supermarché* with Letzie. But by all means, check in with your minions up in the mezzanine and go get some pastries for them if you fancy it.' He drained the last of his coffee, stifled a burp and plonked his cup in the sink. 'Right, I'd better get crack-a-lacking.'

'Hon! Don't forget your breakfast!' She pointed to her homemade muesli.

Claude rolled his eyes at himself, grabbed the ladle and filled a small bowl. Sylvie nodded her approval.

'I'd better get going, too,' she said. 'I'm picking up Letzie en route. See you later, Ori. Oh and keep an eye out for the bunting delivery.'

She left the kitchen, exchanging greetings with Odette as she passed her on the way out.

'Morning, sis. Can I get you a coffee?' asked Claude, his mouth full of muesli.

'*Non, non*, I can do it myself,' she replied, waving him out the way. 'But maybe now we could talk?'

Claude glanced at the clock on the cooker. 'Sure. I've got a lot to do, but all that shenanigania can wait while I sit down and eat breakfast with my sister.'

'I'll give you some privacy,' I said, taking my coffee and heading out of the kitchen.

'*Non, tu restes là!*' said Odette firmly. 'We will sit down together, the three of us.' She peered in Sylvie's large fibre-fest bowl. 'What is that?'

'Fancy some?' said Claude. 'Here, let me dish you up. You, too, Ori. Get something healthy down you.'

He carried a tray with three bowls of Sylvie's muesli out onto the patio, placed it on the table and pulled out a chair for Odette to sit on.

I sat down and looked in my bowl. I wasn't sure about the nuts and seeds, but didn't dare remove them for fear of looking childish.

'So, let's do this.' Claude smiled uneasily at Odette.

Odette took a deep breath. She looked like she was figuring out where to begin.

'We often disagree about our father,' she said.

'True. We do,' said Claude, tucking into his breakfast.

'Yet we agree he was disappointed by both of us, and that he favoured Gerry, yes?'

'Yes,' Claude chewed. 'Agreed.'

So far, so good.

'We agree he was a man of double standards when it came to marriage and fidelity?' continued Odette.

Claude's face stiffened slightly.

'I suppose that's true. Where are you going with this, Odey?'

'Relax, Claude. I'm not interested to draw parallels between you and him about women.'

'Good, cos after the Jacqueline episode I turned over a new leaf – I've been upfront and honest every time I've met a woman. I haven't lied to a woman in decades. You ask Sylvie. She knows all about Hendrika.'

'Who's Hendrika?' I asked.

'She's been a girlfriend of mine for nearly fifty years,' said Claude matter-of-factly. 'She lives in Denmark so we only see each other once every seven or eight years, but it was the first thing I told Sylvie when we got together: *Sometimes, albeit very rarely, I see other women*, I said. *If that doesn't work for you, then it's best we don't get involved.* But she's cool with it.' He looked at me. 'Don't pull that face! What's wrong with what I just said? Sylvie sees other fellas, too! There isn't just one way of doing relationships, you know!'

I wasn't sure what to think. When Mum said he had girlfriends all over Europe, I'd thought she meant *ex*-girlfriends – not *ongoing* ones. Still, if Sylvie had other boyfriends and they were both happy with their arrangement, then who was I to judge?

'Anyway, it's more or less a redundant issue these days cos I haven't seen anyone else in years.'

Odette put her hand on his arm. 'Shut up, Claude. I'm not interested in your love life. You are digressing. Please allow me to continue.'

Irritation bubbled in Claude's eyes. 'Go on then.'

'We agree he was not very respectful towards Albertine, yes?'

'True, but she weren't too respectful towards him either as we got older.'

'I agree.'

Back on safe ground again. Where *was* she going with this?

She took a sip of coffee and continued. 'He was celebrated after the war for his efforts in the resistance, for helping many people flee the Nazis. Agree?'

'Agree.'

'And he *did* help people escape. This was good of him,

it was moral and brave of him. Agree?'

'Agree – can you just get to the point, Odey? I sense disagreement just around the corner.'

'He was not keen to adopt me, he only did so because Albertine insisted on it. Agree?'

Claude frowned. This one wasn't looking quite so straight forward.

'That's the impression I got, I suppose. Although, to be honest, I don't know how keen he was or wasn't. I was younger than you. I don't remember stuff in as much detail as you do.'

'What *do* you remember, Claude?' she probed.

'I remember they had a big fight one day. I don't know what about, but she was screaming at him and threatening to leave, and somehow he talked her round. And then a week or so later, you arrived. They only told us a few days before.'

'And what did they tell you?'

'That the widow of Dad's friend who died in the war couldn't look after her daughter any more. And that we were going to look after her instead, cos that's what your real dad would've wanted.'

Odette put down her cup of coffee and looked him in the eye.

'My "real dad" . . .' she inhaled, 'was your dad.'

CHAPTER TWENTY THREE

The Departed

Claude froze, his spoon almost at his lips. He lowered it back down, missed the bowl and accidentally catapulted the spoonful of muesli across the table. We both blinked at Odette, not sure if we'd heard right.

'What are you on about?' he muttered.

'You mean Great Grandpa Leonard was your *actual birth father?*' I gasped.

'*Exactement,*' said Odette, her eyes fixed on Claude. 'Albertine made me promise never to tell you or Gerry. Our father had made her swear never to reveal the truth to anyone. It was the only way she could make him agree to rescue me. She hated him for cheating on her, but she hate him much more for abandoning me and my mother. But despite everything, she didn't want you and Gerry to grow up hating him – not because he didn't deserve it, but because it would cause you pain.'

Claude's jaw hung open, wide enough for a double decker bus to drive in, as Mum would say. God – *Mum!* Wait till I told her all this!

'I'm . . . I'm . . .' Claude's eyebrows were so knotted, his eyes so screwed up in disbelief, his whole face must've ached. 'I'm a bit confused . . .' He looked like he was trying to do a complicated sum in his head for the first time in years.

Odette sipped her coffee and continued. 'Our father had a "relationship" with my mother that lasted a few years until the arrival of a screaming baby – *me* – who killed the romance stone dead. They continue to work together in the resistance, so he would come to the house every few months, but he never acknowledge me. She explain to me who he was, though, and I would desperately try to get his attention when he came, but it was no use. I would draw him pictures, give them to him, but he would put them down without even looking at them, turn immediately to talk to my mother, give her money and leave as quickly as possible. After the war ended, we saw him less and less – and the money came less and less until it stopped completely. My mother write him many times, begging for help. Meanwhile, her drinking grew worse. Then one day, Albertine intercept one of my mother's letters and, without telling Leonard, came to France to see us.'

Claude's eyes widened. 'The fight. It was about her buggering off for a few days against his wishes.'

I tried to picture the expression on my great grandmother's face as she intercepted that letter. I wouldn't have known what she looked like had it not been for the old photograph I'd spotted at Odette's house. I suddenly felt a tonne of respect for this woman I'd never known, born a hundred years ago, whose DNA I shared. If only I'd inherited her bravery. She sounded like a force to be reckoned with.

'Mathilde told Albertine *everything*,' Odette continued. 'But what offend Albertine the most, was how Leonard showed no compassion for me or my desperate mother. Albertine returned to England and told him she will adopt me. Of course, he went crazy and refuse – as she knew he would – so she said she would divorce him, take you boys and, worst of all, tell everyone his dirty secret. Leonard made some prestigious connections after the war so, *naturellement*, he was desperate to avoid any scandal. But *he* threaten *her*, too: He said that if she tell anyone the truth, he will deny it and fight her for custody. And in those days, he probably would have won. However, his reputation would suffer and he didn't want that. *Vous voyez?*' She looked at us both. 'They *both* have something to lose, so they make an agreement.'

Claude's phone started ringing but he ignored it, instead staring into the distance as if he'd just seen an alien spaceship land in the woods. Slumped back in his chair in the shade of the parasol, he suddenly looked tired, frozen, his thoughts a million miles away. Usually he was strutting lopsidedly around barking orders, cracking jokes or giving you a long and painful history of some famous historic building. Now, he looked old and worn out, like all the life had drained out of him.

'Why didn't she say anything *after* Leonard died?' I blurted.

'Exactly,' said Claude, looking up. 'There was no reason to keep it from us after he was six feet under.'

I imagined the coffin being lowered into the ground. *Good riddance*, indeed.

Odette clenched her fists. 'Because you struggled with life already, Claude! Albertine knew our father did not approve of your choices. No matter how hard you try, nothing you did made him proud. If she tell you this ugly, deceitful thing after he is dead, it would make you more lost and frustrated than you were already . . . How could this knowledge be good for you while you were drifting from here to there, drinking too much and never settling down?'

'But maybe I would've made different choices?' Claude threw his hands up in frustration. 'Maybe I wouldn't have got involved with Jacqueline? I was jealous – you were Mum's favourite and Gerry was Dad's! And I felt guilty for feeling jealous cos I knew what a shit time you'd had, and I knew Gerry never wanted to be an accountant! If I'd known the truth about how Dad had *really* treated you, it might've changed how I saw things?'

Odette shrugged. '*Bof.* Maybe it would have helped you, maybe it would have made things worse. Anyway, I'm telling you now.'

Claude's phone rang again and he whipped it out of his pocket. 'Sylvie?' We could hear a muffled voice rambling into his ear. He interrupted her. 'You decide, sweetpea, I'm just in the middle of something right now – no, wait! You're right, Camembert's a bit stinky – get Brie.' He hung up and sighed. 'Christ, Odey . . . You should've told me sooner.'

'I nearly did. But when you took Jacqueline from me, I closed the door on you.'

'And you never told Gerry?'

'We were not close. We were barely in touch.'

A loud yawn warbled out of the mezzanine window. The boys were up – or one of them was.

'I think I'm gonna go for a walk,' said Claude, standing up and checking the time on his phone.

'You are OK?' asked Odette.

'Yeah, I just need a minute to digest the bombshell you've dropped on me.'

Odette nodded. 'Of course.'

'What shall I get on with?' I asked, feeling like I needed to step up my efforts to help out.

'Clean the bogs, put the rubbish out and unpack the glasses. I won't be long.'

I watched Claude disappear into the barn and exit through the front door.

Odette flopped back in her chair. Her whole body seemed to deflate like Yoda after using the force.

'Are you OK?' I asked her.

She took off her glasses and looked wearily up at the sky. 'Finally he knows the truth.'

'Can I ask you a question?'

'*Oui, ma chérie.*'

'Didn't Leonard treat you any better at all when you went to live with him?'

She smiled sadly. 'He would only speak to me to say, "Go to bed" or "Help Albertine wash the dishes." He would never say, "How is school?" or "Well done for passing your exam."'

'Didn't Claude and Gerry notice he treated you differently?'

'They were just kids. *They* didn't always know what to say to this strange teenage girl when I first arrived, so why would anybody else? Albertine tried very hard to welcome me into the family. She explained to Claude and Gerry that my mother was unwell and my "father" was dead and now I would be their big sister. She showed me love and kindness that I had not experienced before. Mathilde did her best, but she wasn't ready to have a child. I was an accident, and she was all alone. Leonard blamed her for my existence. Accused her of plotting to trap him, made her feel worthless. Perhaps if she'd had my father's support instead of his anger and shame . . . Who knows if things could have been different?'

'Did you see Mathilde again?'

'*Non.* Albertine made me write to her but she didn't always write back. She died a few years later. Albertine was the only person who truly loved me. But I couldn't live with my father's hostility. When I was eighteen, I fell in love and move to Greece. Albertine begged me not to leave, but my father was relieved. Claude and I stayed in touch, but not so much Gerry.'

'I don't understand how your dad could treat you so coldly.' I felt angry for her. This selfish, horrible man had caused her so much pain and got away with it – it made my blood boil. How come *she* hadn't ended up drifting from place to place, taking drugs? She had it so much worse than Claude ever did.

'I was a mistake,' said Odette. 'He didn't like to make mistakes. His own parents were very religious – mistakes were not tolerated. They taught him to believe he would be someone important, and tolerating mistakes – his own or anyone else's – just was not acceptable. His parents were determined to have status and success. For Christian people, they were not so kind or forgiving.'

'Did you ever meet Leonard's parents?'

'No, they die in a bombing raid the year I was born. If they had known their precious son had an illegitimate child with a younger woman . . . They would have died from a heart attack!' She cackled.

'My great, great grandparents sound like total dickheads.'

'The question I often ask myself is: could my father have been any other way?'

I thought about it. She had a point.

'How do you feel about him now?' I asked.

'Leonard? I feel sad for him. He suffer so much.'

'*Seriously?* But he made other people suffer! He made *you* suffer!'

'He suffer in his head, *ma chérie.*' She tapped her temple with her index finger. 'He was not a happy man. When I feel angry, I suffer in my head. When I try to open my heart to him, my mind becomes peaceful.'

I wasn't sure I could be so forgiving of someone who had treated me that way and never shown the slightest bit of remorse. I thought of my dad, of how I'd written him off over the last few years. He was annoying but he was no Leonard. Whatever his faults, I knew he loved me. Perhaps I'd been a bit harsh towards him? And perhaps I'd been a bit harsh on Mum, too? I wasn't sure I'd ever be a fan of #chuckChuck but, her choice of boyfriend aside, Mum wasn't so bad. I knew she loved me, even when she was grumpy. We just needed a break from each other every now and again.

'How do *you* feel about *your* grandfather?' asked Odette.

I shrugged. 'I'm not sure. Claude was a rubbish dad to my mum and he's never really been a grandad to me.' *Till now,* but would it last? He was just doing Mum a favour, wasn't he?

'*Écoute, ma chérie.* I will be dead soon. Who knows how long Sylvie will put up with him, and he has no one else.'

What was she trying to say? That Claude needed me?

'Why worry about him now? You've barely spoken to him in years yourself. He *hurts* people. You shut him out in order to protect yourself – so did Mum. He lets people down.'

'Yes, I know. But he has not had a family in many years. I think he begins to realise what he has missed. And I think maybe he has changed more than I realised . . .'

The mezzanine window flew open with a guffaw of laughter and a loud groan.

'You stinky bastard, Jackson!'

'Can't help it, mate. It was the pepperoni on that pizza.'

There was more guffawing (Jackson) and more groaning (Ravi).

'When are you getting up anyway?' said Ravi. 'It's nearly ten o'clock.'

'I'll get up when you bring us a coffee, mate. Milk, two sugars.'

'In your dreams, bro.'

Odette squeezed my hand and stood up. 'You know, I think I will swim today.'

'Really? What, actually swim – in a swim suit?'

'Yes, why not? With the wet shoes, it is much easier than I thought. You will come?'

'Sure.'

Ravi appeared on the patio, squinting in the sunlight. 'Ori, you should've woken me – I would've got up earlier.'

'It's fine. We were having a family meeting.'

The word "family" felt strange the second it popped out of my mouth. Despite being related by blood, I'd never considered Claude to be "family" in any meaningful way, and I'd only known Odette a week. And yet, thanks to people who'd lived a whole century before I was born (some of whom were dickheads), we were undeniably connected.

And I was beginning to sense that this connection was stronger than just DNA.

CHAPTER TWENTY FOUR

Gravity

The day whizzed past in a blur of activity.

When Claude returned from his walk, his mind was still a million miles away – I'm guessing somewhere in London in the 1950s. He threw himself into his To Do list, staying silent except to give out orders or advice on what still needed to be done.

Sylvie returned from the supermarket with Letzie, and the two of them spent the afternoon beavering away in the kitchen. Odette joined them for a short while to make a *tarte aux pommes* and Ravi helped to chop up vegetables once he'd finished sweeping and mopping the stage. Meanwhile, Sylvie sent Jackson on a mission into Frenac to buy some marker pens and card to make labels for the food so that people could see which dishes had meat and which were veggie. Yet somehow, three hours later, Jackson still hadn't returned from what should've been a forty-minute round trip. I messaged him to find out where he was and got a reply saying he'd taken a few wrong turnings, which was strange because there were only so many wrong turnings you could take before you ended up taking the right one.

In the meantime, it was mid-afternoon by the time I was

on to my final job, sorting out the recycling in the driveway, when Elias turned up in his grandparents' car to drop off some supplies and pick up Letzie. He waved to Letzie through the window and grinned at me as he wrestled a box of plates and cutlery out of the boot.

What was he so happy about? The fact he was going off to explore other places and other girls, free of parents and grandparents? The fact that he'd worked his charms on me and then had the pleasure of dropping me like an empty crisp packet? I kicked myself. I should've played harder to get. I should've played totally unavailable. Closed. Padlocked. Triple password protected. I felt my chest tighten. Then again, how could I regret that awesome kiss in that awesome setting? That wasn't something I'd ever imagined would happen while staying at Grandpa Airhead's house. My body relaxed again.

'How's it going? Looks like you're nearly ready?' He gestured behind me to where the marquee was standing bright and white on the other side of the barn.

'Yeah, nearly there. Just preparing food and waiting for the bunting to show up.' I tried to sound as upbeat as possible. 'And also Jackson's gone missing in action.'

'Oh I just saw him sitting outside a café, eating an ice cream the size of his head.'

'Interesting . . .'

'I waved but he didn't see me. I think he was trying to eat it before it melted.'

'So when's your train?' I asked.

'Tomorrow morning. Nine-thirty.'

I tried not to let my face fall.

'So, is this goodbye or are you joining us for a swim later?'

'I don't think I'll make the swim – I need to pack and my grandparents want to take me out for dinner. If I can come back later I will, but maybe we should say goodbye now, just in case?'

The disappointment rose up inside me again so I swallowed it back down. It stung a little, but not as much as the day before when he'd broken the news about his early departure. Besides, it's not like he ever made me any promises or gave me any false impressions. He'd never been unkind. And I'd only allowed my imagination to run wild *after* we'd kissed, and even then I'd been aware I was doing it. I hadn't actually done anything stupid or embarrassing. So I could handle this. It wasn't a big deal. My heart was intact and so was my dignity (for once).

'OK, well, have a safe journey,' I said, giving him what I hoped was a warm, purely platonic smile. 'Enjoy Italy.'

'Thanks. I thought we could swap numbers and email addresses?'

I was tempted to play it super-cool and say "Oh sure, I'll get Claude to pass my details on to Letzie later," but I doubted I could pull it off.

'Sure,' I said instead.

We took out our phones and swapped numbers.

'I might return to Frenac next summer. If you're here, it would be great to hang out again . . . ?' He smiled and touched my arm, adding, 'I just want you to know that I won't forget the time we spent together.'

My heart softened. 'Me neither.'

'You're pretty special, Ori Reynolds.'

'You're not so bad yourself, Elias . . . er . . .' I'd already forgotten the surname he'd just buzzed through to my phone.

'Dressel.'

'Elias Dressel.'

I felt a little less gutted. He was leaving because of pre-arranged plans – not because he didn't like me. And if I was still this single and friendless in a year's time, then maybe there was a possibility we could pick up where we left off? Although I couldn't imagine Elias would still be single in a year's time, but it was good to know I wasn't just some meaningless fling to him.

He leaned a little closer and lowered his voice. 'By the way, I think you have a fan club.'

I narrowed my eyes. 'What do you mean?'

'Ravi and Jackson. They both like you.'

'*Both?* You're mistaken. Jackson just can't stand being single for five minutes, and Ravi's just a friend. What makes you think that?' I garbled, feeling slightly fluttery all of a sudden.

Elias laughed. 'I'm a guy. Guys know guys.'

I gave him a sceptical look, despite the fact my scepticism was evaporating by the second. 'If you say so.'

'I say so.'

We stood there, holding each other's gaze.

'Stay in touch.' He pointed a finger at me. 'Or else.'

He held out his arms and we hugged like old friends. Weird. I wasn't even sure how to categorise this whole experience. Summer romance? Random snog? Week-long flirtation? Friend with benefits? Long-distance friend with minimal benefits?

Letzie joined us outside, ruffled Elias's head, pinched my cheek, and climbed into the car. I waved them off and went back inside. Odette was sitting at the end of the garden, painting at her easel; Claude was testing the stage lighting; and Sylvie and Ravi were in the kitchen making party food.

'Oh man,' said Ravi, stepping out of the kitchen and shaking his hands.

'What's up?' I asked, forcing my nerves back under control.

'I've chopped so many vegetables, my wrist is hurting.'

'Take a break,' I said.

'There's still a lot to do.'

'You're allowed to take a break, Rav. Sit down, I'll take over.'

Claude looked up from his lighting and editing suite. 'Yeah, take a break, mate. I think we're pretty much done for today.' He flipped a few switches, then stood up and came over to pat us on the back. 'Well done, people. Your work is greatly appreciated.'

The front door opened and Jackson staggered in, dripping with sweat. 'Jesus, it's so bloody hot out there!' he groaned.

'Surely your *ice cream* helped cool you down?' I teased.

'How did you know I had an ice cream?' A sheepish grin spread across his face.

'I'm psychic.'

'Yeah, well, like I said, I got a bit lost, and then I got really hot and I was hungry, so I stopped for an ice cream. I only wanted a small one, but they didn't understand me so I ended up with a multi-scoop leaning tower of Pisa which cost a bloody fortune and melted before I could eat it.'

'Idiot,' laughed Ravi.

'Well, I dunno about you lot, but I'm going for a swim,' said Claude. 'Who's coming?'

'I'm up for that,' said Jackson. 'I'm so hot, I just need to throw myself into a river.'

'Coming, Rav?' I asked.

He shook his head slowly. 'I might catch up with you. Sylvie's going to show me how to make houmous from scratch.'

'Come on!' I punched him on the arm. 'Time to chill!'

'I'll join you in a bit,' he insisted.

As Ravi returned to the kitchen and Jackson went to find his trunks, I turned to Claude.

'Are you OK?' I whispered.

'I'm a bit shell-shocked to be honest,' he sighed, his eyes still glazed. 'All day long my brain's been scanning the past, replaying random memories through this new lens. It's like my childhood just re-wrote itself.'

'Have you told Sylvie yet?'

'Not yet. All in good time.'

'Are you angry with Odette?'

'God, no! I'm angry at *myself*. All the times I've been an utter cock to her – and to my mother – which I feel bad enough about as it is. This just makes it even worse. If only I'd known . . .'

'You probably need to talk to someone about it. Mum says therapy saved her from having a total breakdown . . . She said that going back to her childhood–' I realised what I was saying and quickly switched tactic. 'Basically, she says if she had to choose between her therapist and her boyfriend, she'd choose her therapist every time.' I laughed nervously and hoped I hadn't offended him. (And if only she *would* choose her therapist over her boyfriend.)

Claude gave me a thoughtful look. 'Yeah, well, in the meantime, I'll just have to make do with a therapeutic swim in nature's bath tub.'

As he wandered off to get changed, I cringed. Then I uncringed. It would probably do him good to know that his daughter went to therapy and ranted about her childhood. Then I cringed again. Two revelations in one day wasn't exactly the best timing.

Far too cool to borrow a pair of wet shoes, Jackson was now slipping and stumbling over the pebbly shore as he waded into the water towards me and Odette.

We watched him in silent amusement until she broke away from me in a steady breast stroke. She seemed like a strong swimmer.

'*Dépêche-toi, Claude!*' she called, gliding past him.

Claude was still in a trance, standing ankle-deep and staring down at his reflection in the rippled water. 'I'm coming,' he replied absently.

Jackson swam towards me, stopped, and splashed me in the face. I glared at him.

'Do that again and you're dead,' I warned.

He did it again.

'I wasn't joking,' I said.

'Empty words . . .' he teased.

I launched myself at him and tried to push his head under

but he scooped me up and hurled me over his shoulder. I went under and got an earful of river water. I swam away from him screaming as he chased me.

'Stop! I've got water in my ears! I could get an infection! I'm SERIOUS!'

He stopped and held up his hands in surrender. 'OK, OK, *calmez-vous!*'

'Do NOT come any closer!' I said firmly.

'Fine.' He looked over my shoulder at Claude and Odette who were swimming past each other in different directions. 'Your olds are pretty cool, Ori. My grandparents would *never* swim in a river. A hotel pool maybe, but a river? No way.'

'Spending time with them hasn't been nearly as bad as I thought it would be,' I admitted.

'When Ravi said you'd gone to France, I really started to miss you,' he said, drifting a bit closer. 'You know, me and Ava were pretty much over the day you and me kissed.'

'I'm sorry,' I said automatically.

'Don't be. I'm not. It took something like that to happen to make me realise that me and her weren't getting on anyway.'

I kept quiet. I didn't really want to get back into this conversation again. I watched as Claude swam back to the shore and went to sit down on his log. He picked up a stone and threw it into the water. I guess he needed some plopotherapy after the day he'd had.

'Ori . . .' Jackson's face was suddenly inches from mine. He looked dangerously attractive with water dripping down his forehead and over his eyelashes. I back-pedalled cautiously out of reach. 'Just hear me out, yeah?' He caught my arm and brought me to a stop. I was aware of the current gently nudging me towards him. Surely he wouldn't try to kiss me – not in front of the Boomers? The gap between us seemed to be shrinking. 'Ori...'

Suddenly Jackson pushed me out the way with such force that my knee-jerk reaction was to try to kick him in the nuts. But he'd already swum away from me like his life depended on it. *He was such a bloody child!* Then I caught sight of Claude, charging towards the river and pointing maniacally, as if he'd just seen a man-eating crocodile swimming towards us.

'ODEY! GET ODEY!' he yelled before slipping and landing flat on his back at the water's edge.

Odette – where was she? I looked to where he was pointing and swam with all my might in the same direction as Jackson who was now diving beneath the surface. A heart-stopping few seconds later he submerged with his arm around her, her head flopped back against his shoulder. *Thank God.*

'Oh God, Odey!' wailed Claude behind us.

Jackson began paddling awkwardly with one arm, struggling to steer her towards the shore. I caught up with him and, just as our feet touched the bottom, I reached out and slipped my arm around her waist.

'Is she OK?' yelled Claude, still sprawled out on the bank nearby. Together we dragged her into the shallow water where Jackson scooped her up and carried her in his arms. I helped steady him over the stones until we were back on the shore and Jackson was able to lower her carefully to the ground.

'Odette, can you hear me?' Jackson knelt over her and gently shook her shoulder.

We watched and waited, adrenaline pumping round our bodies, as Jackson shook her again.

But Odette didn't move.

CHAPTER TWENTY FIVE

The Proposal

'Have you brought your phones?' shouted Claude, heaving himself into a sitting position.

'No!' we chorused.

'Shit,' muttered Jackson. He put one hand on top of the other, inter-locked his fingers and plunged the heal of his hand into Odette's chest over and over while counting under his breath. He stopped, glanced nervously at me, then tilted her head back and pinched her nostrils. He took a deep breath and breathed into her mouth. On his third breath, Odette's fingers twitched and she started to cough. Jackson moved back and carefully manoeuvred her onto her side as she spluttered shakily back to life.

'Oh, thank God!' I squeaked, getting up and rushing over to Claude. 'Can you get up?' I asked.

'Is she OK?' he asked, trembling.

'She's breathing. Let me help you up.'

Claude turned himself over like a crab, so that he was on his hands and knees and slowly, holding onto my arm for balance, climbed to his feet. He staggered and I caught him and held onto him until he'd centred himself.

'What's going on?' said a voice.

I looked up, relieved to see Ravi standing there in his shorts with a towel hanging round his neck.

'Have you got your phone?' Jackson and I said in unison.

Ravi delved into his pocket and pulled out a phone.

'Call an ambulance,' said Jackson.

'What's the number?' asked Ravi. 'Is it the same as–'

'It's 1-1-2,' interrupted Claude, motioning for Ravi to pass him the phone.

'What the hell happened?' Ravi squatted down next to me, brushing lightly against me as Claude spoke to the emergency operator.

'I don't know,' I said, feeling flustered again. I grabbed my towel and covered Odette with it. 'Did you see what happened, Jackson?'

'No . . . I just looked up and she was going under.' Jackson reached for his towel, folded it into a makeshift pillow and slid it under Odette's head.

Claude hobbled over and eased himself onto the pebbles next to Odette.

'An ambulance is coming. They told us to stay here. Can you hear me, Odey?'

Odey's eyes fluttered open.

'Sis? You still with us?' Claude stroked her head.

Her lips opened and a barely audible croak seeped out.

'Try again, sis. Louder!'

'Imbecile!' Her eyelids snapped shut.

I stared out the taxi window at the moonlit fields. I could've easily nodded off, but Claude had already done that and was snoring loudly in the front passenger seat.

At the hospital, while they'd run tests on Odette, Claude had limped off with a doctor to get himself checked over for damage. He'd hobbled back along the blindingly-white corridor to Odette's bedside half an hour later, giving me the thumbs up.

The doctor, a tall man with small round glasses and a dark beard, stood between me and Claude and began talking to me in French. I interrupted.

'I'm sorry, could you speak in English please?' I asked.

'So your aunt has concussion from where she hit her head,' said the doctor in perfect English.

Hit her head?

From behind the doctor, Claude raised a finger to his lips, warning me to keep quiet. That's when I remembered him throwing his stupid stones, Odette swimming nearby . . . Could he have hit her by accident? Surely he wouldn't have been able to hit a moving target if he'd tried? Hand-eye coordination wasn't his greatest skill, as his driving had already proved. She must've done it some other way.

'OK . . .' I looked at the doctor. 'But will she be all right?'

'We will give her a scan to see if she has any serious brain injury, and if not, then we will keep her here until we are confident she is well enough to go home. We talked a little just now, and she was able to answer all my questions, so I'm optimistic.'

'OK, thank you. Can we get another chair so we can both sit in here with her?' I asked.

'My advice is that you both go home and return in the morning when we will have more information. We will keep a close eye on her while she is sleeping.'

I glanced at Claude, expecting him to insist on staying put, but he looked burnt out. Stifling a yawn, he saluted the doctor and went over to Odette to give her a kiss goodnight.

'How did she hit her head?' asked the doctor. 'That bruise will be impressive.'

We both glanced at the shiner already ripening on Odette's forehead.

'Um, we don't know . . .' I stammered, trying not to let the panic show in my eyes.

The doctor looked at Claude. 'You have no idea how it happened?'

Claude looked bewildered. 'Total mystery, Doc. Maybe she hit it on a low-hanging branch – there are quite a few sticking out over the water where we were swimming. She disappeared out of sight for a short while.'

The doctor considered this and nodded.

'Actually, could we have a minute alone with her before we go?' asked Claude.

'Yes of course.' The doctor opened the door.

Claude hesitated. 'But first, just a quick question. To me she seems as fit as ever,' he said to the doctor. 'Odey has always been a force of nature, but according to *her*, she ain't got long to live. Something she weren't prepared to elaborate on so I'm not sure exactly what we're looking at. She's not one for tears and mushiness, so er, any clarity you could give us would be much appreciated.'

The doctor smiled kindly. 'At her age, of course time is starting to run out. But the way I see it, we are all living on borrowed time from the moment we are born. None of us knows when we're going to go.'

'Profound. Thanks, Doc. I'll remember that . . .' Claude scratched his hair. 'So one year, two? Three, four?'

'I'm sorry, it is not my place to discuss her diagnosis with you – it is up to her.'

'Ballpark?'

The doctor cleared his throat. 'Odette is resilient. She can handle reality. Her healthy attitude to life is her best defence. So, if she takes it easy – rests, eats healthily, stays hydrated, all the usual rules for healthy living – I don't think she'll be departing from this life just yet.'

'OK, Doc. Vague, but optimistic. I'll take it.'

The doctor nodded and disappeared down the corridor, closing the door behind him.

Claude turned to Odette and gently squeezed her hand.

'Sis, you can hear me?'

'Shouldn't we just let her sleep?' I asked.

'I just need to tell her something first – it's important.' He gently shook her arm. 'Odey, wake up a minute. Just give me one minute, sis.'

One of Odey's eyes cranked open. '*Qu'est-ce que c'est?*' she mumbled.

'I just wanted to say I love you and I'm really, really sorry. I'm sorry about every dickhead thing I've done my whole life and I'm even more sorry about knocking you on the conkerbox

– the stone just flew out of me flipping hand before I was ready to throw it and I didn't see you were right there . . . Christ, I nearly killed you!' He smacked his forehead with the palm of his hand.

'*Imbecile*,' she croaked again.

'I know, I know. I'm a *prize* imbecile.'

Odette's face crumpled. 'Why did you resuscitate me?' she hissed. 'It was perfect! Just perfect . . . The best gift you could give me . . .'

'Er, sorry not sorry?' said Claude. 'I'd kind of like you to stick around a tad longer, if that's OK? I like spending time with my sister.'

Odette sighed. 'I suppose I like spending time with my brother too.'

Her eyelids closed and she was gone again.

Claude and I looked at each other.

'*You knocked her out with your bloody plopotherapy?*' I was right! I couldn't believe it. No, I *could* believe it. Airhead by name, Airhead by nature.

'It was an accident! Like I said, it slipped out of my hand before I meant to let go.'

I blew out my cheeks. 'Wow! You nearly killed your sister!'

'Yeah, all right, kid. Don't rub it in. It's been a bit of a challenging day as it happens.' He limped off down the corridor towards the exit.

Half an hour later, as the cab pulled up outside the barn, I nudged him awake.

'We're home.'

He looked out the window, grunted as he cranked his head from side to side, and paid the driver. As we entered the barn, Jackson, Ravi and Sylvie all jumped up from the sofas, eager for news.

'She's stable,' announced Claude. 'For the time being, that is. Look kids, I'm beyond knackered. I'm going straight to bed. I'll be up early in the morning to go visit Odey first thing.'

'Do you think we should postpone the party?' asked Sylvie, putting an arm around him.

Claude sighed. 'We'll see how Odey is in the morning and take it from there . . .'

'You OK, Ori?' asked Ravi as Claude and Sylvie said goodnight and headed out to the caravan.

A wave of tiredness hit me and I flopped face-down onto the sofa like a skittle, arms pinned to my side, legs straight as a rod. 'Can't move . . .' I mumbled into the cushion beneath my face.

'I should warn you I was sitting there a minute ago,' said Jackson. 'And what with that epic ice cream followed by all the drama, I've been feeling a bit windy . . .'

'Don't care . . .' I replied. *Actually, yes, I did care. That was gross.* I flipped onto my back and looked up at Jackson's grinning face. He smiled apologetically.

'Cup of tea, Oreo?' asked Ravi.

I grinned and he disappeared into the kitchen.

'I'm glad Odette's OK,' said Jackson, sitting down opposite me. 'That was a scary moment.'

I reached for a cushion behind me and levered it under my head so that I could see him. It had just occurred to me that Jackson had saved the day. *Jackson. Of all people.*

'You were amazing,' I said. 'You saved Odette's life. Where did you learn CPR?'

'Duke of Edinburgh Award, year nine. Did First Aid for my new skill.'

'God, I vaguely remember that. I did *baking*. Like that's ever going to save anyone's life.'

'Oh, I don't know. Imagine a world without cake. How depressing would that be?'

'True,' I chuckled. 'It would be very depressing.'

'So baking skills *are* important. Imagine birthdays or weddings *without cakes?*' He threw his arms about excitedly. 'Imagine it's your eighteenth birthday party and someone says, *OK, listen up everybody, it's time to do the bowl of Minstrels now.* And someone brings out a bowl of Minstrels and sets it down on the table while everyone sings Happy Birthday?' He grinned at me. 'It wouldn't be the same, would it? Cake – you could say – is essential for bringing joy and therefore good mental health into the world.'

'Well argued!' I laughed. 'Although I'd be happy with a bowl of Minstrels *and* a cake. Remember what new "skill" Ravi did for his D of E?' I teased as Ravi returned with three cups of tea and set them down on the coffee table.

'Oh yeah, *basketball*,' Jackson smirked.

Ravi sat down next to him with pursed lips, ready for a ribbing.

'Which ought to count as a *physical activity* rather than a skill, don't you think?' I narrowed my eyes.

He groaned. 'As I've already told you many times, Oreo, it's *both*.'

'Hmm . . .' I eyed him doubtfully. 'Bit lame, Ravioli . . .'

'It's *not lame!* Shooting hoops involves skill.'

'It doesn't save lives like CPR or protect mental health like cake though.'

'Scoring a goal for your team brings major happiness to all your fans. And playing basketball is good for your physical *and* mental health, so there!'

'It's not up there with CPR, though, mate,' said Jackson.

'It beats cake!' protested Ravi.

We continued chatting until we started to fade, each of us taking it in turns to yawn and scroll vacantly on our phones.

'I'm going to bed,' I announced, standing up. Jackson put his phone down. Ravi didn't respond – he was already asleep on the sofa, his head lolled backwards and his mouth wide open.

'Yeah, me too,' said Jackson.

I was about to give Ravi's foot a gentle kick, when Jackson intercepted me and steered me into the kitchen.

'I just need to ask you something,' he whispered.

It sounded ominous. 'Okaaay . . .'

'I keep screwing up and not handling things very well. When I kissed you the other day – that was really uncool of me and I'm really sorry. I took advantage of you and, yeah, like I said, I'm sorry. I had my chance with you and maybe it's too late, but for what it's worth, I want you to know that I'm not a bad person. Sometimes I goof around, make uncool mistakes and tend to act my shoe size, but overall I'm a good person.'

I was surprised to hear him acknowledge his shortcomings. I'd assumed he had no idea how immature he could be, but it turned out he *was* aware. And, the bottom line was, he *was* a good person. He'd saved Odette's life.

I looked at him. 'I know you're a good person,' I said.

'Phew,' he replied, mock-wiping sweat from his brow. 'That's a relief. OK, so there's one more thing I want to say to you. I'd really like to kiss you. I mean, I was hoping you would do me the honour of letting me kiss you? I mean, when *you* kissed *me*, it took me by surprise, and then when *I* kissed *you*, it took *you* by surprise, so we haven't actually shared a proper kiss yet – you know, a kiss that hasn't gone wrong. So, like, you could think of it as an experiment, to see whether you feel anything for me or not. And if you don't, then that's fine – I'll know it's not happening and so *friend zone* it is.' A brief nod of the head signalled he'd finished his speech. He lowered his eyes to the floor.

I was taken aback by everything he'd said. I couldn't really argue with any of it. He was being honest, fair and polite. What he said made sense. After everything that had happened, it seemed kind of stupid not to take this opportunity to find out if there really was anything between us.

'By the way I haven't smoked today,' he added. 'I'm giving up – both cigarettes and vape pens. Well, I'm going to seriously try.'

I smiled. 'OK.'

'I'm serious.'

'Yes, I know. I was saying OK to the experiment, not the smoking thing.'

'Oh, right.' He looked genuinely surprised, happy – and *cute*. And slightly lost, like he didn't know what to do next.

We moved towards each other and Jackson put his arms around me. As our lips were about to touch, I suddenly turned my face to the side and went in for a hug instead. Confused, Jackson went along with it and hugged me back.

As we parted, a shadow in the doorway startled us.

'Er, sorry to interrupt,' said Ravi awkwardly. 'I was just going to get a glass of water to take upstairs but actually I don't really need one. I'll see you in the morning. Night.'

He gave a brief nod and walked off quickly in the direction of the bathroom.

Jackson looked at me, baffled. 'What happened? The experiment, I mean?'

'I realised I already knew what the result would be,' I said. 'Sorry.' I gave him a peck on the cheek and said goodnight.

CHAPTER TWENTY SIX

Clueless

'Ta-daaah!' Claude revealed the huge bunch of lilies he was hiding behind his back and presented them to Odette.

She wrinkled up her nose in disgust. 'Pah! Cat poison!'

'Watch out, kitty-cats!' called Claude, making kissy sounds to any cats that might've been lurking under the bed. 'Killer flowers at large! Bought out of love, received with contempt!'

'Hmmph.'

He bent down to peck her on the forehead, careful to avoid her bruise, which was now a purpley yellow colour. 'Be grumpy all you like, I will only lavish you with more brotherly love – which now comes in a new, improved, *biological* formula.'

'Good news about the scan!' I said, sitting in the chair next to her bed.

'*Bof*. Everything else fall apart, it is just a matter of time before the brain goes, too.'

'Maybe, but at least you'll be out of here in no time.'

Claude laid the bouquet on the swivel-tray at the end of her bed and sat down. 'The doc said there's no chance you're coming out today, though. Tomorrow at the earliest.'

'When they discharge me, I want to go home,' she said assertively.

'No problemo,' said Claude. 'I'll take you back whenever you're ready.'

'I miss *mes animaux*. I want to see Saucisse and Sylvestre. They will be wondering where I am!' She wiped a tear from the corner of her eye. I took her hand and squeezed it. 'I have never spent this long apart from them.'

'They're all right,' Claude assured her. 'Your mate Ossie seemed a reliable bloke.'

'That is not the point!' she huffed. '*I miss them!*' A tear rolled down her cheek.

'I'll take you back as soon as the doc reckons you're ready for a long car journey. In the meantime, what do you think I should do about the Grand Opening?'

'What do you mean?' she asked, blowing her nose.

'I mean, I should probably cancel it, shouldn't I? Wouldn't be right to have a party while you're stuck in here.'

'For God's sake, Claude – don't be ridiculous! I *hate* parties. Shallow conversation with boring people and terrible music and too much noise! This is the only time in my life I am glad to be in hospital so I have a perfect excuse not to come.'

I grinned. There it was again – that thing I couldn't quite put my finger on. Odette being Odette, speaking her truth. No shame, no blame, just honesty.

I wanted to be more like that.

Claude tried not to laugh. 'So that's a green light, then, is it?' She gave him a withering look and turned to me.

'*Tiens, chérie* . . . Pass me the water please.' I helped her sit up a bit, took the glass of water from the bedside table and held the straw to her lips while she sucked down thirsty gulps.

'You might not miss the party,' I said, 'but the party will definitely miss you.'

She released the straw and turned her head towards me. 'Look after my brother. He already thinks he is twenty-nine, but after some drinks he will act like fifteen. *You* are more mature than him!'

'I'm still in the room, you know!' Claude frowned and stood up.

'Your body is in the room, but your brain is often somewhere else,' muttered Odette, looking at me with a mischievous glint in her eye.

I sniggered.

'Right, come on, Pinkerama.' Claude cocked his head towards the door. 'It's ten o'clock – time to get back to the ranch and put up the bunting.'

I stood up and kissed Odette goodbye.

'See you tomorrow,' I said.

'I'll be here,' she smiled.

'Love you, sis!' Claude squeezed her arm.

'*Vas-y!* Go!' She dismissed him as if he were one of her dogs being told to *go pipi*.

Back at the barn, it was strangely quiet. The sliding doors were open, and a warm breeze trickled in from the garden.

Sylvie was sitting at the dining table, writing labels for the party food. Someone was in the bathroom and someone – Jackson I guessed – was still in bed.

'How's Odey?' asked Sylvie, looking up as we walked in.

'No damage to the old noggin,' said Claude with a grin.

'Thank goodness for that.' She sighed with relief.

'Right, what's left on me list?' asked Claude.

'I think we've done it all, hon. You can sit down and put your feet up for half an hour.'

'Really?' Claude narrowed his eyes. 'There must be *something* I haven't done yet?'

'Had breakfast?' Sylvie winked at me. 'Sit down, the pair of you. Chill out for a minute.'

The bathroom door opened and Jackson strolled out, fully clothed and smelling lemon-zesty from the shower.

'I didn't think you'd be up yet!' I said.

'I'm up, I'm awake, and I'm at your service,' he replied with a bow.

'I must say,' said Sylvie. 'You boys have been such a help. Don't know how we'd have got it all done without you.'

'It's been fun,' smiled Jackson.

'Put the coffee on, will you, sweet cheeks?' Claude nodded to me and flopped on the sofa.

Jackson followed me into the kitchen.

'So, first things first,' he said in a low voice.

'Oh, she's fine,' I said.

He looked confused. 'Oh, yes! Awesome. That's a relief.'

Odette clearly wasn't what he was referring to by "first things first".

'Last night . . .' He drew closer. I quickly turned my back to him to put the coffee machine on. 'What made you change your mind?'

I tried to find the right words. 'I'm just not feeling it any more . . . I think all the drama I caused just kind of killed my crush, and now my head's just not in the same place.'

There was a bit more to it than that, but I didn't know how to explain it to him without offending him. It had taken me a while to work out that Fantasy Jackson and Real Jackson were not the same person. I might as well have been crushing on a fictional character, because the Jackson of my daydreams was basically an enhanced version of him that I'd invented. The real Jackson was a nice guy and I liked him a lot more than the two-dimensional version I'd invented in my head, but any romantic chemistry I thought I'd felt, had kind of evaporated.

And then there was Ava. If I was to get together with Jackson, even if we just kissed once and nothing more, I knew we'd never be friends again. I wanted, if I could, to make things better – even just a little bit better. Not worse.

'I'm sorry . . .' I said.

'It's OK. I understand.' He looked disappointed, but not annoyed.

'You came all this way.'

'You didn't ask me to.'

'I ruined your relationship.'

'It wasn't working anyway.'

Cue awkward silence.

'Want a coffee?' I asked.

'Yeah, cheers.'

'Shall I make one for Ravi or let him sleep a bit longer?'

'So that's the other thing,' said Jackson. 'He said he was going to text you, but it looks like he hasn't . . . ?'

'Text me? Why?' I put down the cup I was holding.

'He left about an hour ago. He said he'd text you to let you know.'

'What? When did he leave? Why?'

A weird feeling came over me. A sudden sense of disappointment, like going to the cinema to see a film you'd been dying to see, only to get there and find it had sold out. Or being really revved up about going to the beach for a picnic only for it to cloud over and rain. Or when the person whose company you enjoy the most, who's on the same page as you, who gets you, suddenly ups and leaves without saying goodbye.

'Er, not sure. It was pretty early – that's why *I'm* up so early. Bastard woke me up.'

'*Why* did he leave? He didn't even say goodbye!'

'His dad's really short-staffed – he felt like he had to go back and help out.'

'But he didn't need to rush off without saying goodbye!'

'There was a train leaving this morning from Sarlat. There isn't another one till later this evening.'

I stared out the window. Why did I feel so gutted?

'Something tells me you like Ravi . . .' said Jackson cautiously.

'What? I'm just a bit pissed off he left without saying goodbye – that's all.'

'He said he was walking into Frenac to catch a bus to the station in Sarlat.'

'And he left an hour ago?'

I took out my phone and called Ravi's number, but it went straight to voicemail.

'Ravi, it's Ori. We need to talk. Can you call me back?' I hung up.

Jackson looked at his phone. 'The train doesn't leave till eleven. We could—'

I rushed past him into the barn and interrupted Claude and Sylvie kissing on the sofa.

'Claude, I know this is the last thing you want to do right now, but could you drive me into Sarlat? Ravi's leaving and I need to speak to him before he catches his train. It's *urgent*.'

'Ravi's left? Why? Did we work him too hard?'

I dropped to my knees, pressed my hands together, and begged. If Ravi had left because he thought me and Jackson had got together, I had to set him straight. I desperately needed him to know that what he saw was *not* the beginning of a new romance, but the moment I realised once and for all that there wasn't any romance to be had. Why this felt so urgent, I wasn't entirely sure – I just needed Ravi to know he mattered to me, because it was starting to dawn on me how much he really did. I squeezed my hands together extra hard and clenched my eyes shut.

'All right, all right, don't wet yourself.' Claude dragged himself up off the sofa, his joints creaking like the corkscrew staircase. 'Come on then. You coming an' all?' He nodded to Jackson.

'Let's *all* go,' said Sylvie excitedly. 'The more of us there are, the easier it'll be to find him!'

We hurried out the door and jumped into Claude's car.

'Who needs breakfast anyway?' whimpered Claude as he pulled out of the driveway and roared down the lane. 'Let's rock'n'roll!'

'Put your seatbelt on!' I blurted from the back seat. 'And try not to speed, please, thank you!'

'Do you wanna reach him in time or not?' snapped Claude.

'Yes, but I don't wanna kill anyone on the way!'

'Like I said, in over fifty years of driving, I haven't injured a soul!' He exchanged a secretive eye-roll with Sylvie.

'*That you know of,*' I reminded him.

He narrowed his eyes at me in the rear-view mirror. 'Of course it's quite possible I could murder a backseat driver in cold blood – especially one that hasn't even had a *single driving lesson.*'

'Eyes on the road!' I yelled.

Sylvie put a soothing hand on his lap. 'Just drive, hon. The tension is high because the stakes are high.'

He frowned at her. 'Why are the stakes high?'

'Because . . .' she whispered out of the corner of her mouth, 'love is in the air . . .'

'No it's not!' I groaned, glancing at Jackson. 'We just didn't part on the best terms and I need to put that right.'

I noticed Jackson had gone quiet.

I gave him a cheery smile. 'You OK?'

'Sure,' he said unconvincingly.

'I'm sorry about this,' I said to Jackson. 'I just – it's not like *that*, it's just . . . you know, last night, what he saw–'

'It's cool,' he interrupted. 'Don't worry about it.'

I called Ravi's number again, and again it went straight

to voicemail. I left another message anyway. 'Ravi, please don't get on that train. We need to talk. You can get the next one instead. Please just wait for me, I'll be at Sarlat station in the next ten minutes.'

We drove on in silence until Claude shouted, 'Knackers and *piss*!'

'What?' we all chorused.

'Forgot to charge the car yesterday – battery's about to die and the tank's empty an' all.'

He slowed down as the traffic got busier.

'Can we make it to the station?' I asked, leaning forward on the edge of my seat.

'Negatorai, leader one. There's a petrol station a few streets away. If you hop out there, it's a ten minute walk. Quicker if you run, obviously.'

We crawled along with the traffic, my heart racing as I tried Ravi's number over and over, without success. Meanwhile Jackson took out his phone and looked up where the station was.

When we pulled into the petrol station, Jackson and I leapt out of the car like two criminals on the run. It was 10.53 a.m.. Jackson shot way ahead of me in no time. I jogged as quickly as I could (running wasn't my strong point), past the supermarket, past the car show room, across a busy road, down a high street, following signs for "*la gare*" and trying not to lose sight of Jackson.

Eventually I saw the station up ahead and panted my way towards it, a stitch in my side taunting me about how unfit I was. Jackson had already vanished inside. I lumbered along till I reached the main entrance and darted in. It was 10.58. I vowed to myself that if Ravi was still there, I would take up regular exercise from the day I got home.

There were groups of people everywhere. Some locals, some tourists, pulling suitcases on wheels behind them. I looked up at the timetable screen, searching for a train that was due to leave at eleven, but couldn't see one. I did a three hundred and sixty degree pivot. No sign of Ravi anywhere. I ran towards the barriers and scanned as far as I could see along each platform. Then I tried the ticket office, and hovered outside the loos until I caught sight of Jackson walking towards me. It was now 11.05.

He shook his head as he reached my side. 'I think we've missed him.'

I continued scanning all around me. 'God, Jackson, if you'd told me straight away – INSTEAD OF WAITING – we could've got here in time!'

'How was I to know? He said he was going to text you! And you could've run a bit faster – your grandad could probably outrun you!'

I glared at him. I doubted Claude could outrun me, but there was a fair chance Sylvie could. The possibility of being outrun by someone in their mid-sixties was something I clearly needed to address.

'What exactly did you want to tell him anyway?' he asked. 'I mean, can't you just say it in a text?'

I swallowed. I wasn't a hundred per cent sure what I wanted to tell him, other than: *please don't go.*

I shrugged. 'I think he got the wrong end of the stick last night and he left because of that – not because his dad asked him to come home.'

'Why would he leave because he saw us hugging? He wouldn't care about that.'

'How do you know? He might've thought there was more going on than there actually was.'

'He would've said something,' insisted Jackson.

'Really? You think he'd have said, "Hey mate, I'm gonna split, cos I don't really wanna hang around being a spare part while you and Ori get cosy with each other." You actually think he'd have said that, do you?' I tried not to sound annoyed.

'Why would he care if we got "cosy with each other"?'

'Because you guys have been saying *for the last few years* that he likes me!'

'Ori, not being funny but that was *ages* ago. He's long moved on since then. Er, remember Maya?'

'Well other people have said things more recently that make it seem he *does* still like me.'

'Who?'

'Odette. And Elias.'

Jackson shrugged. 'They probably picked up on how much he likes you *as a friend*. He thinks of you as his best mate. When everyone was badmouthing you, he stuck up for you a hundred per cent. I had to stop him and Ava getting snarky with each other before it turned into a row when we were in Cornwall. He likes you as a mate, but he hasn't hinted he feels anything more than that in, like, *light years*.'

'Well he's not going to shout it through a megaphone, is he?' I snapped.

Ever since I could remember, I'd simply thought of Ravi as my reliable, funny, nice but shy friend. We'd pretty much grown up together, through braces and oversized uniforms, skin breakouts and bird's nest hair. And then at some point, Jackson had started to morph into something seriously cute and distracting, and I was so focused on him, that I hadn't noticed Ravi gradually morphing into something else, too.

'OK, calm down. Maybe you're right, maybe you're wrong. You need to talk to him.'

'You don't say!' I threw my arms out.

A couple nearby glanced at us as they walked past. We must've looked like a couple having a row.

'Come on, let's go. He'll be in touch soon. He probably ran out of juice or can't get a signal.' Jackson took my arm and led me out of the station. We walked silently back to the petrol station in the scorching sun, a horrible nagging feeling weighing down on me that I had once again been stupid and thoughtless towards someone I cared about. Someone who I cared about *a lot*.

CHAPTER TWENTY SEVEN

Life Is Beautiful

The garden looked so pretty in the evening light with all the bunting I'd strung up (Sylvie had ordered miles of it) that I couldn't stop taking photos.

Jackson and I had put ourselves on bar duty – even though it was supposed to be self-service, like the rest of the buffet. I guess it gave us something to do other than standing around awkwardly making conversation with people.

The garden emptied out a little as Claude and The Lost Marbles took to the stage inside the barn. They kicked off with a Rolling Stones song and the crowd started singing and dancing straight away. Letzie had taken the frontman role, while Rolf banged a tambourine and strutted around like Mick Jagger behind her. Sylvie did backing vocals and someone else I'd not seen before was on the drums.

'Oh my days – your grandad knows how to get a party going!' Jackson gazed with awe from behind the bar.

'Yup,' I said.

'He's like the coolest septa— er, septua— person in their seventies I've ever met.'

'He's seriously not as cool as you think.'

'How come?' he asked, cramming a slice of garlic bread into his mouth.

'He left my mum when she was a kid. He saw her every other weekend until she was about ten and then he buggered off to live in Denmark, followed by Germany, followed by France, so she hardly ever saw him. He didn't exactly make much effort to keep in touch either. This is only the fourth or fifth time I've even met him.'

'Oh,' said Jackson. 'I thought you and him seemed pretty close?'

'I've got to know him a bit better and he's not *all* bad, I suppose.'

'You should meet *my* grandad. He's from another century. Expects his dinner on the table every night at six. Expects my nan to do everything. Doesn't make conversation with us when we go and visit – just sits there watching the telly or reading the papers. I *hate* him. I only go to see my nan. I don't know why she puts up with him.'

I smiled sympathetically. 'Compared to that, I guess Claude does seem cool.'

'If you've got a "Grandpa Airhead", then I've got a "Grandpa Dickhead".'

We sniggered and it felt like maybe Jackson and I could finally relax and be friends.

'Thanks for letting us stay, Ori. I'm really glad I came,' he said.

'Even though things didn't go the way you expected . . . with us?'

He shrugged. 'Yeah, we've become better friends. So it's all good.'

'I'm glad you feel that way. Me too.'

'I'll be making a move tomorrow, though. Gonna take the train back up to Paris and meet up with my cousin.'

'OK. Do you need a lift anywhere?' I asked, not sure I wanted to ask Claude for yet another favour.

'Nah, you're all right. I'll get the bus from Frenac to Sarlat. I'd better check the train timetable,' he said taking out his phone.

I grabbed a piece of garlic bread before he ate the lot and was about to get stuck into the cheeseboard when my phone buzzed. I yanked it out of my pocket expecting to see Ravi's name on my lockscreen, but instead I saw Ava's. Immediately my heart started pounding. Had she just found out Jackson was here with me?

Ava: We need to talk. When are you back from France?

What did she want to talk to me about? Did she want to vent at me? Should I just go along and take it, like the punishment I deserved? Maybe that's what I needed to do – get it over and done with.

Me: I'm not sure – in the next three or four days.

I hesitated over whether to ask if she was OK, or whether to say sorry again. But what was the point? I'd soon find out where her head was at, and it probably wasn't in a good place.

Ava: There are things I need to say to you. Face 2 face.

Me: OK. As soon as I know when I'll be back, I'll let you know.

I slid my phone back into my pocket and exhaled.

'What's up?' asked Jackson.

'That was Ava. She wants to meet up and talk. Does she know you're here?'

He shrugged. 'I haven't told her. But she's bound to find out sooner or later – you know how word gets around.'

'I think we should tell her before she hears it from someone else.'

'Maybe,' said Jackson. 'But maybe wait till you meet up. No point telling her now.'

He was right. It wasn't the kind of conversation you could have long-distance. And I didn't want to have a drama in the middle of Claude's Grand Opening party. I glanced at Claude as he played his guitar and felt a surprise shiver surge down my spine. His face strained in concentration, lost in the music, it was like the guitar was an extension of his very soul. As he launched into a solo, the crowd went into a frenzy, dancing and cheering. In that moment, I felt proud. That was my grandad.

The crowd clapped and whistled as another song finished and he took the mic to make an announcement. He glanced over at us and waved us towards him.

'Come on,' said Jackson. 'Let's go in.'

Claude beamed at the audience. 'Thank you so much for coming today and celebrating the opening of Studio Marchand, *Performing Arts and Community Space*.' Everybody cheered. 'It's been a long time in the planning, and in the making, and this is basically a dream come true. It's something I've been working towards all my life, although often without even realising it. And I wanted to thank a few people in particular for helping me turn this dream into a reality. First of all to all my fabulous friends – Rolf and Letzie, for helping with the planning – and their grandson Elias, who unfortunately couldn't make the party. I'm lucky to have such knowledgeable friends. I also want to thank my incredibly supportive partner, Sylvie, who I'd be lost without.' He turned to face Sylvie, who waved sheepishly at the audience. 'She didn't realise what she was getting into when she met me, but she's kicked my arse into gear, and helped me get through the rollercoaster ride of building this place. We make a good team.' He blew her a kiss, then scanned the audience till his eyes found me. 'Then there's my amazing granddaughter Ori, and her mates, Jackson and Ravi, who provided some unexpected last-minute help for which I'm extremely grateful. I've been extremely lucky to spend this time with my granddaughter. And I'm kicking myself I didn't make it happen a lot sooner. She's taught me a lot about myself that I didn't expect to learn at this ripe old age, and I hope we get to spend more time together now that we've broken the ice.'

I felt my cheeks fill with blood. *Well that was unexpected.*

'It restores my faith in humanity when I meet kids like Ori and her mates. They're the future, and I'm pretty sure they'll do a much better job of running this planet than my lot or the current muppets in charge.' The audience clapped and whooped, some of them turning to look at me which was a bit embarrassing. 'Don't worry, I'm nearly done,' said Claude. 'There's just one more person I'd like to thank and that's my sister Odey, who's recovering in hospital after an unfortunate accident. There's a lot I didn't realise about my sister, mainly that she's incredibly resilient, wise, and forgiving. We haven't always been the best of friends, but she's another person who has taught me so much. She's been through more than I ever could've imagined and I'm so grateful we've had this time together. Because of her, I've been doing a lot of thinking and, well, I've got a few amends to make. Anyway, I've rambled on long enough. Thanks for listening – on with the party!'

He counted the band down to their next number, and I realised it must be the song he'd named his favourite guitar after: Layla. The crowd were really going for it, which was interesting as just about everyone was middle aged or as old as Claude.

'Whoa, look at him go!' blurted Jackson, as Claude blasted out another guitar solo.

I remembered what Odette had said about him thinking he was fifteen after a few drinks, and prayed he wouldn't try any foolish moves, like skidding along the stage on his knees. It would not end well.

I turned to say something to Jackson, but he was talking to a French girl who looked about our age. From what I could tell, neither of them could speak more than a few words of the other's language.

'You speak Spanish?' asked the girl, hopefully.

'*Si! Hablo español!*' grinned Jackson triumphantly.

I gave him an encouraging slap on the arm and wandered back outside. A lot of empty glasses had been left sitting on the wall, so I started gathering them up. As I was taking some back to the outside bar, my phone buzzed. Hoping it wasn't Ava again, I pulled it out of my pocket with trepidation. *Ravi, finally!*

Hey I'm sorry I didn't call you back. Low battery. Sorry I missed you at the station, too. My dad needed me to come back and help out pretty urgently. Hope Jackson explained. Sorry not to say goodbye and to miss the party. See you when you get back.

Me: I just wanted to explain that what you saw last night wasn't what it looked like.

I paused, cringing, my finger poised over the delete key. Didn't Jackson say something cheesy like that to Ava when she caught us? Oh well, it would have to do – I was in too much of a rush to reply to think of a better way of saying it. I carried on tapping out my message.

I'm not getting together with Jackson. I just wanted you to know that. I wish you hadn't left so suddenly – I wish you were here with me now. 😔

Ravi: You're not getting together with Jackson? Why?

Me: We don't have anything in common. Did you really leave because you had to help your dad or was it because of what you thought you saw?

I waited and watched the bubbles that showed he was replying. And then they disappeared. Was he figuring out what to say or had his battery died? I waited a little longer, then put my phone back in my pocket, disappointed. I took the empty glasses and stashed them under the outdoor table. There was going to be a mountain of washing up to do later.

A loud cheer roared from inside the barn, and the band climbed down from the stage, stopping to chat with people on their way outside to the bar.

'Pinkeroo! A round of bubbly for The Lost Marbles, if you'd be so kind!' Claude said with a wink.

'I'm not sure Ori should be serving alcohol,' said Sylvie. 'You don't want to lose your licence!'

'Oops, good point.' Claude clenched his teeth. 'Didn't think of that.' He jerked his thumb over his shoulder and whistled – an instruction for me to come out from behind the bar while he replaced me. 'Anyway, your talents are wasted pouring drinks, young'un. You'll be running the country in no time.'

What was he on about? 'Yeah right,' I said. 'I have no idea what I want to do and I don't have any talents.'

'Everyone has talents!' butted in Rolf. 'You just need to discover what yours are.'

'Take Christophe, for example,' said Letzie, pointing to their drummer. 'Christophe didn't start learning to play the drums until he was in his twenties, right Christophe?'

Christophe, who looked about ten years younger than the rest of The Lost Marbles, nodded his head. 'And it was just a hobby for many years,' he said. 'Until about five years ago I finally quit my job and joined a band full time.'

'What was your job?' I asked.

'I taught maths.'

Claude passed them each a glass of Champagne and they all clinked glasses.

'A quick toast, if I may!' said Claude. 'To following our dreams, no matter how long it takes. And to listening to our hearts and not any other parts of our anatomy. Bottoms up!'

I raised my glass of shandy, Claude's words making me

shiver. For once he was right – I needed to listen to my heart. It was definitely trying to say something, and it hadn't really had anything to say before (unlike other parts of my anatomy).

As for following my dreams, I was no closer to working out what I wanted to do with my life, or figuring out what my "dream" was, but I'd made a few interesting, random discoveries over the last few weeks:

1. If I could learn how to build a brick wall, there were probably lots of other things I could learn how to do, too. I was thinking I might try and build a bird table to go on our balcony back home.

2. I got a buzz out of watching birds of prey. Who knew?

3. My stay in Boomersville was the opposite of what I had thought it would be. I learned stuff about my family history that made me see things differently. I got out of the social bubble I'd been living in for the last few years and met new people with different lives and different views. It felt good. Basically, life felt like it couldn't get any worse a few weeks ago, and now it felt a truck-load better.

4. People didn't just fall into two categories – good people and idiots. We weren't either/or – we were both. I was a work-in-progress, *not* a terrible person.

5. Just when you think life is terrible and you're the worst person in the universe, and these facts are written in stone, things gradually start to change. I was looking forward to September, to a new start. I wasn't so worried about Ava and the others anymore and I didn't hate myself anymore either. Things would be OK.

6. I quite enjoyed making lists. And might start doing so more often. In a notebook even, where I could keep an orderly, helpful track of things. I mean, what the actual fudgecakes was happening to me?

CHAPTER TWENTY EIGHT
You Can Count On Me

It had been twelve days since we'd first arrived at Odette's cottage and I'd met my great aunt for the second time in my life, and her entourage of animals for the first. Now it was time to say goodbye and I was feeling strangely emotional. Would this be the last time I ever saw her?

'So are you sure you'll be OK?' asked Claude as we stood on the door step saying goodbye the next morning. We'd stopped at a *supermarché* on the way there so that we could stock Odette's cupboards with food, although when we'd arrived at her house, it turned out she already had enough dried and tinned food to see her through a nuclear war.

'Stop fussing. *Les animaux* will look after me,' she said as Saucisse and Sylvestre stood either side of her like a couple of bodyguards. 'Oh, I've got something for you!' Odette hobbled back inside and emerged a minute later carrying the painting of her, Claude and Great Uncle Gerry with animal heads. She handed it to Claude. 'Present *pour toi*. I was going to develop it further but I changed my mind. It is finished.'

Claude laughed as he examined the canvas. 'Let me guess . . .

the chicken is Gerry, the donkey is me and the elephant is you?'

'*Voilà!*' beamed Odette, nudging me. 'I told you he'd understand.'

'I still don't get it,' I said.

Claude pointed to the characters in the painting. 'Gerry was too afraid to follow his dreams, so he's a chicken. Odey is the elephant in the room – having a new sister was never talked about after her arrival, at least, not the *real* reasons why she came to live with us. And I'm the donkey. For obvious reasons.'

'Shouldn't you be a snake though?' I suggested and instantly regretted it for fear of offending him.

Odette cackled. '*Bah, non!* He's not evil, just stupid – sometimes. Just as we all can be. Besides, I'm rather fond of donkeys.'

'Thanks, sis. I'll hang it up above Layla.' Claude tucked the painting under his arm. 'In the meantime, I really think you should come and live with me.'

'Absolutely not!' she scowled. 'You would drive me crazy.'

'You'd drive me bonkers too, but I think we'd rub along OK. There's plenty of space at the barn.'

'So you think I would be better off living in a cupboard in a music hall than in this comfortable, pretty cottage with my artist's studio?' she said.

Claude took her point. 'But you're all on your own here!'

'I *like* being on my own. *You* are the one who needs a babysitter. You never could handle being alone for five minutes.' Odette leaned on her walking stick and rolled her eyes.

'Talk some sense into her, will you, Ori?'

And say what exactly? 'Well, Odette has lots of friends round here, right?'

Odette nodded. 'Yes, I know everyone in the village. And they all know me.'

'So, if Odette needs anything, she can call one of her friends.'

'Well I don't care what you say, I'm dropping in on the way back from Brighton,' said Claude. 'We'll talk about it then.'

Odette sighed. 'There is nothing to talk about, Claude!'

'There's plenty to talk about that we've barely scratched the surface of.'

It felt like Claude could do with some back-up. 'It might be nice to sit down and talk about things properly without so much going on,' I said.

'And say what?' said Odette.

I nudged Claude.

'And tell you what I told everyone at the party about my sister.'

'What did you tell everyone about your sister?' Odette eyed him suspiciously.

'That she's an amazing person, I love her to death . . .' Tears welled up in Claude's eyes and he sniffed them away. 'And I haven't spent nearly enough time with her, showing her how much I care. That sort of thing. That was the, er, general gist of it.'

'Go on, Odette,' I said. 'It would be good for him to break up the journey on his way back, otherwise he'll probably crash the car.'

'Don't be cheeky!' Claude prodded me in the ribs.

'And you can talk properly, without all the craziness of decorating a barn going on around you,' I added.

'*Bof!*' Odette tried to look annoyed but I could tell she was touched. 'Well if you bring me some sesame seed bread, I suppose you could stay again. *Just for one night.*'

Claude grinned. 'So that's sorted then. I'll be back in the next twenty-four hours or so.'

'*Au revoir, ma chérie.*' Odette stepped forward to embrace me. I kissed her on both cheeks. '*Au revoir, Odette.*'

'I hope we will see each other again.'

'Me too. Maybe we can email each other?'

'I would like that,' said Odette. 'And you are welcome to visit whenever you like.'

Now my eyes were welling up.

'Blimey, and I had to practically *beg* for an invitation!' laughed Claude. 'Come on, let's hit the road, Jack.' He punched me on the arm and gave Odette a tight squeeze. 'I'll be back in two shakes of a showgirl's tail-feathers.'

We climbed into the car and Claude beeped the horn as we drove off. 'I say we stop in Honfleur for some *dejeuner* on our way to Dieppe. What do you say, Captain Pinker-rinkerton?'

'I say put your seatbelt on before you have an accident.'

'Affirmative, leader one.' He strapped himself in and saluted me.

***

I texted Mum to tell her to put the kettle on – we were five minutes away.

'Well this place gets more colourful every time I come here,' mused Claude as we drove through the centre of Brighton. 'It's got a good vibe – like a mini-London on sea. If I was ten years younger, I could see myself living here.'

'There's a big music scene here.'

'Yeah, I can tell . . .' he said, sizing up a crowd outside a pub in the North Laine as we sat in a traffic jam. 'You've got all sorts – hippies, goths, dandies, disco-divas . . . This place would be right up Rolf and Letzie's alley.'

'Maybe The Lost Marbles could do a gig here?' I suggested.

Claude grinned. 'That ain't a bad idea, Pinkeroo. That ain't a bad idea at all.'

When Mum opened the door, she grabbed me and squeezed the air out of me.

'Piggles!' she squealed. 'I've missed you so much!'

'Missed you too,' I mumbled into her chest. Although, to be totally honest, I didn't miss her *that* much as I'd been pretty busy having fun.

'Hey sweet cheeks,' said Claude. 'How was Noo Yoik Ciddeee?'

'I've no idea,' she replied. 'But *Chicago* was amazing.'

'That's a nice dress.' He looked her up and down. She was wearing a long, chiffony, floaty thing with white trainers.

'Thanks. Flea market purchase from Chicago. Wait till you see what I found for *you*, Piggles! She glimmered at me.

'Is your fella here?' asked Claude.

'Not at the moment. We're taking some time to reassess where we're at with everything.'

HOORAH! Was #chuckChuck chucked? My face must've given away my feelings.

'That doesn't mean we've split up, necessarily,' she said, eyeing me. 'We're just taking some space . . .'

'How come?' I asked.

'Well he wants us to move to Chicago. But that's not going to happen because my life is here with my baby girl. Also I met his ex-girlfriend. Turns out the end of their relationship slightly overlapped with the beginning of ours, and I'm not too impressed by that.'

Claude sucked in his breath.

'Yup. Not cool,' said Mum.

I gave her a hug. I'd press her for more details after Claude had gone.

'Before I forget, I spoke to your dad earlier. He wants to know if you'd like to spend some time with him next week?'

'OK.'

'Oh, great.' She looked surprised.

'What?' I asked.

'Well you never usually sound that keen. He was starting to worry you didn't want to go over there anymore.'

'I *am* keen.' It was true. I was. I'd been thinking about Dad a lot more lately. We just needed to change things up a bit, do something different. And to be fair, he'd made lots of suggestions of things we could do together in the past, but I'd never shown any interest. 'I'll call him later,' I said, 'and tell him I'm looking forward to seeing him.'

'Great,' said Mum, 'Anyway, let me put the kettle on and you can tell me all about France.'

I wondered who was going to tell her about Odette's bombshell – me or Claude?

'Mind if I sit down?' Claude lowered himself onto the sofa.

'The old Cilla's playin' up after the long drive,' he groaned.

'Sounds like you've been burning the candle at both ends,' said Mum, looking at him almost sympathetically. 'How's Odette by the way?'

'Now there's a funny story.' Claude winked at me. 'But I'll save that for later.'

'Does that mean you're staying the night?' asked Mum, surprised.

'If the invitation's still open?'

'Course it is. I wouldn't expect you to drive all that way and leave immediately. It's just that usually you're zipping off to see some old friend – or old flame . . .'

'I'm done with old flames,' yawned Claude, leaning back on the sofa. 'I think I've met my match – if you'll pardon the pun.'

'Really?' I asked. 'Is Sylvie "The One"?'

'I really think she might be.' Claude closed his eyes. 'Been thinking for a while . . . Might pop the question. Whatcha reckon?'

'What about your Danish girlfriend?' I asked. 'Hendrika?'

Claude waved his hand airily. 'Haven't seen her in years. Haven't missed her.'

Mum and I exchanged doubtful glances.

'Well,' said Mum, pouring hot water into a teapot. 'That's something I never thought I'd hear you say. I thought you were too much of a free spirit to ever tie yourself down to one person? Not that I'm not pleased for you – on the contrary, I think it would be wonderful if you felt strongly enough about someone to want to make that commitment—'

'Mum . . .' I spoke softly.

She turned around. 'What?' She clocked Claude. 'Oh.'

A soft snore vibrated through Claude's nostrils.

Mum handed me a cup of tea and sat down next to me.

'I missed you, Piggles,' she whispered, brushing my hair out of my eyes.

'Sorry I was so grumpy before I went,' I said.

'It's OK. You were going through a tough time. Life gave you some lemons, but the thing about lemons is – as you might have discovered by now – sometimes they have a surprisingly sweet aftertaste.'

I couldn't recall noticing a sweet aftertaste whenever I'd sucked on a slice of lemon. I frowned. 'Do they really?'

Mum laughed. 'No, dopey. I was talking metaphorically.'

'God!' I rolled my eyes. 'Enough with the cringey lemon references! So anyway, yeah, things are OK – better than OK.'

'*Better than OK?* Wow. I want to hear every single detail – quick, tell me as much as you can before Grandpa Airhead wakes up.'

'Well, for a start, Grandpa Airhead isn't as bad as I thought he'd be.'

Mum arched an eyebrow. 'Really? I'm all ears . . .'

CHAPTER TWENTY NINE
Up

It was three days since I'd got back from France and as promised, I'd got in touch with Ava and arranged a time and place to meet.

I'd been a jittery mess before coming out to meet her. Her texts had sounded neither friendly nor unfriendly but, for all I knew, she could've been waiting till we met in order to fire-blast me to a cinder. I wasn't sure what to expect.

I got to the end of the pier first and leaned against the handrail, looking out to sea. While I waited anxiously for her to arrive, I stood there listening to the fun fair rides roaring and blaring out music all around me. As I gazed at the choppy green waves, I imagined Ava pushing me over the railings, and wondered if there was anything sharp and pointy beneath the water below that I could be impaled on.

'Hi,' she said, sauntering up to me and propping an elbow casually on the railings. She didn't smile, but nor did she give me an arctic glare.

'Hi,' I said nervously.

'What the hell have you done to your hair?' She stared at the radical change of hairstyle I'd forgotten all about.

'New chapter, new me,' I joked, hoping I sounded like I was taking the piss out of myself.

'Right . . .' She raised her eyebrows, unconvinced.

'Look, Ava,' I geared up to apologise once again, this time directly to her face. 'I'll never be able to apologise enough for what I did. I have no excuse other than I never stopped to think what I was doing, about whether it was wrong or right, or how much it would affect you. I can't even believe how stupid I was. I'm so sorry I hurt you.'

'I'm sorry you hurt me, too. Still, Jackson was just as bad. Took him a while to fess up that it wasn't all you and he did actually kiss you back,' she said tersely, her eyes following a car full of screaming kids going round the Crazy Mouse rollercoaster. 'Look, me and Jackson weren't the perfect couple I wanted everyone to think we were. We argued a lot. I never felt like he was as into me as he should've been. And he used to get annoyed at me, saying I was always complaining.'

I kept quiet. This was pretty honest of her to admit, but I didn't want to say the wrong thing and wind her up.

She tucked a bunch of ringlets behind her ear. 'Maybe we wouldn't have lasted much longer anyway,' she said. 'But you'll just never understand how much it hurt, walking in on you and him like that. It was like being punched in the stomach.'

I could see the pain in her eyes and felt ashamed that I was the cause of it.

'I'm so sorry, Ava—'

'You were my *best friend*, Ori. Best friends don't do that to each other. Boyfriends come and go but we had something more solid than that. Something sacred. At least, that's what I'd always thought.'

'You're right,' I said. 'I've never regretted anything so much.' I caught my breath. I needed to be completely honest – even if there was no chance our friendship would ever get back to what it was. At least then, if she ever decided to get back together with Jackson one day, she'd know exactly what had and hadn't happened between us. There wouldn't be any more secrets or nasty surprises. So I took a deep breath and went for it. 'I need to let you know that while I was in France, Jackson and Ravi turned up at my grandad's place – unexpectedly – and ended up staying.' I braced myself for being toppled over the railings, but she kept still, waiting for me to go on. I told her how my feelings for Jackson had evaporated, how even though he'd tried to make a move, we'd stayed firmly in the friend zone. Confession over, I exhaled and waited for my impalement in the shadowy waters below.

'Thanks for telling me,' she said after she'd taken it all in. 'I already knew Jackson went to France to find you – Daisy bumped into Ravi's mum on the bus. So I already figured he was hoping the two of you would get together. Just so you know, that also really hurt.'

'I'm really sorry,' I said again. 'I didn't invite him to come or encourage him in any way – if he'd told me he was coming, I'd have told him not to – I swear.'

'So, how come you didn't jump on him then?' she asked. 'I mean, he was single and he travelled all that way to be with you and I'm supposed to believe nothing happened?'

'You can believe what you like, but you know everything now. There's nothing more to tell. Betraying you and losing all my friends overnight kind of killed my crush on him. He was a fantasy, Ava. But I've realised real life doesn't always match up to fantasy. It's hard to explain. I just wish I could rewind to the day I messed up and do everything differently. I don't know why I did what I did. I guess, subconsciously, all the time you and Jackson were together, I just really wanted what you had. I was lonely.' As I said the words, I realised how true they were. I'd wanted love. My mum had a partner, my dad had a partner, my best friend had a partner. They all had someone to hold them and love them while I felt like I had no one. Sure, I had parents, but one lived a three hour journey away and one was usually busy or snuggling up to her boyfriend on the sofa right under my nose.

'So you're saying you don't fancy him anymore?' She looked at me.

'Nope. Do you?'

'You have to be kidding.' She looked at me like I'd lost the plot. 'What about Ravi? He's liked you for ages. He told me he freaked out when Jackson said he wanted to go to France to see you – that's why he went with him, to hopefully get in there first. Of course, Ravi being Ravi, he bottled it.' She shook her head sadly. 'You know, when Maya was flirting with him at the prom, I told him he should go for it – that he should stop waiting around for you. Especially as you were someone who didn't understand what loyalty was.'

Ouch. But I could understand now. Probably better than most people even. 'Fair enough,' I said. 'He totally deserves to be happy.'

'Yeah, but he still likes you. Like *really* likes you.'

'What about Maya?'

Ava shrugged. 'Guess he figured out in Cornwall that there wasn't quite the spark he'd hoped for – not like the spark he has for you. Thing is, I don't think you deserve someone like him right now.'

'Guess I can understand that,' I said softly. I wasn't sure I deserved Ravi's attention either. We'd exchanged a few texts in the last few days with me saying we needed to talk and him saying he was busy working at the garden centre. Neither of us had mentioned his surprise departure from the barn, so I wasn't sure where we stood with each other, but I'd finally figured out where I wanted us to be. We were supposed to be meeting up tomorrow afternoon – if he could get the time off work – so hopefully that was when I'd find out. In the meantime, I needed to know where I stood with Ava.

'Do you think you'll ever be able to forgive me?' I asked.

Ava brushed her windswept hair out of her face. 'I don't know, Ori. It still hurts whenever I think about it – *a lot*. And how will I ever be able to trust you from now on?'

'I promise I'll never do anything like that again. To you or anyone,' I said solemnly. 'I've never felt so miserable.'

She gave a slight nod. A nod that said, "We'll see."

'I miss you,' I said.

'I miss you, too. But I'm not ready to be friends again. Not yet. I don't hate you, but I'm still hurting. Do you understand?' She looked me in the eye.

'Yeah, I understand.' I smiled. 'Thank you.'

She turned to go. 'By the way, I told Ravi I was meeting you here. I said I'd tell you to meet him outside Palm Court at two o'clock.' She nodded towards the fish and chip restaurant further down the pier. 'It's time you two sorted things out.'

'How come you arranged for us to meet?' I asked, confused.

'Well it was *his* idea for *me and you* to sort things out. He's been on about it for ages. So I'm returning the favour. Just let him know where he stands, Ori. He deserves closure.'

She hoisted her bag over her shoulder and walked away, her hair swishing as she went.

I checked my phone – ten to two – and leaned back against the railings, watching people scream on the Waltzer. I knew it was going to take a long time for Ava and me to become friends again, but it no longer felt as impossible as it did a few weeks ago. I felt myself breathe a little more easily again. Until my heart sped up at the thought of meeting Ravi.

He was standing outside Palm Court restaurant, holding a box of chips and looking at his phone.

All of a sudden I had goosebumps. How had I missed what was right in front of me all this time? Although he hadn't been the scrawny kid with scruffy hair and an oversized blazer for a while now, I hadn't really clocked until recently how he made me feel when he was around – happy, comfortable, valued, cared about. He looked up from his phone and saw me, gave me a nod. Those eyes – I realised now that I was paying attention – were pretty intense. I actually felt nervous – not something I'd ever felt around Ravi before. I tried not to let it show.

'Hey!' I said. 'This is a surprise.'

'I got the afternoon off.' He grinned at me. 'I've got chips. You hungry?'

'Always.'

'Let's sit over there.' He pointed to a bench beneath a nearby shelter and we sat down side by side. He opened the box of chips and their hot, salty smell hit me in the face. 'Help yourself.'

'Thanks.' I took a couple and blew on them to cool them down.

'How did it go with Ava?' he asked.

I shrugged. 'Not terrible. Kind of as good as it could go, I suppose.'

'So are you talking to each other? Friends again?'

'I wouldn't go that far,' I said, biting my chip in half and keeping a close eye on an audience of gangster seagulls. 'The ice has been broken, just a teeny tiny tad. I guess I'm no longer in Siberia, but like . . .' I tried to think of somewhere less arctic and not as far away.

'Poland?' he suggested.

I laughed. 'Yeah, I'm in Poland for now. Hopefully I'll be in France or maybe even England by Christmas.'

We smiled at each other and he nudged the chips towards me.

'So is that it now – are you working full time till we start college?' I asked.

'No, just till my dad fills some vacancies. He's interviewing this week.'

'Do you even need to go to college?' I joked. 'You could be your Dad's deputy chief-in-command?'

Ravi's eyes bulged. 'I don't want to work for my *dad!* I'm doing this to keep him off my back and earn a bit of money. Next summer I'll make sure I've got a job somewhere else – *anywhere else.* Maybe do what your German *bf* did, go work my way around Europe.'

'He's not my *bf!*' I elbowed him. 'Never was. But you're right – he's having a good time working in a really cool bar in Italy.' I pulled out my phone and showed Ravi the brief (and so far only) exchange of texts we'd had two days ago.

Elias: Hey Ori. Check this place out. Cool, right?

Me: OK, stop rubbing it in.

Elias: How was the big party? Did my grandfather get drunk?

Me: It was great. Shame you missed it. Rolf was on best behaviour.

Elias: I don't believe it. Better go. Remember your sun cream, ha ha! 😎

Ravi read the conversation and looked at me.

'*Not my bf,*' I repeated sternly. 'But you're right – I love the idea of working abroad next summer. I was thinking I might even go back to my grandad's place. If he won't let me work behind the bar, I'm sure there's other stuff I could do.'

Ravi bit into a hot chip and spluttered as he burnt his tongue. I passed him my Chilly's water bottle.

'So how's Maya? Have you seen her since you got back?' I asked as he glugged from my bottle.

'No. She's visiting family and I've been working. Anyway, we've agreed we're just going to stay friends.'

'Oh,' I said, my heart starting to speed up. 'Well, at least it sounds like you're both on the same page.'

We both grabbed a handful of chips.

'So anyway, you never answered my question,' I said.

'What question?' He frowned, his mouth full of chips.

'The one I asked when you left my grandad's place: Did you leave because of your dad or because you thought me and Jackson were getting together?'

Ravi gave a defeated smile. I'd cornered him at last. He couldn't wriggle out of answering me now. He picked up another chip. A couple of the seagulls crept closer, their eyes on the prize. I nudged him and the chip fell on the floor. A seagull seized it and flew off.

'Hey – that's my lunch!'

'Answer my question!'

'OK, it did have something to do with it.'

I grinned. '*Finally!*'

'What is it you want me to say, Ori?' Ravi looked annoyed. 'Are you getting some kind of twisted satisfaction from seeing me squirm?'

'What? No, of course not!'

'I didn't want to hang around and be a spare part while you and Jackson finally hooked up, OK?'

'But why couldn't you tell me how you were feeling?' I asked.

'And risk freaking you out, losing you as a friend? I've liked you for a long time, Ori. It wasn't a problem to begin with, but when you started liking Jackson, being the invisible one started to suck. I know you know exactly how that feels, but anyway,

I figured the best thing to do was to just be your friend and hope that one day you might actually *notice* me.' He took a deep breath, keeping his eyes fixed on the horizon.

I felt my heart open as I took in what he'd said. I couldn't help smiling.

'I've *noticed* you,' I said, turning towards him.

He kept perfectly still, but a smile was slowly breaking out on his lips. He still wouldn't look at me. 'What?'

'I said, I've *noticed* you,' I grinned.

'Sorry, didn't quite catch that.' He cupped his ear.

'I'VE NOTICED YOU!' I shouted, laughing.

'*Have you seeeeen the light?*' He joked, pointing a preachy finger at me.

'Your American accent is rubbish!' I grabbed his finger and threatened to bite it. 'But, yes, I've seen the light.'

'Hallelujah!' he laughed, leaning towards me. 'About bloody time, *Ori Reynolds*!'

As we were about to kiss, the tray of chips slid off his lap and onto the wooden planks beneath our feet. In seconds we were under a squawking, flapping siege, but Ravi grabbed the tray and tossed the last of the chips towards them.

'Can we try that again?' he asked, sliding his arm around me.

'Affirmative, leader one,' I said. *Goddamn Claude!*

I moved towards him and we kissed. We kissed for what felt like a long time. Somehow it just felt right. Eventually we broke away, grinning sheepishly.

'What are you doing later?' I said.

He shrugged. 'I'm open to suggestions.'

'How about a movie marathon?'

Ravi narrowed his eyes. 'Oh, I see what's going on here. You think that by making me re-watch all the films you haven't yet seen, you can catch up with me? Maybe even overtake me?'

'Get real, Ravioli. I'm already ahead of you cos I've watched films you haven't even heard of!'

'Is that so, Oreo?' He prodded me in the ribs, making me giggle. 'Well there's only one way to settle this.'

'Which is?'

'A spreadsheet with point scoring system.'

'Oh my gosh,' I clutched my heart and pretended to swoon.

'What? You don't think that's fair? I've already got it all worked out with bonus points for obscure films, foreign language films or anything pre-1970s–'

I put my finger to his lips and shushed him.

'Shut up, Ravioli. You had me at spreadsheet.'

The End

ACKNOWLEDGEMENTS

I would like to sincerely thank...

Hazel Holmes for her publishing expertise and passion; Nicki Marshall for her editing super-wisdom; Amy Cooper for her creative design, Erin Jones for the beautiful cover illustration and interior art, Charlotte Rothwell for her all-round support, Jake Hope for his sensitivity insights, Jezebel Mansell and Antonia Wilkinson, and everyone at UCLan Publishing who contributed to the production and marketing of this book.

My lovely agent Lauren Gardner and equally lovely acting agent Justine Smith, Sarah McDonnell, Lorna Hemingway, Julie Gourinchas, John Baker, Soraya Bouazzaoui and Paul Moreton at Bell Lomax Moreton Literary Agency for their feedback, enthusiasm and general support. Thanks also to the awesome sales reps at Bounce who play such an important role in getting books like this one out there.

Deep appreciation to all the lovely supportive authors in the writing community who I'm constantly learning from; all the booksellers, teachers and librarians who help bring books to readers young and old with such incredible knowledge and passion; all the reviewers, bloggers, Instagrammers and TikTokers for giving this book a thumbs-up – thank you, I really appreciate it.

Many thanks to Bruce and Mal (AKA the blues brothers), and Eleonor for providing lots of inspiration, and for each having such a golden sense of humour. Merci beaucoup. Thanks also to my bosom book buddy Jen J for her feedback and support. And a huge thank you to my parents for always being behind me.

And finally, to my beloved Mr H and my two amazing daughters, thanks for being solid sounding boards and the best family anyone could wish for. Love you big time.

P.S. In case anyone was wondering, Frenac is a fictional town, but all other locations mentioned are real.

P.P.S. Swimming in a river is a glorious experience, but always find out about depth, currents and pollution before you take the plunge. And tell someone where you're going.

Twitter & Instagram: @DotDashTash

IF YOU LIKE THIS, YOU'LL LOVE . . .

NATASHA DEVON

TOXiC

Is she your best friend
or your worst enemy?

'Such an exciting
new author of YA fiction.'
HOLLY BOURNE

The Nicest Girl

Set boundaries.
Be honest.
Say no.

SOPHIE JO

THREE GIRLS

KATIE CLAPHAM

BRYONY PEARCE

Black magic just met
its match …

RAISING
HELL

'Delicious and gruesome – will ignite a new generation of vampire fans' LAUREN JAMES

MINA
and the Undead

MYSTERY

Be Kind
Rewind
◀◀

Amy McCaw

YA

VHS

'Mina is back, with bite in this action-packed romp of a sequel.' KENDARE BLAKE

MINA
and the Slayers

MYSTERY

BE KIND
REWIND

YA

VHS

Amy
McCaw

ROSE EDWARDS

*This whole
kingdom floats
on a sea of blood*

*Plough the fields
and it comes
seeping up*

The
HARM TREE

"A rich, compelling epic" MELINDA SALISBURY

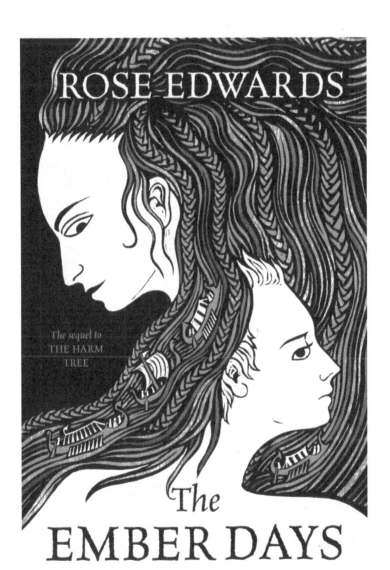

ROSE EDWARDS

The sequel to
THE HARM
TREE

The
EMBER DAYS

"A rich, compelling epic" MELINDA SALISBURY